I0768982

crime writer

crime writer

VINNIE HANSEN

First published by Level Best Books 2025

Copyright © 2025 by Vinnie Hansen

All rights reserved. No part of this publication may be reproduced, stored or transmitted in any form or by any means, electronic, mechanical, photocopying, recording, scanning, or otherwise without written permission from the publisher. It is illegal to copy this book, post it to a website, or distribute it by any other means without permission.

Vinnie Hansen asserts the moral right to be identified as the author of this work.

This novel is entirely a work of fiction created without any assistance from artificial intelligence. The names, characters and incidents portrayed in it are the work of the author's imagination. Any resemblance to actual persons, living or dead, events or localities is entirely coincidental.

First edition

ISBN: 979-8-89820-027-5

Cover art by Level Best Designs

This book was professionally typeset on Reedsy.
Find out more at reedsy.com

To Robbin Stull, mystery fan extraordinaire and my #1 Street Team Member

Praise for Crime Writer

"Vinnie Hansen hits the ground running in her latest novel *Crime Writer*. Novelist Zoey Kozinski is thrown into the heart of a murder investigation when her ride-along with a police officer goes horribly wrong. This gritty novel is laced with clever moves that will keep the reader on their toes until the end."—Allen Eskens, recipient of the Barry Award, the Minnesota Book Award, Rosebud Award, and Silver Falchion Award; has also been a finalist for the Edgar and Anthony Awards

"*Crime Writer* is a riveting thriller. The stakes keep getting higher, and the tension never falters. I highly recommend it."—Terry Shames, author of the award-winning Samuel Craddock mystery series and the Jessie Madison thriller series

"Replete with heart-stopping moments, action, and unexpected realizations, *Crime Writer* is a winner."—D. Donovan, Senior Reviewer, *Midwest Book Review*

One Gun

"Vinnie Hansen's *One Gun* unspools a long, exquisite crescendo of foreboding and dread as clouds gather for a chilling, unexpected climax. Top-notch writing, sensitive touch, and heart-wrenching choices. Hansen is an author to watch."—James W. Ziskin, Anthony, Barry, and Macavity award-winning author

"A riveting book that will tear at your heart as the impact from one gun ricochets through a close-knit community. Hansen's commanding voice weaves a compassionate tale that rings true and clear. You won't be able to look away."—Edgar-nominated author Susan Bickford

"In *One Gun*, Vinnie Hansen weaves a spell with a modern-day tale of suspense, pulling the reader into a riveting quest to see if justice will be served.

"When a gun used in a burglary falls into the wrong hands, a chase begins to find the gun before it and its owner can cause more mayhem. But of course things never go as planned when a gun is involved.

"The beautifully described setting is the central coast of California, where hidden forces drive the have-nots to desperate measures, and the criminal justice system is often on trial along with the criminals.

"A bravura outing by the author of the popular Carol Sabala mysteries."—G.M. Malliet, Agatha Award-winning author of the St. Just, Max Tudor, and Augusta Hawke mysteries

"Vinnie Hansen's novel, *One Gun*, takes a simple concept—a couple disturbs a burglary in progress in their home—and crafts an unusual story where a gun becomes an inert, silent protagonist on a fateful journey that profoundly affects several lives. No one is the same once the gun's journey comes to a close. Although there are many characters in this novel, the voice of each character is distinct and finely drawn, rooting the reader in their role of the gun's journey. I highly recommend this book."—Claire M. Johnson, author of *Fog City*

"One gun. One moment in time. Vinnie Hansen's tense crime novel, *One Gun*, explores the consequences of a single act in thought-provoking and taut detail. Thoroughly researched and smartly written, the book twists its way toward a heart-wrenching conclusion that will leave a reader breathless."—Peggy Townsend, author of Amazon Editors' mystery/suspense pick, *The Beautiful and The Wild*

"The weapon casts a gripping Chekhov-ian shadow over Hansen's tense stand-alone thriller."—*Kirkus Reviews*

"…a compelling cat-and-mouse game as perp, victims, and those caught in-between find themselves on different roads to obtaining or concealing evidence and the truth."—D. Donovan, Senior Reviewer, *Midwest Book Review*

Chapter One

Day 1 – early evening

Heat from the Mobile Data Transmitter radiated onto Zoey Kozinski's arm. The interior of the patrol car cooked, muggy and close. September brought the hottest weather to the central coast of California, anxiety about fires flaring as the oak leaves curled and undergrowth crisped. Thankfully, Officer Austin kept the windows of the patrol car open even as the sun started to set.

"Must be boiling with your vest."

"Better to sweat than bleed." Austin's profile was sharp angles, pointed nose, strong chin.

"How much does that thing weigh?" Zoey already knew, but the officer didn't seem talkative. She needed to crack the façade and dig out some grist to apply to Officer Horne, the character in her book. Her stalled, barely-started book.

"Six pounds."

Officer Austin rolled along Scenic Drive, a main thoroughfare through Playa Maria County. Zoey wished they could listen to music, something to go with driving on a sultry evening, maybe Ella Fitzgerald's "Summertime." Instead, the police radio spat information, filling awkward silence. Zoey jotted down that a list of stolen cars was tucked on the left side of his dash. She'd chosen a night shift, hoping for a modicum of action, but nothing on the radio stirred Austin's interest.

"How do you feel about ride-alongs?" She flipped her legal pad, and the printed-out opening pages of her manuscript winged to the floor. All two of them. A whopping three hundred ten words. She bent down to retrieve them.

"It's part of our Community Policing." Austin kept his focus forward. "To increase civilian awareness of what police work entails."

She didn't bother to write down the canned response.

Austin must be a rookie to receive the crappy assignment of hauling a ride-along, but he didn't look like one. Silver highlighted his short hair. Older than her fictional Officer Horne. Her protagonist, Horne, should be young, freshly free of his training wheels, a more credible character to rush toward a terrible mistake after witnessing the shooting of a fellow officer.

In the margin of the legal pad, she scribbled: *A hot-head. Temper=hubris. Too eager to prove himself?*

Then she wrote *Stan* and put a question mark after it. The name of the murdered officer in her manuscript had appeared in a magician's puff of smoke, typed by her fingers before she was conscious of a choice. Not a common name for guys of her generation, the lost kids born between Generation X and the Millennials. The name had merit—easy to pronounce, but not overly used. Why had it popped into her head?

She slipped her pen through her tangle of red hair and scratched her scalp.

Austin shot her a glance, maybe thinking she didn't know she was using the ink end.

"Writing off the top of your head?"

She smiled slightly. *Witty for a police officer.*

He quirked a brow. "Making headlines?" His tone was dry. No smile. Was he being funny or busting her balls?

Zoey tapped the legal pad. Her next question wasn't on it, but Austin's age and his quips begged for it.

"What did you do before becoming a law enforcement officer?"

Long fingers curled around the wheel, maneuvering the vehicle through the rush-hour clog of Scenic Drive. He scanned the lanes of traffic and sidewalks long enough that she thought he wasn't going to answer.

"I was a teacher."

"Really?" Her voice squeaked with unveiled surprise. Heat rose up her face. With her coloring, there was no playing off a blush. When she was a kid, her Grosse Pointe classmates had pinned her with the nickname Tomato.

"High-school history." In the parking lot, he'd offered a firm handshake and introduced himself formally as Officer Austin, although he'd added with a trace of humor 'at your service.' Over six feet with ropy muscles, he was a bit old for her, maybe forty-five, but a hottie, nonetheless.

"That's a strange career trajectory."

"Not really. In both jobs you deal with a lot of young punks."

As part of the outreach program, he probably was not supposed to refer to members of the community as *punks.* She was making progress.

"In policing I bet you have more flexibility about how you deal with *punks?*"

His lip curled, but he didn't respond.

"So why the career move?"

"In teaching, the more you work, the less you're paid," he said. "Police work offers time-and-a-half for overtime. Ten-hour shifts and four-day work weeks. More money and time for my family."

"Kids?"

"Three."

She felt a twinge of disappointment. Her sex life had been reduced to her Magic Wand, and Austin wasn't wearing a wedding ring, so a bit of fantasy had slipped under her normally guarded door. Since she didn't want a *relationship,* a hot cop could be the ticket. *Married* killed that idea.

And three kids! With the world's exploding population and global climate change, that was self-indulgent. One of her least favorite character flaws—in reality. In fiction, it was a great character flaw.

"My wife's the one who should have made the career move to cop," Austin volunteered. "She's a tiger. Can outshoot me." He shook his head in admiration.

Another twinge. She had a serious weakness for men who complimented women in absentia.

Zoey touched the cool metal of the AR-15 propped in front of the passenger seat. "This is some serious firepower."

The creases in his uniform lifted infinitesimally, a hint of a shrug. "You should see what they have on the street."

She ran her finger down her list of questions. Nothing so far had gotten the juices flowing. "What kind of handgun do you carry?"

"Smith & Wesson. Officers with more seniority get Berettas. The most senior officers have Glocks." Jealousy tinged his voice. "But if you want a better gun, you can buy one. I'm looking at a Glock."

The crackling voice of dispatch relayed a report of a middle-aged black male dealing drugs in Playa Maria Park.

Austin swung off Scenic onto a street that cut along the seedier edge of downtown, where the homeless population dwarfed the number of university students. He slowed at the park.

Dusk had sifted into darkness, but streetlights illuminated the perimeter of the grass. Young men played basketball in a well-lit court. A lone man leaning against a light pole straightened at the cruiser's arrival. Austin put the windows up, parked the car, and plucked a wood baton from the base of his door. "Remain in the vehicle."

Another patrolman rolled up and joined him. She noted details. *Suspect's dreadlocks glisten in bluish light. Tan pants bag around skinny legs.*

Austin questioned the man, while the other officer patted him down and dipped into the pockets of his army-fatigue jacket. With the window closed, Zoey sweated.

In the end, the man bumped away and swaggered toward the basketball court.

Talking together, the officers watched him, then turned in the direction of the vehicle. Austin nodded. The other man laughed. They were talking about her. The inside of the cruiser steamed like a sauna. Austin was letting her marinate in a patina of sweat.

Zoey opened the passenger door, which prompted Austin to step toward the cruiser. Before he plopped into his seat, he thunked his baton into its spot.

"I asked the suspect if we could search him, and he said no," he started before Zoey even asked. "But he has a Search Clause." Austin cleaned his hands with foam sanitizer. "That's a bargain he made for probation. He relinquished his right to probable cause."

She scribbled the information. This was good stuff, strengthening her knowledge of the law.

"But you didn't find anything?"

"Maybe he sold out."

Dry humor. Deadpan delivery. Her favorite. To curtail a blush, she cast her eyes to the pocket of his door.

"Don't most officers these days carry whip-batons?"

He gave her a look.

Amazing eyes—way greener than her own. He yanked the baton from its spot and held it across his lap, the top grazing her thigh.

Phallic symbol, for sure. The air inside the car shifted subtly.

"See all those nicks?" he said. "My T.O. gave this to me, said the riff-raff on the street notice the dents. They're mostly from getting in and out of the car, but hey," he returned the baton to the door pocket, "they don't know that."

He gave his hand a second squirt of the sanitizer. "I tell you one part of this job I don't like. The grime. You'd have to get up close to appreciate how much that guy…how grubby he was." Austin started the car. "Tell you the truth, I'm more afraid of an accidental needle poke than a gunshot."

"Was he dealing?"

"I imagine." Austin put down the windows. Fresh air rushed into the compartment. "He doesn't have any other means of income."

The radio called Austin to roust a panhandler near the entrance to the freeway. *Civilian complaint.* Austin zoomed back up to Scenic. At the intersection before the freeway entrance, he stopped at a red light with the rest of the traffic. The girl panhandling on the median spotted the cruiser, folded her sign, and meandered down the sidewalk.

Austin turned and rolled along the street across from the girl. In spite of a curvaceous figure packed into tight jeans, with her wavy brown hair hitched into pigtails, she looked all of fifteen. The girl ignored them.

Zoey twisted toward Austin. "Are you going to stop?"

"She's not doing anything illegal now. She didn't even jaywalk." He sped up. "We got her off the median."

"Yup. Sure did." He knew, and she knew, that as soon as they were out of sight, the girl would return to her spot.

How do they negotiate spots? She wrote. *First-come, first-served?*

If she asked Austin about the girl—did he know her—what was her story—she sensed he'd blow off the questions. The police department had picked the wrong officer to give ride-alongs. Austin lacked a gregarious, empathetic personality.

Zoey tried to unpack how she'd arrived at this conclusion. Maybe because he'd chosen policing over teaching. Police work had to be more frustrating than high school teaching, certainly less rewarding.

She shook her head. *Don't assume.* She asked about the girl.

"Espie Gonzales."

"You know her?"

"Yeah." His forefinger tapped the steering wheel a few times. "She lost her baby in that shooting."

"Oh, that's her." Zoey strained to see the girl disappearing into the darkness. Her tragic case had dominated the front page.

"Hell of a way to start this job." Officer Austin looped around the block back to Scenic Drive. Rush hour traffic had thinned. "I was there earlier when they arrested her piece-of-shit boyfriend, too."

She was sure Officer Austin was not supposed to say that. Zoey chewed on her pen and scribbled an idea: *Stan dies b/c he harbors a secret?* She doodled hashtag symbols on her paper.

Maybe Austin recognized zoning-out behavior from all those past students because he volunteered, "As a mystery writer, you're probably looking for something more exciting. Let's see if I can find a car to pull over."

Within two minutes, he pointed out a white sedan. "Burned-out taillight." He unclipped his seatbelt.

"Why are you doing that?"

"Your car is your coffin. Cop training 101. If someone jumps out of a vehicle, you don't want to be fumbling with a seatbelt."

She unlatched her seatbelt, too. He didn't object.

He called in the license plate, citing the letters phonetically. "Old model white sedan. Make unclear. One male." He concluded the call with their location and lit up the patrol car.

The driver continued along Scenic toward the outskirts of town. Austin tapped his airhorn. The silhouetted head, wearing a hat, lifted as though checking the rearview.

The dispatcher reported back on the license plate. No red flags.

Austin used the airhorn again. But the white sedan tooled along. The number of businesses thinned. Traffic dwindled.

Muscles jumped in Austin's jaw.

Zoey jotted. *Wants authority obeyed!* No wonder high school kids drove him crazy. *Austin like Camille?* Camille, her mother, was a first-class control freak.

He eyed her notepad and frowned. Closing the windows, he put on the siren and left it on, wailing, but this could hardly be called a chase. They were traveling thirty miles per hour.

"Why isn't he pulling over?"

Austin didn't have an answer, at least not one he could utter with her in the vehicle. Finally, he said, "Could be absorbed in his cell phone."

That was not the reason. She was an eagle at spotting drivers using a device, and, in this case, the hat would have accentuated any dip of the head. He was not using his phone, and his actions were sure to piss off a cop, especially this cop—an authoritarian personality with an audience to impress. Zoey planted her Keds against the cruiser's floor and stretched her torso, staring at the car ahead, anxiety percolating up her legs.

"His car could be sound baffled." Austin's voice tightened as he offered the flimsy possibility.

Rationalizing. Even if the driver couldn't hear, he could see the cruiser lights. The situation reminded her of the pursuit of the Bronco carrying O.J. Simpson up the 405. That day in June 1994, she'd come into the house after swapping mix tapes with her middle school friend. Her mom, in impossibly white Capris, so raptly watched the television that Zoey popped one earbud of her Walkman in the middle of Warren G's "Regulate" to see what was up.

She heard the song now in her head as the white sedan left Playa Maria proper. Scenic Drive opened onto the coastal highway along the Pacific, an empty stretch of dark two-lane highway. The driver put on his blinker. She sighed in relief. The car crunched onto the steeply graded gravel shoulder.

Austin pulled in behind it. She slouched down in her seat, taking notes on the pad propped against her thighs. Her heart hammered. A routine traffic stop, but it felt off. *Austin pissed.* She drew an anger emoji. And he had not called for back-up.

Too macho? she wrote.

She shrank in her seat as Austin approached the sedan, his hand on his weapon. She scribbled details. The car's window glided open. The man stuck his head out, glancing back.

At the turn of the driver's head, Austin crouched and drew. A gun muzzle appeared out the window opening.

Three pops split the silence.

Austin collapsed onto the asphalt.

Zoey's stomach lurched. The white car roared to life. Its tires spat gravel and squealed onto the pavement, the back-end fishtailing. She opened the passenger door, her pulse throbbing in her head, the world awash in swirling blue and red. Her shoes skidded on the gravel. She caught herself by grabbing the door. With the tilt of the car, the door continued to fly open, whirling her toward the drainage ditch.

Regaining her balance, she crept forward, the night so quiet she could hear the distant whoosh of the ocean. Or was the whoosh inside her head?

Officer Austin lay splayed on the edge of the pavement. He'd landed so the exit wound faced her, the back of his head a bloody pulp.

She swallowed bile and recoiled behind the cruiser. There was no way he was alive.

Her body felt floaty, unreal, tethered only by the pain of pebbles under her knee.

A red sports car passed, headed toward town. The driver slowed. Hope surged in her. Help had arrived. She started to rise on wobbly legs.

The car zoomed off, leaving her.

She forced herself to draw a breath but couldn't get it beyond her throat. Austin had been hit at close range with something high caliber. Leaving the cruiser door gaping open, she leaned across the seat divider and grabbed the police radio, her hand shaking wildly. She tried another breath, but air kept going in and out in sharp jags.

The radio would be faster than her cell phone, skirting any telecommunicator and going directly to dispatch. Officers in the area would hear the transmission. She wanted someone to come right now.

The radio suddenly squawked to life in her hands. Her heart slammed her chest.

"555, are you 10-4 on your stop?"

Hell no. Nothing was 10-4. She keyed the mic.

Another set of headlights zoomed toward her. Maybe when she'd gotten out, the killer had spotted her and was returning to take care of loose ends. Her whole body shook. Shrinking down, she identified herself to the dispatcher.

"The ride-along?" the suspicious voice snapped. "Where's Officer Austin?"

"He's been shot!"

An intake of air. A tiny pause.

The car in the opposite lane sped by. A white car! Its bright lights were blinding, the driver in too big of a hurry to be bothered with the odd appearance of a lone police vehicle at the side of the road, overhead lights flashing. Or maybe the driver didn't slow down because he already knew what was there.

"Where are you?" the dispatcher's voice steeled into all business.

Zoey wished she had the dispatcher's nerves, hoped she could get through her report before fainting or puking. Sweat slicked her palm. "Edge of town on the coast highway headed north, about a mile past where Officer Austin called in the stop."

"Help is on the way. Stay put."

As though she were going to do what? Run up the deserted, dark highway?

The white car that had sped by flipped a U-ey and roared back toward her, skidding to a stop behind the cruiser.

The sedan's lights remained on bright. Her stomach shriveled. A man strolled toward the cruiser.

Maybe she should run.

Chapter Two

Day 1 – night

Zoey pulled at the AR-15. It was stuck. Or locked. She flopped across the seats and grabbed Austin's baton.

Slithering back to her seat with the heavy weapon in hand, she raised her head to peek over the dash.

The man loomed above Officer Austin's body. "Holy shit!" He tugged earphones down around blond hair flowing to his shoulders. His tight yellow pants glowed like neon in the weird lighting. He spun toward the cop car. She froze.

A black patch covered one eye. No wonder he drove with his lights on bright. Was it even legal to drive with one eye? Zoey lowered her head, hiding, fingers quivering around the base of the baton.

The man wasn't acting like a shooter.

What the hell do you know about how shooters act, Zoey? Maybe he is acting just like a shooter, one who is legitimately stunned he's killed an officer.

His car was a white sedan.

Hunkered down with her legs protruding from the open door, Zoey tried to reassure herself that white was the most common car color.

Gripping the baton, she slipped from the cruiser. Her chartreuse Keds slid, rattling over the pebbles of the steep grade.

The man's head swiveled. He jumped back when he spotted her. Each beat of Zoey's heart throbbed in her head. She shrank behind the engine compartment, her mouth dry.

"What the fuck?" The man ducked down on the other side of the hood. "Do you have a gun? Did you shoot this cop?"

She peeped around the rubber smell of the tire. Glistening blood surrounded the gaping wound in Austin's head. She drew back, her stomach revolting. Vomit rose in the back of her throat, but nothing came out except a cough of acidic liquid. Sirens shrilled in the distance.

"Listen to me!" She sucked in cold coastal air. This guy was not the shooter; the shooter wouldn't stick around, would he? She placed the baton on the gravel next to her. Then she waved her hands in the air above the wheel well to show the long-haired man she was unarmed. "My name's Zoey. I didn't shoot anyone." *Except in books.* "I'm the officer's rider." She felt relieved to have another human to share this horror, to carry some of the emotional load.

"I don't know what that is," he called from the other side of the car. "Stay over there."

"I'm a writer!"

"You just said that."

"Not rider—a wriTER! Doing research."

"Just stay over there."

A screaming parade of law enforcement vehicles raced toward them. The higher pitch of an ambulance and the impatient honking of a fire truck joined the cacophony.

Dizziness spun through her.

Do not faint. Do not act like some damsel in a romance novel.

The long-haired guy stayed tucked down. She duck-walked back a bit, towing the baton. She lifted herself and saw him through the windows of the cruiser, whipping out his phone, turning in a full arc—toward the oncoming rush of vehicles, toward Officer Austin's body. He rose enough to capture her, gradually uncurling from her shelter.

Her relief lasted until the first patrol car slewed to a stop on the highway. The officer leapt out, weapon drawn, using the vehicle for cover. "Hands in the air! On your knees!" he screamed.

She dropped the baton and followed the order.

"You behind the car, move forward!"

Vehicles jammed up the road, blocking any car that might come from either direction.

The guy from the white sedan, long legs in yellow pants, had dropped down in front of Officer Austin's cruiser. When she scooted forward, he scowled at her as though this was her fault. An officer hooked him up behind his back.

Gravel on the highway's shoulder pressed into her skin through the holes in her jeans. Pain stabbed through her rotator as another officer yanked her arms back.

"I'm Officer Austin's ride-along," she protested. "I called this in." The officer frisked her.

Yellow Pants tipped his head up and said, "And I'm a Good Samaritan. I stopped to see if I could help."

The cop behind him placed a boot on his back and shoved him to the pavement.

"What the fuck, man!"

She imagined the push to the ground not only hurt but also had scratched up the earphones. The officer kicked the guy's legs apart and patted him down.

The officer behind Zoey frowned at his partner's back but didn't say anything. He muttered to her, "We'll sort this out later."

Meaning what? She didn't appreciate the roughness but understood. The men had arrived on the scene with their comrade dead on the pavement. The officer who'd put on her cuffs, tall with a broad back, lumbered toward his boys in blue, a loose chaotic circle, ebbing in around the dead body that had been their mate. Shouted commands moved them back, some of the officers tiptoeing, trying not to contaminate the scene. Others with weapons drawn secured the perimeter as though the shooter might still be around.

Vehicles continued to arrive, sirens shrieking.

She exhaled. Now that she was safe, her writer mind kicked into high gear, absorbing details. A cop in front of the chaos, a strobing silhouette, used his flashlight for the unsexy task of stopping and redirecting traffic. Headlights and emergency lights lit up the fog.

For the moment, she and the Good Samaritan had been abandoned, cuffed and searched, but unsecured, which seemed like a mistake. But in the craziness of a situation like this, how could there not be mistakes?

The Good Samaritan raised himself back to his knees.

"How you doing over there?" Zoey swallowed hard against the coffee-flavored acid in the back of her throat.

"Not what I planned for my evening."

The sarcasm pulled her attention from the drama. The narrow black band of his eyepatch sliced a diagonal across a high, very pale, forehead. She wondered if he was going to be sick. The cup of his eyepatch had been knocked off kilter and sat too far down his cheek.

"Jimmy." He wiggled an ear in an effort to lift the eyepatch.

"Zoey."

A squat officer stepped from the hubbub. "And I'm Sergeant De La Torre." He grasped her bicep and helped her to her feet. "You're Officer Austin's ride-along?"

She nodded. "Zoey Kozinski."

Jimmy shot her a sharp look.

Like a Southern gent, Sergeant De La Torre took her elbow and steered her—not roughly but forcefully—toward the back seat of Austin's vehicle, barking over the roof for an officer to situate the other witness in a patrol car. Austin's baton lay, abandoned, by the side of the road.

The indignity of being demoted to the hard, plastic back seat hit Zoey along with the primal, animal-odor of the human body, not eliminated by cleaner. Sergeant De La Torre allowed her to drape her legs out the open door while he peppered her with questions: type of vehicle, color, direction of travel.

She told him. "And the taillight was out. That's why Officer Austin pulled him over."

"Did you get a look at the license plate?"

"Officer Austin called it in." But he must know that and the other things, too.

"I'll be back."

The sergeant closed her into the back seat and strode toward the group. Officers huddled around him. The cruiser's reds continued to wash the scene with color. Men dispersed from the circle to their cars and tore off in both directions even though she'd told De La Torre that the white sedan had headed north.

Sergeant De La Torre returned to her, his notepad out. When he opened the door, cool air flowed in, the dampness fresh and invigorating.

De La Torre didn't waste time. "Was the driver alone?"

"I didn't see anyone else."

"Male?"

"Yes."

"Black? White? Latino?"

"He was wearing a hat."

"A cap?"

"No. A hat." Something flitted at her brain, teasing like moth wings, but she couldn't catch it.

"Anything else?"

She shook her curls, overcome with the sudden thought of Officer Austin's wife and three kids. *Ohmygod.* Tears filmed her eyes.

The sergeant closed his pad. "You'll have to wait here for the homicide detective. I'll put on the air so you don't suffocate."

Through blurry eyes, she spotted a photographer from the *Playa Maria Reporter* prowling the edge of the scene, nudging as close as he could to the coroner and cluster of crime scene investigators. The photographer had been named Playa Maria Artist of the Year so she recognized him, not that she could remember his name, or much of anything, at the moment.

Chapter Three

Day 1 – night

Seated at his desk, Ray dropped his head into his hands and scrubbed at his bald head. His subordinates called him Adolph, which irritated him only because Hitler was German. Ray was proudly Italian. Otherwise, the nickname meant he ran a tight ship, so the moron standing across the room profoundly disturbed him.

It was peak season, they were short-handed, and he'd been here for fourteen hours. *Now this. Catastrophic. Unfuckingbelievable.*

The dirtbag should never have been let into the operation, but paying only fifteen dollars an hour, you couldn't get picky. And this kid *Johnny? Jerry?* had scampered up and down ladders like a monkey.

Given the situation, probably better he couldn't remember his name.

Ray's stubby fingers took refuge on the shelf made by a blue polo shirt stretched over his belly. "Let me get this straight." To quell his panic, he pressed his hands tight against his stomach. "Instead of *maybe* getting busted, you shot a cop?"

The kid kept his distance and his silence, but didn't hang his head or indicate remorse. He didn't even seem scared, which was fucking unnerving.

Ray had had misgivings from the get-go, suspected the kid sampled the merchandise. And obviously he didn't keep his car up. *Getting pulled over for a taillight.* Stuart, his right-hand man, should have noticed that when they packed the units into the trunk. Of course, the loading itself could have pulled the wire loose.

"What kind of business do you think this is?" Ray's hand lost control and flew out, fingers splayed. "I'm just a pot grower." His stomach roiled.

"Illegal pot grower."

"Say what?" Ray pressed up onto his fingertips. *Unbelievable.* "It's pot! Nobody gives a shit about that. But they sure as hell care about cop killers."

"Wanna call the cops?" The kid smirked.

Little shit. If all Ray had going was the weed, he might have called the kid's bluff, but with legalization, venture capital had swept in to snap up permits, glutting the market and driving down his prices. What could a businessman do but diversify?

Ray wiggled open his desk drawer. His Colt slid forward. He stared at it, weighing options. The kid had his own gun and apparently didn't have hang-ups about shooting people. Ray clammed a small groan in his throat. There was also the fact he'd never shot anyone, not even in Vietnam, thanks to his high school typing teacher who'd taught his thick fingers to fly over typewriter keys.

He'd fired over the heads of vagrants trying to steal his plants. You had to protect your product. The thieves knew that—respected that. But killing people? He waggled his heavy head. Well, if it came to that, he had acreage, tilled earth, and farm equipment—ways to dispose of a body.

"How many times did you fire?" he asked.

"Huh?"

"To take out the cop?"

"Once."

"Once?" Ray scratched his stubble-covered jowl and glanced again at the Colt. Maybe the kid was lying, maybe he got lucky, or maybe he was one hell of a shot. Ray hadn't survived in the cannabis industry by taking unnecessary risks. With a thick thigh, he nudged the drawer shut. "We have to get your car out of sight."

"How am I supposed to get around?"

Ray slammed a fist on the dusty mahogany. The lamp jumped. "You've killed a cop, and that's your concern? *How am I supposed to get around?* Jesus

H. Christ!"

"Well where should I take it?"

"You," Ray pointed a finger, "aren't taking it anywhere. Every cop and his brother is looking for that car." The pull chain on the lamp ticked against the stained-glass shade. He grabbed the base to quiet it. Suzette, his first wife, had made the thing, back when they were young and in love.

"If everybody's looking for it, how do we move it?"

"After you and Stuart do some body work," he pointed to a baseball bat in the corner, "we'll spray it black and tow it."

"But that's my mom's car."

Ray scoured his forehead with his hands. *Unfuckingbelievable.*

"Where will it go?"

"Not your business." For a reason Ray couldn't fathom, maybe inertia, a dangerous thing, he kept talking. "My friend has a barn."

The idiot shifted his weight again from one scuffed cowboy boot to the other. Maybe he'd grown up in the country, hunting since he was in diapers. That could explain the bull's eye on the cop.

"Can you trust this friend?"

"That's what I'm wondering about you." The kid didn't reply. *Not chatty. And a good shot.* Two redeeming qualities. "We were in Vietnam together." Over there, Ray had been in hairy situations, but this, right here, topped them all. His head bobbed in silent agreement with himself.

The cops would be combing the countryside for that car, now parked at his Brussels sprout farm with his cannabis grow less than a half mile away. He groaned aloud. Switching the packing warehouse was easy enough— clear out the product and throw in produce boxes. The stink of the sprouts would mask the residual pot smell. And, seriously, the cops had so much countryside to cover, that if they even came, at most they'd only want a quick look to confirm there was no car hidden inside.

The real hassle was shutting down production at peak season.

Ray swung his chair to indicate the baseball bat. "Time to get to work."

The kid didn't move, like he was stuck to the pine floor. "We have a problem," he said.

"No shit, Sherlock." Ray scratched his scalp, scabby from too many years in the sun, in spite of the hat he now wore.

"Besides the dead cop."

Ray's head throbbed. He needed a drink. "There's more?"

"There was a woman in the vehicle."

"Don't tell me," Ray said. "You had your mother along."

"Not in my vehicle. In the cop's."

"A criminal?"

"No." The kid tipped his head sideways. "In the front seat."

"A partner?"

"Nuh uh. Playa Maria cops ride alone."

"A witness, though?"

He nodded.

Ray lurched forward so fast his legs propelled the chair back. It banged against the wall. "A fucking witness!" He sliced the air with his hands. His stomach churned like he'd eaten gluten.

The shooting was one thing; getting caught, entirely another. He was a businessman. A purveyor of primo weed. A third-generation Playa Marian.

The chair trundled back to him, a realization rolling on its wheels. As much as he groused about his life—his ex-wives, his spoiled adult children, the direction California had taken with legalization—Ray liked strolling downtown and greeting people from buskers to city council members. The idiot in front of him threatened all of that. He'd shot a cop just because his load had contained some white Southeast Asian heroin. Ray wanted to fly across the desk and strangle him, but opted for kicking the chair aside and pacing, trying to think. Sweat bit his armpits. "She's gotta go." What other choice was there?

"I agree, Boss."

"Don't call me *Boss*." Ray strolled to the wet bar, but instead of pouring a shot of tequila, he snapped up his Louisville Slugger. "Find out who she is and clean up this mess."

"How do I do that?"

Ray tapped the endcap against the wood floor. Did the punk need him to spell it out? "You seem good with a gun."

"I mean how do I find out who she is?"

There was that smart-aleck smirk again. "You must have at least one low-life friend with a police scanner. Maybe the passenger's name came up." Ray's free hand assailed the air, like his Italian mother's used to, in inarticulate frustration. "Or maybe read the newspaper." Ray lifted the bat into swinging position.

A pistol pointed at his head before he even registered where it came from. The polymer was a shocking aqua. It looked like a toy, and yet, the kid had killed a cop with it.

"3-D printed," he said proudly.

"Untraceable?" That part was good, Ray thought, unless he was about to be offed.

The kid's head bobbed.

Ray snorted, even though the plastic barrel could deliver a bullet as easily as a metal one. "Shooting me would be ill-advised." He extended the bat.

The kid crept forward and with one hand, yanked it from him, the ridiculous aqua weapon trained on Ray's face. "How am I even going to get back to town?"

"After you make the alterations to the car, Stuart can drive you."

"Then how am I supposed to get around?"

Now Ray did pour the shot, straining not to slosh it. There was something wrong with this kid. Next, he'd ask how he was supposed to explain the missing car to his mommy. He was a dangerous moron, though, who pivoted in cowboy boots to keep the gun beaded on Ray's head. Ray dug in his pocket for his wallet and tweezered out some Franklins. "Rent something."

The kid let the bat clatter to the floor and snatched the bills without lowering the handgun. "And if I don't take out the witness?"

"You know the rest of that story."

Stuart kept tabs on their employees—knew where they lived.

That would be the faster, cleaner option. But letting an off-the-rails crazy clean up a mess of his own making seemed substantively different to Ray than he, himself, ordering a hit. *Murder.*

He shook his head. None of this belonged in his life. He was a gentleman farmer, not a mob boss.

And he was not someone who asked a friend to hide evidence. They'd been young bucks together, doing wall-sits by pressing their backs together, holding each other up way before Vietnam. These days, they hardly spoke, but they were still propped against one another in shared grief. He was pure shit to take advantage of that.

The drink burned its way down his throat. He would have preferred to savor the top-shelf tequila, but you couldn't do that when playing tough guy in front of a loose cannon pointing a firearm at your forehead.

"Find her," Ray growled, "and do what needs to be done."

Chapter Four

Day 2

At half past two in the morning, Zoey bumped down the dirt road to Harvey Shaffer's weed farm. Legal medical marijuana, according to him, but she doubted it. Harvey was not the type to weave through the bureaucratic maze for a permit.

Zoey's SUV rocked to a stop in front of her Toy Box home, fifty feet to the side of Harvey's old farmhouse. Since Harvey let her park the trailer on his property for free, she didn't press him about his marijuana fields.

"Tweakers circle us growers like a bunch of hyenas," he'd said. "Watchin' for an opportunity to rip us off and make a fast buck. Another person around discourages that."

At five-foot-two, she didn't pose much of a threat. More likely Harvey's largesse sprang from his "thing for redheads."

She wouldn't have sex with him in a million years. He was older than her stepdads. But if he wanted to engage in lustful fantasies in exchange for a free hook-up to his septic tank, who was she to argue? As long as he kept it in his head. And in his pants.

At the moment, though, Zoey welcomed the nearby presence of Harvey and the first thoughts in hours not related to the death of Officer Austin.

She jumped down from her Honda Element and shivered. The heat of the day had sucked cold fog up into the mountains, and the resinous smell of Harvey's plants hung in the silent miasma. No wonder old-timers called it skunk weed. Harvey's fence was meant to conceal his grow, but the marijuana had grown too tall and the odor was too strong.

She blinked, her eyes gritty like they'd been scoured with sandpaper. At a strange noise, they popped open. She peered into the night, the tops of the marijuana plants silvery and the redwoods dark silhouettes like a woodcut print.

The grating sound, muffled in fog, drifted up from behind Harvey's house. Her ears pricked, but the quiet of mountain forest resettled around her. Possibly Harvey was working in his barn.

Zoey stepped from a single concrete block into her 140-square-foot refuge. The various movable ottomans, upholstered in neutral gray, seemed as foreign to her as Stonehenge.

How did she start to return to normal?

She turned in a slow 360—the row of three cubical ottomans forming a living-area couch, the single counter of the kitchen, the ladder up to her loft, an ottoman on either side of her table, and back to the sliding glass door out into the darkness.

She entertained the idea of going right back out the door, driving to Brianna's apartment, and snuggling up to her local best friend. Spoon against Brianna's big butt.

Zoey checked the time and then plugged her phone into the charger on her table. Every writer has a pet peeve, and hers was a character's mobile phone losing connectivity at a pivotal moment, putting him—or her—in peril. Right now, the plot of her life was at a pivotal point. *So keep the damn phone charged.*

With leaden arms, Zoey stripped off her clothes and removed stackable racks from inside one ottoman, a fancy name, she thought, for upholstered storage cubes. She placed her folded jeans on the bottom rack. The armpits of her tee reeked of nervous sweat. She pulled open the hinged lid of the other cube at the table and stuffed in the stinky shirt along with her pink thong and matching bra.

The horror of the evening stiffened her resolve to stay in control, to stay organized. That was the key to living in a tiny house anyway, exhausted or not.

She yanked on the bathroom sink's faucet, pulled the flexible extension from its hidey hole, and clipped the faucet into a wall bracket. Showering was one occasion when she appreciated being short. Warm water washed away the grime of the cruiser's back seat, the staleness of the interview room, the imagined bits of brain and blood clinging to her skin. But it couldn't rinse away the gun. *Bam, bam, bam.* Ricocheting now inside her skull. Officer Austin falling. The extra blackness of his blood on the asphalt.

Her heart hammered. She snapped off the water and reached for her towel to escape the cage of memories. While drying off, she tried deep breathing.

She unfolded her ladder, scaled the rungs to her loft, and flopped down naked on the futon, bone-tired and wide-awake. Across the room, through three small hopper windows, tendrils of fog muffled the susurration of a tanoak.

Even contemplating sleep was ridiculous. She switched on the lamp atop the nightstand and opened a drawer full of personal items. Closed it.

From the nightstand's shelf, she selected *November Road*. Read the first lines. Read them again. Nothing computed. The words wouldn't arrange themselves in her brain. Instead, the crime scene unspooled again, an avalanche rush of adrenaline behind it, tumbling boulders of sadness. The dead officer. His wife. His three children.

Fishing her pajamas from under the pillow, Zoey slipped them on. She scooted across her twin-sized mattress and sat at her electric piano. She should thank her mom for the years of piano lessons, but she'd hated them as a kid. Camille had trotted her out like a trained circus seal to perform at cocktail parties. Then a nanny had whisked her off to bed.

She found herself now pounding power chords for Joan Jett's "I Hate Myself for Loving You." In her teens, it had given her great satisfaction to discover this other use for her talent. With a jolt, she remembered the She Cats had a gig at Poorboy Brew. *Tonight.* She was going to need mainlined caffeine to perform for two sets.

Scuttling down the ladder, she wrangled one of the ottomans closer to the table and sat, cross-legged, on top of it. The cube's whiff of dirty clothes meant she'd have to break down soon and hit a laundromat. *One more thing to do.*

On her laptop, she googled the *Playa Maria Reporter*. Playa Maria probably hadn't lost a police officer in twenty years. This was going to be a huge story. But the online edition didn't have anything up yet, and events had happened too late to make it into the morning print edition.

Zoey's fingers rattled the laptop keyboard, and then she opened her work-in-progress.

She groaned. On the ride-along, she'd taken copies of the first two pages to read while waiting—to keep the scene vivid in her mind—but her questions and all the ideas she'd jotted down were on a legal pad that had slid to the floor of Officer Austin's Crown Vic.

Once the homicide detective laid his eyeballs on those, he'd want to interview her all over again, wondering why she was writing a story that started with an officer down. A pretty striking coincidence if she said so herself.

When he'd grilled her at headquarters, the detective—Detective Bowman—a man with a grooved face like a pug's, had been professional, but the interview had dragged on and become so repetitive, she'd wanted to scream.

He'd asked several times how many shots she'd heard. By the last time she said "three," she was starting to doubt herself.

"Don't you believe me?"

"Officer Austin sustained one wound." The detective pressed his index finger to the center of his forehead.

She winced. "The other two must have gone wild."

Yet neither had pinged into the cruiser. Traveling unimpeded through the night, how far would bullets fly? The manpower they expended on a search for them rested solely on her insistence that there'd been three shots. And her response changed the profile of the suspect from a marksman who'd capped an officer with a single shot to someone who happened to hit his target.

By the time Bowman asked her why Jimmy had stopped, she'd lost it. "I don't know—maybe because there was a dead body in the road."

From her crime writing research, she knew criminals sometimes did return to the scene. *But seriously? A one-eyed guy named Jimmy?* She wouldn't name a villain Jimmy in a million years. Still, this line of questioning raised a specter before her. "What if the shooter saw me?" she asked.

The detective shooed away the idea with the swish of a hand, too much on his plate to entertain the hypothetical.

Now Zoey glanced uneasily toward the sliding glass door of her trailer. Light from the loft spilled down, silhouetting her, and the laptop illuminated her face. For anyone outside, she was a sitting duck.

No one can find this place. Zoey repeated the words like a mantra.

She stood up, too fast, head spinning. Propping herself against the kitchenette counter, she poured a shot of whiskey, hammered it, and then rinsed the shot glass.

Resettled in front of her laptop, she streamed Charles Brown, her favorite pianist, regretting her space allowed for only a tiny Bose speaker. Good sound, though, for a unit the size of a toothpaste box, delivering every tickle of the ivories in "Black Night." Nice to listen to something besides the She Cats' punky girl band sound. She followed the notes—hoping for an escape into a magical space occupied by sound, but she crashed back to the table and the night in front of her. The alcohol and music failed to loosen the coil in her pit.

She tapped open Instagram. Nothing like social media for a distraction. Thank God her mom was self-centered. Camille had once given Facebook a try, but didn't like that being a friend on social media took energy, like being a friend in real life.

Zoey stared at the screen, then switched over to Facebook, even though her friends there ran from older to ancient. She felt too weary to compose a coherent synopsis of what had happened on Highway One. As a writer, she couldn't post any old piece of crap. So she diddled, skimming through posts, listening to Brown's blues, waiting for sleep to slip into the realm of possibility.

A friend request appeared. From Jimmy Patak. *Mr. Good Samaritan?*

A spidery feeling crawled the back of her neck. She kept a low profile, and yet this stranger, who'd entered her life only hours ago, had found her.

She clicked his name, almost desperate for a postmortem of the night's events. Jimmy was a good candidate. The only candidate, really. She wouldn't be able to unscramble the intense and convoluted evening for Brianna if she tried. Plus, it was the middle of the night.

But why was Jimmy Patak contacting her? How? She remembered Jimmy cutting his eyes toward her when she gave Sergeant De La Torre her full name. But to have the presence of mind to store it? And to send a friend request?

A little weird.

Or bold?

She liked bold.

Jimmy's page had the look of a troll's—no banner, no photo, no posts. *WTF?*

Had he opened an account to contact her? Was that stalking? Could there be a one-eyed villain named Jimmy, after all?

Was the friend request really from Jimmy?

Was crime fiction making her too cynical?

Chapter Five

Day 2 – before dawn

uriosity beat out Zoey's caution. Facebook was only a virtual connection; it wasn't as if Jimmy would know where she lived. She approved the friend request. A private message appeared as though he'd been waiting.

You're Z. Kozinski!!! Big fan. Loved Craze.

Craze was her suspense novel about five young people living on the edge who formed a theft ring that tightened around their existences like a noose.

She responded: *Fans rock. (I'd sprinkle a million or two exclamations, but I'm not a fan of them.)*

But you like hyperbole, he returned.

Smiley emoji.

You don't look like your headshot, he wrote.

I look like my mom in that photo. Long story.

One that made Zoey shudder. She used the headshot, though. A professional photo shoot (arranged and paid for by her mother) wasn't something Zoey cared to repeat, even when Camille crashed her book events and basked in the confusion of readers mistaking her for Zoey.

Was tonight crazy or what! Jimmy wrote. *Exclamation worthy, I think.*

Can't get the images out of my head, she typed.

It wasn't surprising that Jimmy was up if the night had affected him the way it had her. With every creak in the Tiny House or rustle in the trees, a shot of adrenaline jacked her wide awake.

Are you going to write about it?

She shook her head even though Jimmy couldn't see her. Good thing. No doubt her mop of curls had passed Carrot Top stage, and by this time, the pouches under her eyes could each hold up a peanut.

Cupping her chin, she tapped her lips with two fingers. *Would she write about it?* The words of Alice McDermott sprang into her head: "A good writer sells out everybody he knows, sooner or later." She swallowed. She closed her eyes, and glistening specks of Austin's brain flitted behind the lids. Saliva gathered in her mouth. Nausea curdled in her throat.

The writer part of her brain chastised her—told her the inside scoop on the shooting of a police officer was potential Pulitzer material, especially if investigative reporting helped track down the killer. She preferred fiction, but her non-fiction *Cannabis Cutter* had sold better than her novel.

Her computer pinged. *You still there?*

Heartless to write about it, don't you think? she typed.

No. Cathartic.

Hyperbole? Cathartic? She worked a hand through her hair, the wiry strands sticking out inches from her head. *Were you an English major?* she asked.

Nope.

A rap on the door made her jump, knocking her laptop sideways. Outside the sliding glass door, a dark shape hovered. She ducked. There was nothing to protect her but the laptop screen. Her heart pounded like a drum inside her head. The figure moved sideways as though trying to get a bead on her.

If someone means to harm you, he wouldn't knock, Zoey.

With a few steps, she reached the door and slid it open. "You scared the holy crap out of me."

Harvey stroked his bushy mustache. "Is that any way to greet a concerned citizen?" Brawny arms crossed over a faded Willie Nelson tee-shirt. He backed off her step to the ground, one of his clodhoppers tied halfway down its tongue. "You okay?"

Cold air funneled around her. "Just writing." Since she'd met Harvey while researching *Cannabis Cutter*, he almost qualified as an old friend. *Certainly old.*

He squinted up at her. "Never knew you to burn the midnight oil."

"You either."

"Rambo's in a mood."

As far as Zoey was concerned, Harvey's Doberman was always *in a mood.* The piano run of Charles Brown's *Trouble Blues* floated on the air behind her. Below her, Harvey waited for a response, hands tucked up near his armpits. He reminded her of the actor Sam Elliott, one of her mom's favorites. Back in the day, Harvey had probably been a stud muffin.

She shivered, aware of her nipples, erect under the cotton of her night shirt. Harvey was generous as hell to share his septic tank, but that was all she wanted to share with him. "It's been a night, Harvey. Too much to discuss it now."

"Okey doke, then, Rachelle," he said. "As long as you're okay."

Who the hell is Rachelle? A senior moment, she guessed.

She banged the door shut, locked it, and thought about getting curtains, but generally no one visited. Partly because Harvey didn't want people around his farm and partly for a host of her own reasons. On a private mountain road, the place was about as off the grid as possible in the Twenty-first Century, but even at that, Harvey had a secret hunting cabin. When he disappeared, she'd thought he was going there, but maybe he had a girlfriend named Rachelle.

She returned to her computer. Thank God Harvey's clearing on top of a hill allowed for a decent internet connection.

Uh, goodnight? Jimmy's new message said.

She wrote back: *Still here.*

But the line of communication had gone dead. Strands of soulful blues riffed around her. For a moment, she regretted dismissing Harvey. The night felt large and she felt small.

She climbed to her loft, tumbled onto the narrow futon, and eventually drifted into a restless sleep.

Barking woke her before dawn. Harvey's watchdog, Rambo. Harvey worried about plant thieves or the "fuzz." More likely a raccoon was exciting the dog.

The racket intensified, coming toward her trailer. Zoey bolted upright in bed.

Chapter Six

Day 2 – early morning

Almost as suddenly, Rambo's barking receded, headed back toward Harvey's house. The thudding of Zoey's heart receded, too, but she lay completely awake, thinking about the driver in the white car who'd killed a cop in cold blood. Who'd left a family fatherless.

She rolled out of bed, clambered down the ladder rungs, and pressed her face to the sliding glass door. The dog had not tripped Harvey's motion-sensor light. Shadowy shapes of redwoods circled their cleared plot, and Harvey's white house glowed eerily.

Something banged. Zoey startled. Sounds bounced in the woods, so she couldn't tell where the noise originated. She crossed to her only back window and peered into the darkness. There might be a shimmer of light coming from Harvey's barn. He did put in crazy hours during harvest.

But what if Jimmy were the shooter? What if he'd tracked her via her laptop's location?

Mulling over the idea, she put on the electric water kettle, poured dark French roast grounds into a single-serve filter, and flipped open her laptop. She fought the urge to check if Jimmy had written. Fought the urge to post her experience. Fought the urge to call Brianna. Fought the urge to see if the story of the shooting was online.

The contract for her book *Craze* had been a two-book deal. She seriously needed to get something going on the second book. Her agent, Helga

Bosworth, would be contacting her soon, saying, "Whataya got, Kiddo?" with a New Yorker's impatience, especially for what she called Zoey's *little dramas.* If Zoey even checked the internet, it would swallow her. She'd never meet her daily word count.

She fixed her coffee and ported a steaming mug to the table. At least she had an idea. Her character, Officer Horne, would break protocol, rush toward his fallen fellow officer, Stan, and get shot by the deranged man in the domestic-violence house. She typed, the fresh image of a shattered head dribbling onto her Word document.

She stopped, sipped, and read over her writing. Maybe she should change the scene to nighttime to use the creepy effect of strobing lights. She changed "house" to "domicile," a more police-y word, but then she had "domestic" and "domicile" in the same phrase. *Argh.*

Zoey rested her head in her hands. Rambo's yapping had destroyed her slim hold on sleep. Now her head felt like the inside of a vacuum cleaner bag clogged with lint and debris.

Eyes back to the screen, she read the scene yet again, whispering aloud. She scratched vigorously at her scalp, trying to stimulate some blood flow to the brain. At least emptying her churning emotions onto the page was calming, helping her to detach from the shooting. *Cathartic*, as Jimmy had said.

Now, away from Detective Bowman's intimidation, she felt certain the shooter had fired three times. *Pop, pop, pop.* She pulled herself upright on the ottoman. One of those bullets could have hit her. Her body could be at the coroner's right now, along with Austin's.

Reaching blindly for her coffee, she slopped liquid onto the keyboard. Zoey spun, grabbed a paper towel from the counter, and dabbed in the grooves between the keys. Turning the laptop upside down, she shook it. Brown liquid sprinkled the table.

If she could crawl back into her writing, she could escape the images attacking her brain—the real one of Austin sprawled on the highway, the imaginary one of her own corpse slumped and bloody in his cruiser.

A vivid imagination. She sighed. *The occupational hazard of being a writer.*

Or, the precursor for being a writer.

She righted the computer and wiggled a twisted paper towel between the keys. Writing provided a portal into a deep, secret, safe spot. She could exit her life and discover hours later that she was still in her pajamas. Even music didn't provide such a great escape.

Picking up her mug with both hands, Zoey guided it to her mouth. She skimmed the new material yet again. In the past, she'd regarded her writing process as a disorganized mess. Then she'd learned her process had a name—*Emergent Design*. Get stuff down and see where it goes. Outlining would be more practical, but to her mind, it limited where the plot might go. Emergent Design worked for her.

It drove her agent Helga crazy.

Her cell phone rang. The Playa Maria Police Department.

"Zoey," she answered.

"Detective Bowman."

She peeked at her computer. Eight o'clock. How had that happened?

"I'd like to ask you a few more questions about last night."

"Okay."

He cleared his throat. "The road where you live doesn't show up on our computer."

"Why do you need to find it?"

"Thought I'd save you the bother of coming downtown."

"You want to do this in person?" Her voice cracked. Thank God they hadn't been able to locate Harvey's place. "I'll come to the station."

Maybe the police department wouldn't care about a weed farm they stumbled upon during a homicide investigation, but if they did, a raid at peak season would destroy Harvey. His living depended on frugality, secrecy, and working like a dog. And, in the prohibitively expensive Playa Maria, her living depended on his.

"What time would you like me there?"

Bowman hesitated. "How 'bout an hour?"

"How about eleven?"

"That'll work." Dissatisfaction edged his voice.

Zoey's nerves tingled. Why would the police want to interview her at home? Another wrinkle to worry about. Harvey claimed he was legit—about as convincing as the argument for Bigfoot. The permit process had alienated growers with a lot more patience for bureaucracy than Harvey. She knew from her *Cannabis Cutter* research that Harvey disliked rules—except his own. Those he considered a code.

She took a gulp of coffee that had gone cold and bitter as she scanned the last bit of her Word document. Her protagonist, Officer Horne, witnessed the shooting of his friend Stan, moved into the open, and was shot, but Zoey couldn't catch the thread. *What next?* The answer hung like a fruit high in a tree, hidden by leaves. Or maybe, behind the leaves, there was no fruit at all. She heaved a sigh and checked for a message from Jimmy.

Nope. She considered possibilities: A. He'd been the last one to leave a message, so the ball was in her court. B. He might be at a job like a normal person. C. If he didn't have to go to work, after being up until three a.m., he might still be sleeping. Or, D. He had ghosted her.

She sent Jimmy a quick message. *Wanna meet up today?* Now that she had to go into town anyway, she might as well get a better sense of him in some place public and full of people.

Since she'd slid into the online vortex, she braced herself and opened the electronic edition of the local paper. The photo and headline, LOCAL OFFICER SLAIN, landed a punch to her solar plexus.

The previous night returned in full force—Officer Austin's ruined skull, the car zooming toward the scene, the shrilling sirens. Her heart revved up like a racecar. Sweat beaded her forehead. As fast as the feverish sensation gripped her, chills replaced it. Her body shook.

She tried to focus her eyes on the computer screen. Officer Stanley Austin. Another jolt. *Stanley? As in Stan!*

She jumped from her seat, flicking her hands and arms to rid herself of the information. Sweat trickled down her temples. Maybe if the guy's name were common, like David or Michael, she could wave it off as coincidence. *But Stan!* That was too weird—like she'd cursed Officer Austin, written him a deathblow, a *coup d'gras*. She rubbed the goose bumps on her bare arms and struggled to pull in air. "You did not cause this, Zoey," she whispered. "Be rational."

Stan was not *that* uncommon. It wasn't like she'd named her character Peyton, and then the officer shot was named Peyton.

She took three rubbery steps to the small back window. Harvey's grow spread in rows from the rear of his house, with a few plants running up along the side. The slope and the elevation of her Tiny House on wheels allowed her to see over the fence and glimpse Harvey bobbing among the tops of his plants. The buttons pinned to the crown of his hat glinted in the sun.

Relieved not to be alone, she slid open the window, though she didn't necessarily want to talk to Harvey.

Even from that distance, he turned toward the sound. Maybe he'd been alerted by Rambo. Out of sight, the dog would be hunkered beside him, ears pricked. Harvey wiped his forehead with an arm. He didn't wave to the trailer window. Maybe he'd felt rebuffed by her last night. Or maybe he was tired. He'd checked on her in the wee hours, no doubt Rambo's barking had woken him, too, and she'd heard that banging before dawn. *The barn door?* The farm was too damn much work for one man, especially someone who must be pushing seventy. She slid the window all the way open with a satisfying *thunk* and sucked in the fresh air of the redwoods.

Harvey glanced in her direction and tipped the brim of his raffia hat.

Zoey went back to the table and steeled herself to continue the online article. The piece mentioned a witness, but not her name. Thank God for small favors.

No known motive.

And then the heart-wrenching part—the survivors. The wife, Christine, his high-school sweetheart; a son, Robert, in his first year at Cal Poly; and two daughters, Grace and Elizabeth, students at Playa Maria High School.

Stanley Austin had been forty-three years old. A teacher for nine years before becoming a police officer. She wondered what he'd done in his twenties and if he'd gone into education more as a way to support his young family than as a calling.

She put keywords into a search to see if anything else came up.

A YouTube video!

Her chest heaved in short, quick spasms. Rubbing her breastbone, she waited and then clicked play.

The camera made a slow, blurry pan of the crime scene, ending with a shot of her—eyes wide, hair wild, face streaked red and blue from the police lights.

Jimmy! Her fingers curled. If his neck were there, she'd strangle it. He hadn't even given her a heads-up.

The last thing she needed was her face connected with a crime and broadcast to the world.

Chapter Seven

Day 2

Jared's skin prickled. His breath came jagged as he huffed along Scenic Boulevard. Two miles across town. Sucking in pollution from four lanes of traffic. Adolph, the boss, had no friggin' idea everything he was going through.

It wasn't like he'd wanted to shoot a cop. But all those charges—fraudulent use of a license plate, illegal possession of a firearm, transporting controlled substances.... Not just weed, but the baggies of heroin Stuart had tucked in the wheel well.

His boots smacked along the sidewalk. Now there was this. He didn't want to shoot the girl, either. If he was going to shoot someone, it should be that dickwad, Adolph.

Or maybe his high school biology teacher, who'd referred him to the school psychologist. Or better yet, Mrs. Godinez, who, right in the middle of conjugating *echar*, had turned from her whiteboard, froze, and with a look like she might vomit, ordered him to take his finger out of his nose.

Back then, his mother came to his defense, complaining to the vice-principal that there had been no need for Mrs. Godinez to humiliate him. The vice-principal agreed, and afterward Jared had made a point of picking his nose whenever Mrs. Godinez looked his way. *Fuck her.* Fuck anyone who gave him shit.

But what could he do in this situation? If he didn't shoot the girl, Adolph would have him killed. And seriously, Jared thought, wouldn't it be easier for Adolph to off him and use him as cannabis fertilizer? A small backhoe was parked right beside the Brussels sprouts shed. Who would pay any attention to disturbed soil on a friggin' farm?

Jared had exhausted his list of people who might own a police scanner. Even in his world, that had been a grand total of two, one who was crazier than him and the other who'd like to whoop his ass. Neither had tuned in last night.

Out of breath, he slowed to a stroll. On the far side of the highway, garages, a yogurt shop, and a senior housing development; on this side, brush and trees, like civilization dropped off the edge of Scenic Boulevard. Coolness drafted out of the ravine, drying his sweat.

Stuart, Adolph's main man, had a scanner, but if Stuart had been listening last night, the boss wouldn't have been so surprised when Jared showed up.

Now, because he couldn't keep making incriminating calls on his mom's landline, he was hoofing it across town to Bill's Place, home of what must be the last pay phone in Playa Maria County.

The boulevard curved back toward the center of town. He stepped into the gutter to get around someone who'd set up a cardboard-and-tarp home on the sidewalk.

He reached the customers lined up in front of Bill's Place, waiting for one of the red booths or tables inside. As he cut up to the front door, a beefy guy said, "Hey, buddy."

"I'm not getting food," Jared muttered. "Just using the phone."

The place was packed and humid, smelling of coffee and pancakes. Jared slipped into the phone booth at the back and called the police department, digging the rotary dial, proud that he knew how to use it. A clipped, female voice answered.

"Uh…." He flushed. This reminded him of when Mrs. Godinez used to spring questions on him. In class. In Spanish. "Uh…."

The official-sounding woman repeated that he'd reached Playa Maria Police Department. "Can I help you?"

He blurted, straight-up asked who'd been with Officer Austin when he was shot.

Cold silence. "Who are you?"

He slammed the receiver onto its metal cradle and hurried from the diner, bumping into a man who'd been summoning the next lucky group to get a table. Jared's breath caught. The friggin' dude looked like a young Adolph.

Quit trippin'.

Across the street there was a bus stop but Jared kept moving along Scenic until he spotted the bus coming that would take him back across town to Target. He ran full out to catch it at its next stop. Until he had a line on the witness, it was better, he figured, to save the money Adolph had given him for a rental car.

At Target, he bought a burner phone, thinking about the money draining from the damp pocket of his shirt. He walked home, smoking a blunt to relax. Zero effect.

The house was quiet. It was just him and his mom, and she put in long hours at the county building. Every so often she griped, "Your dad said he didn't want to be married or have kids. Be nice if he thought of that a little earlier."

Jared didn't care. His dad was a dickwad who used to "take him" from time to time. About the only good thing he ever did was teach him to shoot.

He sank into the couch and watched the second hand *click, click, click* around the wall clock. Waited for the front door to open.

It was a carpool day, so the car hadn't been an issue in the morning. But now he would have 'some explaining to do.'

* * *

"Totaled?" She stood there with her pudgy hands planted on her hips. "Where is it then?"

"Towed." He stayed slouched down on the couch, trying to play it off as not a big deal.

"Towed where?"

"Maybe it's a blessing in disguise." He parroted one of her pet phrases.

"You've been wanting a new car."

She frowned down at him, the brown cushions absorbing his exhaustion, his long legs splayed under the coffee table.

"So my car is totaled?" Her eyes narrowed. "But you're fine?"

"Do you want me to be hurt?" He jacked himself up and let his voice rise, as though angry and wounded. "Is that it, Mom? Wish I was dead?" He yanked at the front of his slinky shirt. The snaps popped open like a line of firecrackers. His mom retreated.

Their relationship had been this way for a while. Probably since he'd gotten his growth and filled out. He looked down. Except for his legs. They were still skinny.

Even if his mom clamped her mouth and trundled away to the kitchen, he knew she didn't believe him. Cynicism weighted her ass like sandbags—all those years as a court reporter, sitting, typing, absorbing the worst about people, filling her with heaviness. Her steps clomped.

He stood up. Disappointment radiated off the stoop of her back. She washed her hands, squirting soap and more soap.

When he edged up to her, she stiffened. Would it matter to her, he wondered, if she knew his life was in danger? Not from Adolph. That guy was a pussy. But Adolph had workers a person should pay attention to. After all, Jared was one of them, and he'd offed a cop. But that had been a one-time thing—almost an accident—he wasn't like that. Adolph's main man, Stuart, for all his Kiwanis haircut and polo shirts, he was like that—a stone-cold psychopath, who'd enjoy taking care of the situation if Jared didn't. But Stuart wouldn't be going after the girl. He'd be coming for him.

Chapter Eight

Detective Bowman didn't look like he'd lost sleep, but with a rumpled face like his, who could tell? He ushered Zoey into his office—basically a cubicle with a door—rather than an interview room. "Coffee?"

She seated herself on a stiff metal-and-fabric chair and shook her head. She respected coffee too much to drink the swill a police department would serve. Besides, her stomach churned.

The detective's overture seemed too friendly, amping her wariness. He'd already done a computer search for the road on which she lived. As she'd told him last night, she didn't have a house number, only a P.O. box.

If the PMPD had been able to locate her, would they have simply shown up at her trailer? What else had they checked?

Her mother said she was too jaded. Zoey didn't think so. Or, if she was, Camille had a lot of nerve to say it, being the primary cause of Zoey's loss of faith in humanity.

"Let's get down to business, then." The detective spun his chair around, hitched up his pant legs, and sat. His aftershave spiced the small office. "Thanks for coming in."

"Sure," she said, even though she often streamed crime shows and found herself propped in bed, muttering at a character on the computer screen: "Don't talk, you idiot. Just say 'I want a lawyer.'" But here she was, about to talk to a homicide detective without uttering the magic words. Like the characters in the shows, she was acting from the naïve place of *Why shouldn't I cooperate? I haven't done anything.*

In spite of the computer on Bowman's desk, papers threatened an avalanche from both sides. Last night, a police officer had escorted her to an austere interview room. The detective's office managed to be bleaker, the light of day highlighting the gloom of a floor-to-ceiling modular office with no décor. But the move to his office was a positive sign, wasn't it?

Zoey locked her bare arms across her torso, knowing the gesture squashed her cleavage into the scooped neckline of her blouse, but the room was chilly. She tried to stay still, but her index finger rubbed the reptilian texture of her tattoo.

Bowman trained steady eyes on her face. He cleared his throat. "A few details have emerged since last night."

Her freckled arms tightened over her blouse, the one she wore for book signings, a flowing pear-green number that accentuated her eyes. The chair kept her rigidly upright, but she tried to wriggle taller. At times it seriously sucked to be short—like when you were going eye-to-eye with a police detective. She waited for him to get on with it.

Bowman scratched at his hair, buzz-cut like a military man's. "So, you said last night you're a writer."

"Yes."

"*Cannabis Cutter. Craze.*"

"Yes." Even if the detective had just clicked on Amazon, that was more investigation of her than she wanted him to do.

He took a slug of coffee and grimaced. "You made a wise choice." He parked his paper cup. "This tastes old enough to drive." His index finger traced the groove curving from his nose to the side of his mouth down to his chin.

His shaving, Zoey thought, must require a lot of lifting and stretching of skin. He seemed old for an organization where a person could retire comfortably at fifty-five.

"I guess you save your words for paper."

She smiled, a quick little pull back of the lips that she couldn't stop.

Bowman leaned back into his chair. "That was quite a story you left in our patrol car."

Zoey touched one of the musical notes inked on her arm. "That's my WIP."

"Say what?"

"Work in progress."

The detective inhaled and exhaled, long and audible. "How did you come up with that name—Stan?"

Is this when she should say, "I want a lawyer"? Her heart pounded beneath her arms. "I've been wracking my brain about that."

Now the detective crossed his arms over permanent-press blue. He leaned back even more, his chair squeaking. "And?"

She bit her lip, wondering if she should continue. "For research, I read local crime coverage. Maybe I previously saw Officer Austin's name, and my subconscious filed it."

"Maybe."

"Last night wasn't my first encounter with the police." She braced herself for what was coming.

"Interesting word *encounter*," Bowman said.

"Not really." She dug deep for the charm some claimed she possessed. "Now, *happenchance*, that's an interesting word."

"This is a murder investigation, Ms. Kozinski." Bowman tipped forward, his eyes drilling into her. "Of a police officer. A family man." Each word hit like a bullet.

The sound, the popping of the gun, blasted again in Zoey's ears. Her right eye spasmed. Heat seared through her. She tried to pull a breath. "I'm sorry. I haven't slept." She hugged herself, gripping her torso more tightly.

"So, what about this assault and battery charge?"

Anger bubbled up in her, welcome in a way, because it dispelled the impending panic. She thought of the ways—the hundreds of ways—Camille had damaged her life. She'd written about it indirectly, had changed the circumstances around and used the material in *Craze*. That had been cathartic. But the toxic fallout of her relationship to her mother kept raining down.

"The San Francisco DA decided not to pursue that charge when my mom said she wouldn't testify. As you know." Zoey planted sweaty palms on the narrow arms of her chair and leaned forward. "Do I need my lawyer?" She dipped one hand into a pocket of her slacks, taking out her phone. She didn't have a lawyer, but knew one—the wife of the She Cat's drummer.

Bowman settled his hammy buttocks. "No need for that," he replied calmly. "Just a couple more questions."

Her muscles ached against the upright back of the chair. "Let's keep the interrogation about the slaying of Officer Austin then."

The detective had no business asking about the incident with her mom. He was doing more checking into her background than necessary unless he was suspicious of her. But then he had to check out anyone at the scene, and the notes she'd left in the cruiser hadn't helped matters. She couldn't remember everything she'd jotted on the yellow pad. But the pages she'd printed out of her story opened with the killing of a cop named Stan, enough to make anyone wonder.

"There's info written on the paper you left in the cruiser," the detective said, as though he'd been swimming in her stream of consciousness. "Did you make those notes during the ride-along?"

"Yes."

"Did you have reason to believe Officer Austin was a...." He stuck a finger in his ear and wiggled it, "...*hot-head*?"

"No." Her response sounded too vehement. "That was an idea for my character." The detective's stare intensified. She could almost see him thinking *the lady doth protest too much, methinks.* Or, some non-Shakespearean equivalent.

"How 'bout *harbors a secret*?" He leaned toward her. "Did Officer Austin share something with you? Did you learn something that might shed light on this shooting?"

"No! No. Absolutely not." She popped out of her seat. *Shut up, Zoey. Stop talking.* But she couldn't. "I'm telling you, I was developing a character. The Stan name was pure coincidence."

With a hand patting the air, Detective Bowman motioned for her to sit, and she perched on the chair.

"I'm not much for *coincidence.*"

"Neither am I. It's anathema in fiction."

He squinted hard at her as though he thought she was being a smart ass again. "As a crime writer, you know the law about impeding investigations?"

She returned the coldest stare she could muster. "That suggestion is downright offensive."

The detective was unfazed. "You wrote *Austin* seemed *pissed*. Not *Stan*. Was Officer Austin *pissed* when he made the traffic stop?"

She hesitated, gauging the significance of her response. What would it mean to the department? To the investigation? To Austin's family? To Bowman's apparent suspicion of her? "Officer Austin seemed agitated—irritated—that the car hadn't stopped." She added quickly, "I don't blame him."

"You said the car was a white sedan." Bowman's voice remained neutral, but a thick finger brushed along the side of his mouth, back to the deep crease.

His tell, Zoey thought. She nodded to indicate she still agreed with her statement. The car was a white sedan.

"And the left taillight was out," he added.

"Yes."

"Have you remembered anything else since last night?"

"The taillight was rectangle-ish. Horizontal."

The detective reached back for a small pad of paper. He swiveled forward and made a note. "Did the car double back?"

Her heartbeat quickened. "I don't know. Why?"

"Police dispatched from Half Moon Bay drove toward our crime scene while our cruisers traveled north."

"And nothing?"

"He either went to ground or doubled back before we arrived on the scene." A finger floated down his marionette wrinkle like a raft drifting on a lazy river. All the way to under his jaw. "*One* white sedan we know about for certain."

"Jimmy's?" Her voice cracked.

"Jimmy, huh?"

"But he stopped," she protested. "At the scene. What kind of killer would do that?"

"You know the answer to that."

A psychopath, wanting to witness his carnage. To relive the thrill of the crime. To experience all over again the rush.

Or, someone who wants to clean up a loose end. She shivered. "There are lots of roads off Highway One. Ways to disappear into the mountains." Why was she jumping to Jimmy's defense? She knew nothing about him. He'd posted that disgusting video and hadn't responded about meeting up.

The detective watched her like he was wondering the same thing.

"You have the license plate number," she said. "Officer Austin called it in."

"How long before *Jimmy* showed up on the scene?" he asked.

"Not long enough to swap plates, if that's what you're implying. It couldn't have been more than five minutes."

Bowman didn't respond.

"And what about the not-working taillight?" she asked. "Did Jimmy's car have a taillight out?"

Bowman tapped his notepad. "Anything else you remember about the car?"

Did the detective not believe her? She remembered, with a sick feeling, that Austin had not told dispatch his exact reason for the traffic stop. The PMPD had only her word about the taillight. Did they have some bizarre theory—based on her notes—she was in cahoots with Jimmy.... But if that were the case, why would she have told them the car was white like Jimmy's? They had to realize that made no sense. She shook her head.

"That's a negative?"

"I feel like there's something, something floating right over here." She waved her hand at the right side of her brain. "Some important detail, but I can't grasp it."

"That happens with acute stress situations like this one. If the memory comes, inform us. Immediately."

Like she didn't know what acute stress disorder was. Warmth crept up Zoey's neck. The flush brought with it the taunt from childhood schoolmates: *Tomato! Nah-nuh-nah-nuh-nah-nuh. Red as tomato! Squishy as tomato. Icky as tomato.* Each fresh taunt cramped her tummy until sometimes her mom had to send whatever nanny or caretaker they had at the moment to fetch her. The memories fanned the heat into a flame. Some people, like Harvey, thought her blushing was adorable, but she would sacrifice a pinky to get rid of it. Zoey cleared her throat. "I was thinking about why I couldn't tell you the make of the car."

"And?"

"All those white sedans look alike, but as a writer, I notice detail." Her throat was dry, her voice croaky. "And since you have my papers, you can see I took notes. I think the back metal logo was missing. Which makes sense. The car was a beater."

The tip of the detective's pen pressed into the pad but didn't move. "Are we in the realm of fact or fiction?"

Zoey tamped down her temper. Did he think her writer's imagination was running wild? His imagination was the one needing an edit. He'd questioned her as though entertaining the idea she was some violent person who attacked her mom and now had participated in the murder of a police officer. To what end?

Bowman wiggled forward in his seat. "The plates were stolen from an old lady's vehicle kept in an open carport. She didn't even notice her plates were missing. We're working on the theory the shooter was driving the same model car."

"Which was?"

He regarded her. "I suppose for you," he said, unable to squelch his scorn, "this is exciting material for a book." His tone was a warning—the model of the car along with other details of the crime—were none of her business. Officer Austin mattered. She didn't, except as a witness or a suspect.

She stood, the chair skidding on the tile. She lifted her chin defiantly. "When will I be able to retrieve my notes, Detective Bowman?"

"When we decide to release them."

"I guess you'll be in touch then." The muscles along her jaw ached.

Bowman rose wearily. "I apologize. That was uncalled for." Dark circles ringed his eyes. "Could we get directions to your house, Ms. Kozinski?"

She shook her head. *No way in hell.*

"Thank you for coming in." He extended his hand, but she ignored it and flounced out, fighting angry tears. It was childish, but she couldn't help herself. The ride-along had been the worst night of her life. She'd come down here, and for what? To be insulted? To have it implied that she couldn't be trusted for a myriad of reasons—the trauma or a wild imagination or some nefarious plot to kill a police officer. To have it be almost directly stated that she was a heartless bitch, who'd only care about the killing as *material* for a book.

Outside the station, she used her phone to check Facebook. No response from Jimmy about meeting up. She stalked down the broad, stately steps. A breeze had kicked up from the ocean a half mile away, ruffling the flags. In spite of the sunshine, a chill shivered down her spine.

She wasn't a bad person because she wanted her notes. The scrawls on those papers embodied her next step. Her inspiration. The right word or two could prime the pump, and a thousand words might come gushing out, providing an escape from her current hell. Without the notes, she felt dried up. And trapped. The cops were holding her brain hostage.

Chapter Nine

Before Zoey reached her house, her cell phone rang to Billy Gibbons' "Sal y Pimiento," as different as possible, she thought, from her mom's "Habanera" from *Ballet Carmen*. Her face flushed with humiliation at the memory of the interview dredging up the one time her conflict with her mother had become physical, when Zoey had lost it.

The caller ID announced Helga. Her agent. She let the call go to voicemail. She was driving over a dangerous, rutted dirt road, after all. She returned the phone to the junk holder between the seats.

She slammed to a halt outside her tiny home—a trailer, really, since it sat on small tires—but a cool trailer with a façade of the three fiberglass sections painted red, aqua, and yellow. Above them, the part that slanted up to her loft was done in cedar shingles.

The phone rang again as she slid from the car. Thank God it wasn't Helga trying back.

"What's up?"

A husky voice said, "Tonight Brianna wants us all to wear our red anklets and red shirts." Part of the She Cats' popularity stemmed from no one quite believing this voice came out of lead singer Sabrina Wilson's skinny body.

"Got it." Before crossing the scrub grass, Zoey leaned against the warm metal of her Element and inhaled the freshness of the surrounding redwoods. She was exhausted, but the gig offered a respite.

"Why're you sniffing?"

"Forest bathing."

"Huh?"

"Sucking up phytoncides to lower my blood pressure."

Zoey waited, not for Sabbie to ask about phytoncides—because she wouldn't—but because Sabrina wanted something more, or she would've texted.

"You know what Kath—"

"I can't talk now, Sabbie. Sorry." Zoey disconnected. Sabbie would be pissed, but there wasn't any other way. Sabbie spewed verbal diarrhea, and her beefs with Kath, the She Cats' drummer, never ceased, probably because Kath was gorgeous, and Sabbie perceived her as competition, never mind that Kath had been married for several years.

Her phone vibrated with an incoming text. Sabbie was a lot like her mom and couldn't take a hint. Camille, Zoey thought, should have been the front for a band, capitalizing on her narcissism the way Sabbie did. Lead singer made a perfect outlet for the need to take center stage.

Zoey resisted looking at the message, pushed away from the warm metal of the car, and focused on the fence that ran behind her house, from the edge of a wooded ravine to the side of Harvey's house. The dirt lot in front was missing Harvey's rusty truck.

A crow cawed into the silence.

Billy Gibbons started singing again. Zoey felt like flinging her phone into the ravine. You could mute it, she chastised herself. With the isolation here, maybe it was a good thing people called, although there was no ID on this call. She didn't recognize the number.

She answered at the same moment she entered her house and remembered the red clothes she needed for the gig were swilling in the cube for dirty clothes.

"Yeah, Millard Cranston here." The identity of the caller thudded her back to the reality of the murder. Millard Cranston was *Playa Maria Reporter's* finest.

She took two steps to the hamper cube and pushed around dirty clothes with her free hand, angry with herself for answering.

Most of the paper's reporters fell into three categories—ambitious ones that moved on to the big leagues like the *L.A. Times*, good ones who stuck around because they liked Playa Maria, and journalists who sucked and couldn't find work elsewhere.

Millard Cranston didn't fit any of these types. He was a strong writer who seemed to detest everything about Playa Maria—the beaches littered with tourists, the culture like a county fair, the homelessness an apocryphal blight. He took pride in being a curmudgeon. And why not? His abrasiveness had made him a local celebrity.

"How can I help you, Millard Cranston?" Her words were pleasant, but her tone wasn't. She fished the red socks and red tee-shirt from her laundry.

"Looks like you'll be in the paper for something other than your books." He obviously meant the police shooting, and yet the man sounded gleeful.

"I don't think so." She sniffed the musty tee-shirt. "I didn't agree to any interview."

"Helga Bosworth might have something to say about that."

"Is that how you got my number?" She spread the tee on the table and tried to iron it with her hand, the rhinestone She Cats bumpy under her palm. Helga wouldn't give out her number—with one gaping exception— free publicity. The downside of having an agent who acted as though she were also a publicist.

Cranston chortled. The sound should be sold to Hollywood to dub for their villains. "So whatdayasay?"

"Meet me at the Suds 'n Duds laundromat on Scenic." She may as well get it over with or she'd have hell to pay with Helga, who was probably already tempted to drop her. "Two-ish?"

"*Ish?*" His voice dripped contempt. She imagined him rolling his beady eyes. "Two."

She bundled her dirty clothes into a dirty bath towel. She considered cancelling with She Cats. They mostly played covers of rocking girl bands from the Bangles through Garbage that could get by without keyboards. But if she didn't go, she'd be stuck in her house, her mind obsessively looping the horrific image of Officer Austin lying by the road. She'd be alone to fume at the way Detective Bowman had questioned her and to castigate herself for leaving her papers in the police cruiser.

Playing music would distract her at a time of day when her brain was too fried for writing but it was too early for sleep. If she could ever sleep now that Bowman had reinforced the idea the killer might have driven by the crime scene. Might know of her existence.

Still, going to a gig, having life march on with a semblance of normality, was whacked.

Zoey weighed the options. The gig included a free meal. Because Sabbie considered her anorexia a lifestyle choice, if Zoey went early, she could take comfort in the company of her bandmates—the closest thing she had to family—without Sabbie's presence. And she hadn't eaten breakfast, hadn't eaten anything since before her ride-along with Officer Austin.

Her phone rang again. Another unknown number. Not marked as spam. Unusual. She was protective of her cell number.

Fool me once. She didn't pick up.

After a moment, she checked her messages. Helga hadn't left one. Had Helga rung to give her a heads-up about Cranston, or for another reason, like wanting to see a first chapter?

Sabbie had texted *"cunt"* in response to Zoey cutting off her call. That didn't matter. Even though Sabbie was the lead singer, Brianna ran the band, and once they started rocking, Sabbie would be basking in the attention of the crowd, not thinking about Zoey.

There were no other messages. She'd picked up the call from Millard Cranston. The last call, the second unknown number, remained a mystery.

In spite of the YouTube video and the big question of how he could have obtained her number, a part of her hoped the call had been from Jimmy.

* * *

Zoey leaned against the laundromat dryer, the warmth pleasant against her back. Millard Cranston entered, frowning when he spotted her. She didn't trust guys with beards, not even hipsters who sported them as a style. What were they hiding?

With Millard Cranston, the full gray beard not only hid his face, but could conceal a derringer. It came all the way down so it covered the top of the palm tree on his black rayon shirt.

Cranston propped himself against a washer. It wasn't in use, but when he placed his tiny tape recorder on top of it, the device hopped around anyway, a machine down the row passing along its vibration. He shifted the recorder to a stainless-steel table.

"You got here early." His voice was even more scabrous than usual.

She'd never intended to arrive after him. She'd changed out of her nice blouse into a sweatshirt, swapped out her sandals for Keds, and grabbed a stick of string cheese because that was all she had on hand, and then headed for town with her bundle of laundry.

She ambled over to the table and parked her Klean Kanteen filled with strong coffee. "No chitchat. Let's stick to business."

Cranston pulled a notepad from a pocket of his cargo pants. "Yeah, you have a reputation as a tough nut. Guess that comes with writing crime fiction."

She squinted at him, her eyes grainy. "Is that a question?"

The reporter placed the pad on the table and stretched unencumbered hands out from the side of his body, as though illustrating the length of a fish he'd caught. "*Cop Killing Witnessed by Crime Writer.*"

"That the best you've got?"

"*Famous Author Witnesses Cop Killing.*"

"Better." She glanced toward the dryer. "But I'm not famous, except maybe in Playa Maria, and I'm not very famous here."

"You make a living from writing."

Barely. And Camille would argue with even that. Zoey ignored the thought and retorted, "So do you."

"Yeah," he said, "and I'm pretty well known."

"Could we get on with it?" She worked a pink scrunchie from her pocket and hitched her mane into a ponytail. "It's not like you guys get to write the headlines anyway."

Cranston shot a look at the dryer, her shirt and socks bright in a wetly clotted mass. "Doesn't look like you're going anywhere soon."

Doesn't mean I want to talk to you. The guy wore Birkenstocks, which should be against the law, especially if you had thick yellow toenails.

"Ready?" His finger hovered above the record button.

"Go ahead." She sighed. One way or the other, tomorrow her name would be in the *Playa Maria Reporter*.

Cranston ran through the same questions she'd answered at the police station, hammering her with the nightmare—the body, the blood, the lights.

He could record away. Once he revealed that she lived in Playa Maria, other details concerning her hardly mattered. They wouldn't change what had happened or what was about to happen.

Chapter Ten

The yeasty smell of the Poorboy brewpub enfolded Zoey, the noise of the crowd echoing off the high concrete walls and huge stainless-steel tanks. As she sat at the bar, Brianna's arm circled her shoulder. "You look like shit."

"Feel like it, too." Zoey ordered the IPA, and the barmaid swung toward a tap. "But at least my shirt is nice and fresh."

Big and steady, Brianna was a typical bass player. "What's up?"

"The cop killing."

Brianna bobbed her head. By now the whole town of Playa Maria had heard the news, although not her part in it. "Drug-related," Brianna pronounced.

"Where did you hear that?" The barmaid plunked down the beer. Zoey leaned over and sucked up the first taste without lifting the mug. It was hoppy, almost as bitter as grapefruit. She licked foam from her top lip. "That fuck boy who's been sniffing around you? Isn't he Harbor Patrol? How would he know?"

Brianna shrugged. "The Boys in Blue talk to one another?" She tried Zoey's beer and wrinkled her nose. "Ugh."

Zoey considered the drug connection idea. How would the police have established that? Was it merely an attempt to ascribe a reason to the horrendous event?

"You going to write about it?" Brianna leaned forward, pendulous breasts grazing the counter. "Hey, Skye," she addressed the bartender, "how about a pale ale and the special?"

"You got it."

The place was filling up. A lot had happened during the short span after the sound check when Zoey had been packing up equipment she wouldn't need.

Kath's wife had joined her at the other end of the room. They were engaged in a conversation that didn't look like it should be interrupted. No surprise there. Kath's wife slaved at a draining Family Law practice while Kath drummed at random gigs. Even at a brewpub, they looked like an illustration of opposites, the wife in a slinky blouse; Kath in ripped jeans and an ancient Bikini Kill tee. Kath pressed buff arms into the counter and lifted herself, her big eyes searching across the room. Zoey turned away and sipped her drink, not wanting to be drawn into their conflict.

After the sound check, Andrea, the lead guitarist, had disappeared out the back to get stoned. No surprise there, either. And Sabbie would leave them warming up the crowd and enter late as the prima donna rock star she thought she was.

Her surrogate sibs, Zoey thought.

The bartender delivered Brianna's pale ale, on the house for the band. Brianna slipped her a dollar tip. A glow lightened Brianna's hazel eyes, signaling the go-ahead for whatever Zoey had to unload.

Zoey bent close. "I was there. At the shooting." The six words fluttered her stomach.

"Whatdaya mean?"

"I was with the cop doing a ride-along for research."

"Are you kidding me?" Bri's eyes widened. She leaned in even closer so they were practically touching foreheads.

"I'm not. But I can't talk about it now. It's too much."

"No shit." Bri's stare bored into her. "Are you sure you should be here?" She pulled back a couple of inches to assess Zoey.

"I was fine during sound check. Seriously, I can't wait to start playing again. Drive the nightmare out of my skull."

"Okay, then." Bri's red lips puckered. "When you're ready, I want deets." She tipped forward so their foreheads did touch. A sort of kiss.

Zoey spun forward on her stool and took another sip of the hoppy IPA. She wanted to get this party started. She tapped her foot on a ledge under the counter, a detail a short-legged person fully appreciated.

Bri's plate arrived—locally produced sausages, steaming and peppery, with a thick brown slab of buttered bread.

Faint with hunger, Zoey stared at the food, but couldn't imagine eating. Even the bit of mozzarella she'd had earlier lumped in her stomach.

Bri motioned to the waitperson. "Bring this girl some bread before she falls off her stool."

* * *

When Sabbie gyrated in her black leather mini and tossed her blonde hair, no one cared her bones could snap like pretzels. The woman was five-foot-seven and didn't top a hundred pounds, but like Krazy Glue, she fastened eyeballs.

To call the performance space a *stage* would be way too generous. It was more of a step-up rise in the floor, with shiny beer vats corralling Zoey closer to her piano than she liked. But right now, she was content to be squeezed in the back with Kath, who'd managed to throw on her She Cats tee at the last minute.

Kath was drumming, tossing her shorn black hair, as though beating out the latest argument with her wife. "Queer" from Garbage was like her anthem, anyway. Zoey pounded a simple power-chord progression with the rock organ voice on her keyboard. All she had to do was lay down a pan—the same three chords over and over—so she didn't have to concentrate. She spotted Jimmy when he entered, his head above most of the crowd.

She hit a G major, instead of the minor, jarringly wrong, but quickly corrected. Brianna gave her a look and a little smile. No one else indicated they'd noticed.

Jimmy lifted his chin at her in greeting.

This brewery attracted people his age, but she would have noticed him if she'd seen him there before. The eye-patch thing was hard to miss. On the other hand, she never came to Poorboy Brew unless the band was booked. He could be a regular for all she knew. He leaned over the drinkers at the bar and ordered without studying the selections.

As the band finished the song, Sabbie twirled the mic-stand like a baton.

The thunk of the stand hitting the floor banged Zoey back to her senses. Even if Jimmy was familiar with the brewery, it was damn coincidental that he was here now. In Playa Maria there were more breweries to choose from than yoga studios.

He must have seen her event listing on Facebook. What would that mean? Did it count as stalking when she'd left the ball in his court? When this was a public space? When something sparked at seeing him?

She remembered Detective Bowman's words: *One white sedan we know about for certain.*

The implication was crazy. If the shooter had an eyepatch, she would have noticed. But would she have? She hadn't seen the guy's face. He'd turned, but not fully. The only light had been from the patrol car.

A memory flitted by like a fragment of a dream she couldn't quite recall. There, but not there.

Flinging her hair over a shoulder, Sabbie twisted to face the band. "Jump to *Check Mate.*" Turning, Sabbie swung her hand down in a dramatic cue. Kath hammered out the four-bar drum intro, Sabbie's narrow hips grinding. Sabbie pedaled a single note for two more bars, a low-throated growl. Then the band crept in.

Check Mate was Sabbie's own song, the band's signature piece. Zoey hated to admit it, but it was a great tune. *Soulful.* A set-closer.

Jimmy's head swiveled toward Sabbie. The guy may have been an idiot for posting that video, and he had already irritated Zoey in a half dozen ways, but jealousy stabbed her. A surprise. She thought she was over everyone staring at Sabbie.

Everyone except one guy in the back. He was staring at her. *What the fuck?* She shivered. No one fixated on the keyboard player. *Maybe another keyboard player?* Or, one of those guys like Harvey with a thing for redheads.

When the band finished the set, Jimmy threaded through the crowd toward her. The bar counter separated them. Jimmy couldn't squeeze between the patrons occupying the stools and their clusters of friends. He wouldn't be able to hear her over the rumble of conversation—it was hard enough for people to hear the amplified band. She pointed to the side door near him and mouthed, "Outside." She disappeared behind the huge cylindrical vessels of local brews to take the back exit.

The back door almost smacked into a couple locked together against the brick exterior. The man's mouth didn't stop sucking the woman's neck.

Zoey slid past them. A tall fence loomed on the other side of the dark alley, making the corridor a narrow canyon filled with the pungent smell of marijuana.

"Hi."

She jumped at the disembodied voice.

A shadowy form prowled toward her. She'd expected Jimmy to wait near the side door with other customers spilling out for fresh air. She glanced back, relieved at the presence of the couple, even though they weren't coming up for air.

"Why are you here?" she blurted.

"Wow," Jimmy said. "Friendly."

His figure took shape—long hair, slender body. Broad shoulders that she hadn't noticed at the scene of the shooting. There was probably a lot she hadn't noticed.

"I'm not known for friendliness." She brushed by Jimmy toward the lighted parking lot.

"Believe it or not, I'm not stalking you. I came for a beer," Jimmy said. "And some music."

She blushed, glad it was dark and her back was to him. Maybe he was telling the truth, and she was acting like an idiot. This was Poorboy Brew's band night, a popular destination for Gen Xers and Millennials. And Playa Maria's population of 65,000 hadn't obliterated a small-town feel; if she were in a crowd, chances were she'd run into someone she knew.

Still, she turned to face him and said, "I don't believe you."

He shrugged. "I like your band."

"I like your shirt."

His arms folded across the yoke and shiny white snaps. *Easy to rip open.* He stood awkwardly for a moment before leaning back against a greenish Prius.

The crowd, thirty feet away, pooled around the light at the pub's side door. She would have preferred to be a little closer to them. "I thought you drove a white car?"

"My friend's," he said. "We came together."

"I didn't see you with anyone."

He lifted his brows, wiggling his eyepatch. "You're as bad as the cops. Are you this suspicious of everyone?"

"Well, where's your *friend?*"

He jerked a thumb toward the side entrance. "Inside."

"Let's go. I want you to point him out."

"Her."

"Point *her* out." The words burred with irritation for having been foolish— again. How totally presumptuous to think he was pursuing her. He hadn't responded to her invitation to meet up. And he'd come here with a girl, in the girl's car.

"She's just a friend," he said. "Less than that." He finger-combed one side of his long hair, tucking it behind an ear. "I barely like her." He flashed a charming smile.

"Point her out."

"Seriously, dude." He aimed his chin toward the crowd. "Unless someone lifts her up, I can't *point her out.* She's shorter than you are."

"I have to get back to the band."

"I saw your *Still here* message," he said. "And when I got home from work, I saw your invite. Guess I got the wrong idea."

She turned to face him. "So you *are* stalking me?"

"No, I totally came for a beer. I was stunned to see you. But I didn't think you'd mind seeing me."

"That YouTube video was whacked."

He tilted his head. "Why?"

He was asking seriously, and it stopped her. *Yes, why, Zoey, other than your own shock and embarrassment?* Officer Austin's family already knew about the catastrophic event. Every other day people were posting videos of horrible accidents and police shootings. It had been an impactful event for Jimmy, part of his life. Why shouldn't he post it? He didn't know she was in hiding from her mother. And what did that matter now that she'd be on the front page of the *Playa Maria Reporter*?

"The cop's family might see it," she said. "He has kids."

"I didn't think about that." He tugged at the string of his eyepatch. "I was all caught up in processing my own trauma. You know they swabbed me for gun-shot residue like I could be the killer?"

She hadn't known but wasn't surprised. "The whole thing was traumatic." She glanced toward the entrance to see if people were reentering for the second set. "I think I have PTSD." She furrowed her brow. "I might have to see someone."

"Like a therapist?"

"Yeah."

"Dang. I was hoping you meant me." He grinned.

She ran her eyes from eyepatch to long hair, down the tight jeans ending in Converse sneakers planted against the asphalt. An appealing package. And the one person who could understand the shock of her experience.

He reached out his arms. Against her better judgment, she stepped forward.

Chapter Eleven

Day 3

Jared nursed his second Venti Pumpkin Spice Latte. It contained sixty-four grams of sugar. No wonder it was delicious. Better than his grandma's pumpkin pies.

He dipped up a bit of whipped cream with his straw and licked it. Outside, a steady stream of cop cars rolled by, officers on their way to testify at the courthouse next door. He smirked at how unsuspecting they were, how unaware that he was sitting right here, under their noses.

Still, his skin crawled. Jared jabbed the straw up and down. This was serious shit. And the search for the girl…woman…was taking more effort than he'd expected. He'd started with people search programs that yielded lots of worthless stuff like her February 2nd birthday, but no address in the area, only a P.O. Box. He rolled his head, neck popping, wondering when Adolph would sic Stuart on him. If Ray was the patient type, they wouldn't all call him Adolph.

He should have shot Ray in his office when he had the chance. That was his problem, according to his mother—a lack of initiative.

He distracted himself by checking out the other customers. Seriously, could you tell a criminal duded up for court from a defense attorney in a bad suit? The older guy with the ponytail, for example. Public defender or aging hippie busted for an illegal grow? There was a lot of that now. The big money of legal pot pressuring law enforcement to clean out illegal farms.

Jared tried the drink again. Sucking hard on the straw, he siphoned up gurgling remains. A lawyer—*definitely a lawyer*—a short lesbian with freshly barbered silver hair and a tailored suit—shot him a disgusted look. "Fuck you," he mouthed. It wasn't illegal to relish the last bits of an expensive drink.

He curled over an ancient iPad, tapped away on the letters, then poked the straw up and down in the cup trying to dislodge any bits of pumpkin spice latte clinging to the sides. The cup remained dismally empty, and they cost a friggin' fortune. But he needed the sugar rush. He'd hardly slept, springing awake to check the local paper online.

And boom. His lucky day. There it was—her name: Zoey Kozinski. The witness. The loose end.

He'd come down to the coffee shop to celebrate and to continue his search, riding with his mom on the bus to her courthouse job.

She said she didn't mind the bus, but he thought she said that because she didn't want him to tag along. Maybe thought he was riding with her out of guilt? The route ran a straight shot to the courthouse, and she took the bus from time to time—when he needed the car or when an exciting case was sure to jam up the parking lot.

Before the bus door had folded shut, she'd added firmly, "You don't need to do this." She sat and smoothed her skirt. His mom must be the last woman on earth to wear pantyhose. "It won't make any difference." She meant about her feelings.

He'd leaned his head against the glass and watched the businesses of Scenic Drive flow by as they rode in silence.

In the coffee house at the corner of the courthouse parking lot, he'd made his way through his first latte without a clue. This Zoey Kozinski was one careful woman. You could tell by the images. Professional shots. Book events. Nothing casual. Nothing at her home.

Her Facebook presence was devoid of personal information. No address. No phone. No e-mail. The people search had revealed her college and old addresses in Michigan and San Francisco, but she remained an alien with green eyes. Eerily beautiful eyes that revealed nothing. Like the surface of pond water. *What's down there? What kind of fish am I gonna catch?*

The links that came up on other searches were articles about her books, about her launches—her website showing book covers and buy links. His eyes rested on the title *Cannabis Cutter.* Did she like weed?

Nothing led to a current address.

And now, at the end of his second Venti, Jared giggled with pleasure and blew specks of pumpkin spice latte out his nose. He wiped it with a napkin and shuffled his boots on the tiled floor. Pay dirt! Zoey Kozinski was part of a band. She Cats.

He googled. She Cats had a site.

And a schedule.

He slapped the top of the table in victory. Then he drummed it, earning a few dirty looks.

His attention returned to the screen. The band modeled themselves after oldie girl bands like the Go-Go's. A YouTube video showed them performing a rocking version of the Runaways' "Cherry Bomb." Too bad they'd just played that gig. They had nothing scheduled for two weeks.

Would this turn into a friggin' three-latte quest?

The site listed the band members and showed a photograph of them, a bunch of hotties, especially the lead singer. They were not likely to be as careful as this Zoey Kozinski. He typed the name for the first person listed, Brianna Brown, the bass player.

The search pulled up a line of images on the screen. Clearly only one of the Brianna Browns could be the bass player in She Cats. The name might be common, but the Brianna Brown in the band picture was a Big Woman, tall with big tits. He'd like to sink his head between them, rest in that cushiony softness, her strong arms wrapped around him. She rocked him, and his mouth latched onto—

His sagging head hit his chest. He righted himself. Even with all that caffeine and sugar, his eyelids wanted to close. He clicked around on the iPad. Forget about looks. Only one Brianna Brown lived in Playa Maria. It took him two minutes to track down an old party invitation.

And bingo, an address.

Not a specific one. The guests were invited to the Sea Breeze apartment complex for a "music jam birthday celebration." The invite's image showed a long U parking lot around a wide swath of grass. Palm trees at each end and a gazebo with picnic tables in the middle.

He didn't have Brianna's apartment number. He tried FastPeopleSearch, but that muddied the search instead of helping. Time, he decided, for the rental car and surveillance. If she lived in the development, she would be easy to spot. From there, it was one small step to Zoey Kozinski and the end of his problem.

Chapter Twelve

Zoey stared blankly at her computer screen. The computer screen stared blankly back. Nothing would come. It wasn't because of the late gig or Jimmy, although the parking lot flirtation played around the edges of her thoughts.

His kiss had been delicious enough that Brianna had come out to haul Zoey back into the brewery. But it was more than the kiss. When Jimmy's arms encircled her, she sank against his warm support, ear to his chest, his heart thumping into her.

"Argh." She bounced her fingers on the computer keyboard, rattling the keys without typing. *Admit it. He's a distraction.* But the big distraction—the real distraction to writing—was the damn video he'd posted.

This morning, she'd watched it over and over. Each time, at the end, the image of her distressed face greeted her along with a powerful flutter in her gut.

At that moment, when Jimmy had captured the image, she had been realizing something. Now she didn't know what it was. *Blotto. Zero. Zip. Nada.* The more she strained to seize the memory, the more elusive it became. It was like trying to grab a moth—to capture it would be to crush it.

She sipped her coffee. Tapped stockinged feet restlessly against the floor. And then there was Millard Cranston's article that would come out today. Was already out. She would be identified. Zoey shivered. No wonder she couldn't concentrate on her manuscript. Plus, the cops had her notes.

She needed something to help her focus. Fast. She couldn't keep avoiding and stalling with Helga.

Maybe hypnosis? Hypnotherapy. Kath had used it to quit smoking, and she'd had a two-pack-a-day habit to occupy her fingers when she wasn't drumming. Of course, now she went around drumming on everything—her lap, chair legs, other people's shoulders.

Zoey googled hypnotherapists in Playa Maria and searched for good Yelp reviews. Found one that sounded good. Two hundred dollars for the initial consultation, which seemed like a lot and very reasonable at the same time.

A recording answered, a woman's voice, a comfortable, calm alto. At the beep, Zoey left a message that didn't sound at all like the articulate woman she liked to present to the world. She should have thought through what she was going to say, but if she'd spent too long prepping, she might have chickened out.

At least she'd gotten out her two most important questions: Could this woman, Maureen Magill, help her with the anxiety, growing out of control like Audrey II? And could she help her with recall?

She needed to remember the night, to aid the police in finding the killer before the killer decided to come after her.

A rap on the glass door made her heart jump. She twisted around on the cubicle ottoman. Harvey stood there, bearing a plate. Persimmon bread, no doubt.

She kept the phone to her ear as she slid open the door. "This is really nice of you," she whispered, even though Harvey was just offloading the stuff. His tree was laden with orange globes, and he couldn't shuck off the raw fruit to anyone. Not wanting to waste the persimmons, he'd been baking for the last few weeks, as if he didn't have enough going on with his marijuana harvest.

Zoey pointed at the phone to make sure Harvey got the message.

"Okey doke," he said.

She accepted the plate—warm from the slices—and started to shut the door with her upper arm. Harvey reached up and closed the slider for her.

His tall frame loped off across the worn earth. She angled herself to watch him. Instead of entering his ramshackle white farmhouse, he kept going, which seemed odd. He turned out of sight onto the road that led down to the big barn in the back. Why not just cut through his house?

She set the plate and her phone on the counter. A cardamom scent, like cinnamon with wings, rose to her nose. She hadn't eaten since before the gig. She gobbled a slice of the bread, her mouth stuffed, when her phone rang. She gulped and washed down the cud with cold coffee, coughing a hello.

"Whatayagot, Kiddo?" Helga rasped.

"Not much." *Nothing* was more like it.

"I understand your life has been rather exciting," Helga said, "but I need the opening." The woman unnecessarily cited a passage of the contract.

"I'd have more if you hadn't sicced Millard Cranston on me."

Helga coughed. "Send me something tomorrow." She hung up.

The woman was a complete bitch. And one of the best in the industry.

* * *

Forget Helga. Forget the book. She stuffed another bite into her mouth. She had to take care of herself.

And just then the phone rang, the caller ID coming up as Magill, like a sign from the universe. The hypnotherapist not only had a cancellation for that morning, but could begin treatment today—if Zoey was so inclined— after the intake interview. And yes, she could help with what seemed to be developing into possible PTSD. But, the woman cautioned, they needed to take one step at a time. And yes, she could help with recall.

* * *

By the time Zoey pulled into the warren of nondescript brown medical buildings, her head felt like a balloon trailing behind her on a string. Something was off. *A sudden onset of the flu?*

Legs quivering, she crossed the parking lot. Was Jimmy the shooter, after all? Could he have drugged her in some way? She whirled at a sound behind her, a man crossing the parking lot in her direction, his footfalls hurried, as if he was trying to catch up to her.

Who is he? What does he want? She quickened her pace, her heart racing. His footsteps slapped faster.

"Hey," he called. "Excuse me, Miss."

She pivoted. The man huffed toward her, his hand stuck inside his jacket pocket.

A gun?

She quickened her pace. Little good that would do if the man wanted to shoot her. She should duck behind a car.

Her name was in the paper today. *The witness.* The guy could be the killer, come to tidy up.

"Hey!" the man called more insistently. "Hey, excuse me!"

Why was this man—about her age, paunchy, already losing his hair— charging up to her? She froze in confusion. Her brain felt like it was taking flight. What was wrong with her?

The man jogged to her side. "Do you know where Dr. Chen's office is?"

"Why you asking me?" In spite of the cool nip in the air, sweat gathered on her forehead.

His hand came out of his pocket. Her heart jumped. He waved his phone at her. "All out of juice."

Oh, right, the dead battery thing. "That's such a fucking cliché."

"Whoa, lady. There's no need to talk like that." He put up his palms and stepped back, stumbling off the curb. "I just thought you might know."

Panic shot through her. Did she know where she was going? Where was 2C? She spun around. Maybe Maureen Magill was a plant like at a comedy show, the whole thing a plot, to put her under and then….

Hyperventilating, she squinted at the buildings. The therapist's office was right in front of her. She pushed open the door into a waiting room, a wicker basket of magazines between two seats. Piped-in Chopin. There was a pass-through window to a reception desk, but no one sat on the other side.

A woman emerged from an inner sanctum, her black shoes big as a clown's. Zoey traced lines of burgundy corduroy up to a halo of gray Medusa hair filling the doorway. The woman was taller than Brianna, probably six foot. And while Brianna curved in complement to her stand-up bass, this woman stood like a redwood tree, and looked an authentic sixty years old. Zoey twisted and tested the doorknob to make sure the door hadn't locked behind her.

"What's wrong?" the woman asked.

Zoey placed a hand over her chest, her heart like a beast trying to escape its cage. "I may have eaten cannabis?"

"Sit down. I'm Maureen Magill, the hypnotherapist. Are you Zoey?"

Maureen Magill radiated serenity, from her soft sweater to her face. She fished a foil pouch from a dish on the pass-through counter.

Zoey sat up on the chair. "What's that?"

"Chamomile tea," the hypnotherapist said. "My guess is you're having a reaction to the pot." She filled a mug with hot water from a canister on the counter. "Is that typical for you? Or, this could be an offshoot of everything that's been happening to you. Paranoia is not uncommon with PTSD."

"I don't normally eat cannabis. I don't even smoke anymore."

"Paranoia is not a rare response to marijuana. Especially when a person ingests it."

"I know." But knowing did little to control it.

Maureen Magill extended a white mug, the tea bag floating in it. "Was this medical marijuana?"

Zoey shook her head. "It was an accident." In spite of piecing together what had happened, she stared suspiciously at the tea.

The hypnotherapist smiled faintly and folded onto the other chair. "That's my objection to edibles." The woman set the mug on the table between them, the grassy scent of chamomile wafting with the steam.

Zoey sprang up. "I have to go."

The therapist stood. "You can't drive in your condition."

"I just did." But reaching out a hand, she lowered herself again. She swam in an eddy of dizziness.

Tea would be good. She eyed the drink. She'd watched the woman prepare it, ripping open the foil and running hot water from the spigot. When could she have doctored it? There might have been something in the cup already. *That's paranoia, Zoey.* The thought was completely nuts.

She took a tentative sip.

"Very good," the therapist coaxed.

Zoey's muscles released slightly, her shoulders dropping.

"Under the circumstances, we won't be able to start treatment today."

Shoulders hunched, jaw hardened, Zoey silently cursed Harvey. What had he been thinking to give her persimmon bread with dope in it?

The therapist moved to fix a cup of tea for herself. "We could try the intake interview. If you want." She stretched far over the counter to retrieve forms and a pen as though reluctant to pass through the door and leave Zoey alone. "Would you be okay moving into my treatment room?"

"I'd rather stay here."

"If we do that, I'll have to lock the door," the therapist said. "Would that be okay with you? It will only be locked from the outside."

That seemed likely to be true. She nodded her assent.

"You can call me Maureen, if you'd like."

In the reception area, Maureen conducted the intake process, the fragrance of her peppermint tea dominating the chamomile.

Zoey slowly unfurled into the soft cushions of the chair. "Do you ever turn people away?"

"About one out of every five."

"Why?"

"They're simply not good candidates." Maureen bobbed her head thoughtfully. "And maybe another couple decide themselves that they don't want to commit the time or money." She ran an unadorned hand through hair that seemed as unmanageable as Zoey's. "If I didn't think this would benefit you, I'd tell you right now."

"Can you see me tomorrow?" Zoey asked. The therapist's soft voice had reassured her, melting away the paranoia and offering a path through the hell-scape that had become her life. Maureen was from her mother's generation, but the two women could not have been more different.

"I'll see if I can shift around a couple of things in my personal schedule,"

Maureen said. "If I can open a space, I'll give you a call. How are you feeling now?"

"I'm coming down."

Zoey promised to rest in her car. Outside, the sun was high and bright, the heat dry. The leaves of the eucalyptus along the parking lot looked gray with dust. The whole area needed rain.

The cab of her SUV was hot. She cracked the window, reclined the seat, and soaked up the September sunlight pouring through the windshield. She already felt better than she had in days.

When she blinked awake, the time shocked her—late afternoon. Since she was already in town, she sped off toward Trader Joe's.

The emotional lift from the therapist, her nap, and loading up two shopping bags with fun food, didn't last through her trip home. As though jarred awake by the bumps in the road, a light on the dash blinked on, a tiny red icon in the shape of an engine. That could not be good.

She prayed the SUV wouldn't stop. The sun already slanted behind the tops of the redwoods, creating the early twilight of forest. If she had trouble out here, no one would be passing by any time soon, and in these tall trees, cell service was spotty.

She slowed to a crawl. Threads of mist snaked from the trees and drifted low across the dirt road. The red light winked off, and then, faster than hope could arrive, came back on.

Maybe a loose wire?

When she crested the hill and her tiny house sprang into view, relief flooded her.

She stopped in front of her trailer, swung down from the Element, and retrieved the grocery bags from the cargo hold. All that space for hauling around her music gear—and a certain coolness factor—had been big selling points, but it wasn't a great vehicle for the mountain roads—too top-heavy. Not enough power.

She packed groceries into her under-the-counter refrigerator before turning her attention to the plateful of persimmon bread. She smashed a slice with a fork, which wasn't necessary. Marijuana buds curled conspicuously from the bread. She balled the mutilated slice in her hand and slammed out the door.

The fence behind her trailer that ran from Harvey's house to the ravine was meant to hide his operation. A big sign on the wood planks displayed a picture of a Doberman and the warning: *Is there life after death? Jump this fence and find out.*

An absurd sign. There was no side or back fence around Harvey's field. Unless Rambo was chained, no one needed to climb the fence to meet his maker. Rambo could come charging at any point. And Harvey had explained—more than once—that Rambo was "highly skilled," and would "detain" rather than "maul."

"With a jaw force of three-hundred and five pounds per square inch," Harvey said, "who needs to bite."

Fortunately, as part of Rambo's daily landscape, Zoey stirred less excitement than a chipmunk. If he was outside, he'd bark anyway, to alert Harvey someone was approaching the house. No sound today.

Harvey either thought no one would enter his property from the back and side canyons, or he was too cheap to enclose the half acre of farmland at the top of his rugged five acres, property that had been in Harvey's family for a century—according to him. Zoey appreciated the fence, though. With it and the breezes drafting away from her trailer, sometimes she didn't smell his plants at all.

Motion sensor lights blazed on. Harvey's GMC truck of silver and rust stood in front of his steps. Rambo barked from inside the house.

She crossed the sagging porch, yanked open the squeaky screen with her left hand, and raised her fist full of persimmon bread. Harvey cracked the door before she could knock. Beside him, Rambo gnashed his teeth—not his usual response to her. The dog must have perceived her anger. The raised fist.

"Red." Harvey smiled and hushed Rambo. "How'd you like the bread?"

"Are you kidding me, Harvey! You gave me stuff with weed in it." She opened her hand to display the wad.

Ears pricked, Rambo growled low in his throat.

"Rambo," Harvey said. Rambo backed off, but bared his teeth and snarled. Harvey latched onto the dog's collar. "Hey, now, Rambo, you know Zoey."

The dog whined like he regretted he couldn't have a piece of her.

"Come on, Red," Harvey said. "I don't give away product. Not even to my favorite people." He patted the dog on its haunches until Rambo sat in submission. He released his hold. "I'd go out of business. It's hard enough with prices in the shithole."

This was Harvey's standard lament—the ways legalization had hurt business. Although he was legit, of course.

Zoey elevated onto the balls of her feet. "You don't believe me?" This pissed her off more than the cannabis-laced bread. She cut an eye to Rambo. If the dog decided she was a threat, he could lunge at lightning speed. Harvey called him his "forty-five-mile-per-hour weapon." But she couldn't stop. "Look at the evidence." She thrust her hand at Harvey.

The dog sprang. She jumped back.

"Rambo!"

Rambo snapped up the bread.

Zoey shook, glad her fingers were intact. The dog slobbered and swallowed, gauging his master with dewy eyes.

"Well, the evidence *was* right here," she said. "You know I don't react well to weed. I spent the morning in a state of marinoia."

Harvey fiddled with his moustache, glanced behind him, and then bent toward her hand where a crumble of bread remained. "I'm sure if I gave you bread with weed in it, you would have noticed before you ate it."

She shook her head, remembering how preoccupied she'd been, cramming the bread in her mouth, rinsing it down with coffee to answer the call from her agent. "You did, and I didn't."

Harvey extracted a pair of reading glasses from the pocket of his flannel shirt and slipped them on. He picked up the tiny remaining blob of dough and smooshed it between his thumb and two fingers, examining it. "I'm sorry about that, Red. I used my high THC strain in that batch." He glanced mournfully at his dog. "Rambo's going to be stoned."

A scuffling sound came from Harvey's kitchen. Shoes scraping the floor.

There hadn't been any other car in the driveway with Harvey's truck. Zoey tried to peek around Harvey and through the archway.

Had Harvey brought home a "date?" *Maybe that Rachelle woman?* She stood on tiptoes, stretched her neck, and glimpsed the round oak table set at the back of the kitchen, Harvey's dining area. A black cowboy boot pointed to a fat tube, shaped like a bullet and standing erect, almost as tall as the table leg. Beside it was a beaker and other equipment. A veritable small chemistry lab. The sole of the boot slid restlessly back and forth, making the noise she'd heard. *Not a woman.*

"Maybe I should go get the rest of the bread for you." She put a little flirt in her voice, curious now what Harvey was up to. "Don't want to waste *product.*"

"Bring it in the morning." Harvey glanced toward the kitchen. "I *am* sorry about the mix-up. How're you feeling now?"

"I'm fine." His sincerity drained her residual anger and left only curiosity. She felt like pushing past him to see what was going on. But between Harvey's muscles and Rambo's jaw, she wouldn't make it one inch. She retreated down his steps, the motion sensor spotlighting her.

Harvey stood in the doorway, watching her go. "Night, Honey Bunches of Oats."

He hadn't said a word about the article in the *Playa Maria Reporter.* But if there was one person in the world who wouldn't be paying attention to the news, who considered all media biased and untrustworthy, it was Harvey.

Harvey. Her heart felt heavy with disappointment. She had an idea what he might be up to. Hadn't she written *Cannabis Cutter?*

Only sixteen years ago, dabbing—inhaling the vapors from marijuana concentrates—had arrived on the scene, a possible moneymaker for a struggling farmer like Harvey. But the process for extracting concentrates— honey oil, wax, and shatter—could be explosive.

With the underbrush parched from drought and ready to ignite, a fire could reach her trailer in a flash.

Her whole life right now was one big cluster fuck.

Chapter Thirteen

Sun slanted through Zoey's three small hopper windows and striped her fuzzy blanket with bars of yellow. A glorious day. Framed by blue sky, tanoak leaves beyond the panes sparkled in the autumn light.

She climbed down from her loft and made a single serving of coffee before her day started to suck.

Instead of meeting her word count, she found herself online—again—this time searching for a new place to park her tiny home should Harvey decide to make wax or shatter. Or honey oil. All potent cannabis concentrates. It really didn't matter which one. She had no desire to be blown to bits if he started making extracts. And she had no power to stop him—except by ratting him out to law enforcement. In which case, she'd surely have to find a new place to live.

Disenchantment with Harvey tugged down her lips. When she'd interviewed him for *Cannabis Cutter*, right here on this farm, his passion for growing weed had captivated her. He'd been happy to share his opinions, and Harvey held a billion of them. He was a regular philosopher on cannabis.

"I grow from seed." He'd puffed up his chest. "Plants are thirty percent more vigorous that way," he'd claimed. (She'd learned that although his beliefs were one-hundred-percent sincere, Harvey's figures bore checking out.) "That's important in this area," he'd told her. "The marine layer creates less than optimal conditions."

Harvey thought growing in hothouses, or even planters, was for "sissies." He grew in gopher-wire-protected trenches, "right down in Mother Earth." He'd smiled down at her. "How can your cannabis have a terroir if it's planted in potting soil?"

She hadn't known weed had *terroir*. That, to her, was a word for wine snobs. She'd scribbled madly on her legal pad, trying to keep up with his enthusiasm. "Folks here like to know how stuff is grown."

"These aren't the greens the farm-to-fork movement had in mind," she muttered.

He either didn't hear her or ignored her. "I like getting my hands in the dirt—makes me happy."

Zoey remembered wishing that her chosen path of writing would deliver the same simple bliss. But she shared Dorothy Parker's sentiment: "I hate to write, I love having written."

"If you grow from seed," Harvey had told her, "each plant is like a snowflake, with slightly different qualities, and you can seed-select to create the product you like. Like the plants over there," he'd pointed a dirt-encrusted finger toward his farthest row, "very floral."

Scrolling down the computer screen now, sadness weighed on Zoey. It was easy to understand how someone could be tempted by the money in extracts. But the practice undermined her image of Harvey as a purist, a farmer who didn't even use pesticides.

She tugged an earlobe. If he moved into making extracts, she'd have to revise her idea of him. He'd be just another drug dealer.

He's always been a drug dealer.

She tilted her head the other direction. She could ask Harvey about the equipment she'd seen under his table. When he wanted to talk, he could be downright voluble. But his behavior last night indicated this was not one of those times.

Zoey focused on the computer screen. The task at hand. If she stayed in Playa Maria, the only inexpensive mobile home lots were for seniors, 55 and over. For everybody else, spots ranged from $250 to $2500, the latter with ocean views, totally sweet, but unnecessary. The cheap ones were depressing, narrow slots of concrete. And even they would take a chunk of her earnings. No free hook-ups, that was for sure.

Admit it. You're spoiled.

Maybe she was getting ahead of herself. The evidence was minimal—only a stranger in Harvey's kitchen and a few items like a person might use for extract production. Maybe she should have more faith in her original conception of the man.

But where was his visitor's car? Had Harvey told him to park in the back, out of sight? And why didn't he want her to see the person?

If she asked him these questions, she wouldn't be able to trust the answers. In Harvey's Code, no one had a right to stick his nose—or her nose—into his business. If a person did, it justified any lies he might tell.

Zoey drummed her lips. If she ever saw Harvey leave and take Rambo, she could poke around a little.

In the meantime, she had a book to write. She called Detective Bowman and asked again for her notes from the patrol car.

"We're not prepared to release them," he said. "They're part of our ongoing investigation."

"I really, really need those notes," she said. "Could you make copies for me?"

"You don't seem to understand that we're investigating the murder of a police officer here."

"I do understand that, sir."

The detective stuck to his guns. The refusal didn't feel like police procedure. It felt personal. Like he suspected her. Or blamed her. Or made her the lucky recipient of his anger over Officer Austin's death.

At the thought of Officer Austin, the image knifed through her—his body sprawled on the asphalt. The gaping wound. The vicious end to his life. His wife. His children.

Her chest tightened. She twirled her body on the storage cube as though she could escape the onslaught of emotion.

A figure stood at her door.

She startled and squinted into the glaring sun.

Outside the glass, her mother posed, decked out like she was going to shop at Nordstrom's. Zoey had feared her mother might see the newspaper article, but the sight of Camille, hand-on-narrow-hip, still surprised her and set her heart racing.

She crossed the room in four steps and slid open the door. "What are you doing here, Camille?"

Her mom stepped up into the house, and Zoey's energy drained. In her experience, Camille walked into a room and owned it, as though entitled to every space she entered. Three-inch heels raised her above Zoey and managed to make her look tallish. If only, Zoey thought, she had inherited Camille's bones along with her short stature. It was the same with the hair. She'd gotten a whacked-out shade of her mom's red curls. As Camille gazed to the table, galley kitchen, up to the loft, her hair swept with the movement. "I've never seen a get-up like this."

"How did you find me?" Even the police hadn't located her, but then, since she was a cooperative witness who responded to phone calls, how motivated had they been? They had their hands full trying to track down a cop killer.

Her mom turned her head away. "I like the little sitting area. The ottomans can obviously be moved together to make a bed."

"It's too tight in here for visitors."

Camille's outlined lips smiled slightly. "Oh, darling, I'd never dream of staying here." The eyes—a beautiful turquoise—widened a fraction. "I just came to check on you, sweetheart."

In spite of her years of training, Zoey loosened the grip over her heart for a second. Right now, with all the stuff that was happening, here was someone checking on her. Who else bothered to check on her? *Well Harvey. Brianna. Jimmy.*

"You're all over the news," her mom trilled.

And there it was—the sucker punch. Bald and bare and right in the gut. Of course, this was why her mom had come, dolled up to be on camera. Probably shocked to find herself dressed up and in the middle of nowhere. No news crew in sight.

Be fair, Zoey. Camille doesn't go to Whole Foods without looking ready for a photo op.

Her mom brushed past her and opened a kitchen cabinet.

"Why don't you make yourself at home?"

Camille gave her a tight smile, bag of coffee in hand. "I wouldn't have to if you knew how to be a hostess."

"This is *my house,*" Zoey said. "Not a Red Lobster."

"House?" Camille lifted sandy-blonde, perfectly-arched brows and tipped her chin toward the loft. "How do you even get up there?"

The media had not revealed Zoey's address, so her mom, like Millard Cranston, must have wheedled info from Helga. Zoey rued the day she'd gotten advice from Helga when buying the tiny home.

Camille and Helga had bonded back at the photo session for Zoey's headshot, both hovering, brushing strands of hair from her face, commenting on angles and light, driving the poor photographer crazy. Helga had appreciated that Camille was a fellow sophisticate, a cosmopolite like herself.

They were certainly alike in the way they insinuated themselves into Zoey's life when it suited them.

"You're not being very gracious, Zoey." Her mom pulled out a mug from Powell's Books, but stopped mid-air when she saw there was no coffee pot, only a single-serve plastic drip cone filled with cold grounds. "Your behavior is not worthy of your name."

Her mom was referring to her middle name—a name Zoey loathed, one of many things with which Camille had saddled her.

Camille abandoned the mug on the counter. Her full polka-dotted skirt—pearl dots on a turquoise that matched her eyes—swished her knees as she crossed the room and positioned herself on an ottoman in *the little sitting area.*

Zoey wished the upholstered cubes had casters so she could push the ottoman and dump her mom out the door. But the one time she had pushed her mom—no, not *pushed,* simply barred her unannounced entrance to the San Francisco flat Zoey shared with other students—the event ended in disaster. Camille's heel broke, her ankle twisted, and she sprained her wrist while catching her fall. Only the day before yesterday, Detective Bowman had scraped the scab from that chapter of their history, so it felt raw.

Camille stared out the slider. "It's rather isolated here."

"I like it that way."

"Oh, sweetheart, what did I do to make you like this?"

Zoey plopped down in front of her computer screen. "Let me count the ways," she muttered even though the question was rhetorical. The answer, in her mother's mind, was *absolutely nothing*. Zoey slipped her laptop and cell phone into her mail carrier bag. If she took these two things, her mom couldn't do too much damage. She stood.

Her mom quirked a brow. "Are you going somewhere?"

She scooted past her mom to the door.

"Dressed like that?" Camille's soprano voice rose to a squeak.

Zoey hesitated. Maybe she should change out of her pajamas. She opened the cube she'd been sitting on and stuffed clothes into the pouch.

Her mother watched.

She slipped on the flip-flops parked by her door, banged shut the glass, and slapped across the yard toward Harvey's, stirring plumes of powdery dust behind her. Rambo barked from the field before she was halfway to the house. "Harvey!" As if he could hear her over Rambo's excitement. It didn't matter. The dog had alerted him to a visitor. On the other side of the fence, Rambo's yap followed her until it rushed forward and was muffled by the heavy whack of the dog door.

Zoey waited on the porch. A couple of minutes later, Harvey cracked the door. Behind him, the Doberman obediently sat, dark eyes zeroed in on Zoey.

What would happen if her mom laid eyes on Harvey? She considered Sam Elliott a heartthrob—the reason Zoey knew who Sam Elliott was—and Harvey definitely resembled the actor.

At the moment, though, Harvey looked tired and his eyes were red-rimmed. During trimming, tiny bits of plant matter stirred into the air. And of course, Harvey being Harvey, he resisted eye protection. "I'm getting mighty popular these days," he said.

Her heart fluttered. Was she too late? Had her mom come to Harvey's door before going to her trailer? Camille could eat someone like Harvey alive. It didn't matter that Harvey had served in Vietnam and grew weed and might be considering dangerous extract production—he was an innocent.

His lanky body leaned against the door frame, one gloved hand dangling a pair of expensive trimmers.

"Can I use your shower?"

"What's wrong with yours?" He pushed away from the door frame, rolling his shoulders. Trimming, he'd told her, was tedious work, worse than hunching over a computer. He squinted down at her.

"My mother's here."

"Oh, the Wicked Witch of the West."

In a weak moment, she'd divulged too much, thinking Harvey deserved an explanation for why she wanted to set up camp on his mountain farm. She'd shared about a piano recital when she was eight years old. She froze halfway through "Starlight Waltz." Near tears, her lacy collar raw against her burning neck, she'd looked to her mother in the front row and found not encouragement, but a woman wilting with disappointment.

Now, even though Harvey waited for it, she wasn't about to elaborate on her mother's arrival. She blushed at having shared the piano recital memory, such a white, privileged trauma. Unworthy of anyone's sympathy.

Harvey gave his mustache a pensive stroke. "You know the thing about parents?"

"What's that, Harvey?"

"One day they're gone. They become mysteries. Then you wish you'd asked them a hundred things."

"Name one."

"Wish I'd asked my mom why her parents built this house in the middle of nowhere, and am I like them?" Harvey was serious, his voice full of nostalgia.

He cleared his throat and waved her in. "I wondered about the car in front of your place. Never known you to entertain." He wiggled his eyebrows suggestively.

"If you knew me to *entertain*, you wouldn't let me live here."

"Suppose that's right."

The pine planks creaked as she moved into his living room. She thought of words she would use to describe the house: funky, ramshackle, comfortable.

"You know where it is," Harvey said, "but it doesn't have a lock."

"I trust you."

A grin lifted his mustache. "You shouldn't."

Before she could respond, he spun on a boot heel, and headed for the door, Rambo's toenails clicking behind him.

Chapter Fourteen

arvey had installed a shower where a tub used to be. There was no fan, so Zoey cracked the small window inside the stall. Music, coming from the barn, spilled in. Harvey had the Stones cranked up. Strains of "Paint It Black" beat down with the water.

Dark mold traced the grout between the tan tiles, but the pelting spray from a full showerhead felt luxurious.

Harvey's bathroom didn't have a towel rack, just a peg on the back of the door. His field hat hung on it. Zoey lifted a threadbare, damp towel from under the hat and wrapped her wet hair. Dripping on the floor, she opened the vanity under the sink. It held a Costco-size supply of toilet paper, a can of Ajax, a bottle of Lysol, and a toilet brush. *No towels.* She should have thought this through a little better.

She cracked the bathroom door. Warm damp air steamed into the hallway. Across from her was another door, hopefully to a closet with some towels.

Leaving wet footprints, she hurried, naked, across the hall. The door did lead to a closet, a tank on the floor and a stack of facemasks on a shelf. *Well that was easy. No more investigation needed.* Harvey planned to make extracts.

The upper shelves of the closet were stacked with blankets and folded towels, neater than she would have expected. She pulled out a towel that was see-through in the center, quickly wiped her feet so as not to leave more tracks, and then wound the material around the crucial real estate.

The next door in the hallway was beckoning her. Harvey and Rambo were out of the house, and she was in it. When would that ever happen again?

Nudging the mystery door open with a hip, she peeked into a master bedroom. It smelled of dust, dog, and marijuana. A sliding glass door—clearly an upgrade—opened the room toward Harvey's field with a view of the trees beyond. If she walked into the room, she'd for sure leave tracks on the dusty pine plank floor.

There were no paintings, only one large, incongruous macramé-and-shell wall hanging. A brass bed, covered with a quilt and a large tan dog bed, took up most of the space. An intriguing clutter topped an ancient, sturdy-looking chest of drawers. The array included a framed photo of a young woman.

Zoey cinched the towel more firmly around her body, grabbed the door frame with both hands, and leaned into the room for a closer look. Red glinted at the end of the bed. A shiny new fire extinguisher.

Well, there you go, Zoey. If Harvey planned to make oil, he'd want a good fire extinguisher.

She remembered, though, that she'd seen a fire extinguisher in Harvey's barn when she'd done her research for *Cannabis Cutter*.

So, maybe, Zoey, she admonished herself, Harvey is just upgrading his equipment. Since he already had a fire extinguisher, getting a new one didn't mean anything.

What is with all the denial?

She twisted back toward the hall, the towel working loose, but the photo on the dresser tugged at her. Black and white, it suggested another era. She squinted. The very young woman wore a simple dark-colored blouse that didn't indicate any particular time period. The photo was a formal studio shot, three-quarters profile, the face oddly familiar.

Zoey placed the ball of one foot inside the room. Maybe if she tiptoed. She lifted the foot. An amorphous oblong smudged the dust.

She raised her head and froze. Harvey was outside in his field.

If he looked toward the glass door, he'd see her half-naked and hanging in the entrance to his bedroom.

Lurching back into the hall, she clutched the falling towel and closed the door to its original position, praying Harvey hadn't spotted her and wouldn't notice the toe prints on his floor. What kind of friend was she to repay his kindness by prying into the private parts of his home?

She scurried to the bathroom. What would she tell Harvey if he'd seen her?

Zoey yanked out gray sweatpants from her mail carrier bag. She'd forgotten to pack underwear, so she'd be going commando. As long as her mom's rental car occupied the driveway, she wasn't going back to her house. Nor did she want to stick around to be questioned by Harvey.

The shirt she'd brought was too bulky to tuck in. Draping it outside the thick sweats would make her look fat. Such was life.

She mopped up the floor with one towel and hung them both on the peg. Harvey would know from the two towels that she'd been in his hall closet. He could make of it what he would.

Baggy shirt flapping, she hurried toward her car. Rambo leapt at the fence, and her heart jumped. The dog had developed a new aggression toward her. Was he reacting to the fact she'd come from Harvey's house? Would the dog come tearing around the end of the fence?

Midway, the Doberman's pounding ceased as though Harvey had him tethered.

Safe inside her car, Zoey took time to let her heart settle and to dab on lip balm.

Her mom opened the sliding door of the trailer, shaded her eyes with a hand, and peered, frowning, at Zoey.

Zoey executed a three-point turn and drove too fast down the rutted driveway to the narrow mountain road. Her speed required her to focus on the curves. The engine icon lit up. By the time she reached the intersection with the highway, she'd chewed off enough coconut-flavored lip balm to concoct a piña colada. She sat at the stop sign. *Where the hell are you going, girl?*

Away from Camille.

Hate to tell you, but that's not a destination.

Her car might not even make it to town. She turned off the engine, set the brake, snapped open the overhead storage compartment, and took out the car manual.

The booklet listed several possibilities for the dashboard warning light. One was a loose gas cap. She hoped that was the reason because she didn't understand the others. In the rearview, the road spooled empty behind her. She wasn't holding anybody up and didn't expect anyone to be coming down the private mountain road. Except, maybe, Camille. If she saw Camille's rental car approaching, she could simply drive away. Provided her SUV started again.

A car on the highway slowed up to allow her to enter traffic, then roared forward as if disgusted with her apparent oblivion to his thoughtfulness.

Zoey climbed out and checked the gas cap. It felt secure, but she unscrewed it, put it on tightly, and climbed back in the cab.

She turned the key. The motor fired. The light came on. Wash, rinse, repeat. Same result.

The road behind her remained deserted, so she checked her phone, leaving the engine running. Nothing from her agent. Nothing from Jimmy. No message from the hypnotherapist. And Brianna? Brianna must be dead not to be razzing her about her brief hook-up with Jimmy in the parking lot. The void on her phone gave Zoey an eerie, Twilight Zone sensation, like The Rapture had happened and she'd been left alone in the world.

At this point, she would have welcomed follow-up questions from Millard Cranston, *Playa Maria Reporter's* finest. Across the T-intersection, redwoods towered, majestic and impenetrable, while she sat in her car, small and invisible. Vulnerable. Marooned. An only child grown into an alone woman.

She glanced down. The red engine icon had not magically disappeared. She should head some place where it would be easier to get help if the car stalled, somewhere that was not this mountain road.

But first she called the police department again.

Detective Bowman took her call. He invited her to come on down. *Right now.* She could have her papers.

"I'll be there in twenty minutes."

If my car makes it.

Her neck hairs prickled like a dog's ruff. Why Bowman's sudden about-face? Something was up. A break in the case? She swung the vehicle onto the highway and headed for the police department.

Chapter Fifteen

The old Playa Maria Police Department building had been destroyed in the 1989 earthquake. Even though that was thirty years ago, a vestige of newness clung to its replacement, a Spanish-style edifice located rather grandly atop a knoll.

On the night of the shooting, Zoey had been escorted in through the back door, passing a labyrinth of rooms and cubicles.

Today she was buzzed through the front door into the reception area for the general public. Detective Bowman came out to greet her from a room to the side of reception—a rendezvous office for volunteers—as though he'd been waiting for her.

He gave her a brusque greeting, his manner as business-like as before. His face as wrinkly. His clothes as boring. Still, Zoey's internal alarms blared.

"How you holding up?" The detective touched the groove beside his mouth.

The nervous tick. It could be from the stress of going three days without hauling in a suspect. "I'm managing," she said.

But something else was off. He failed to register any surprise at her sweatpants and baggy shirt, so different from her previous attire. He'd struck her as an old-school guy not attuned to political correctness, who might have made some remark, but he was holding himself sternly in check, worrying that groove like he meant to wear it deeper.

"This way." He motioned toward a side door.

A detective would notice how different she looked. She had no makeup on. Her hair was damp and uncombed, the curls frizzing out of control. He was trying too hard to be neutral, his back stiff as he led her past two filing clerks into the inner sanctum. *Why?*

The answer waited in Bowman's office. A woman rose when they entered, although she swayed like she might collapse back into her chair. She propped herself with a hand on one of the stacks of folders at the edge of Bowman's desk. The slippery pile threatened to slide out from under her.

The woman was as tall as the detective, maybe five-ten, and athletically trim. But no wonder Bowman hadn't commented on Zoey's appearance. This woman looked a hundred times worse, her face drained of color, eyes shiny, the end of her nose red, her dirty blonde hair cinched into a bedraggled ponytail.

"Mrs. Austin," Detective Bowman said, "this is Zoey Kozinski, Stan's ride-along."

Dizziness swam through Zoey. "Stan's wife?" *Christine.*

Detective Bowman wedged himself into his chair and turned so he could see her and Christine. "Stan's widow."

The bloodshot whites of Christine's eyes set pale blue irises into high relief. Pin-prick pupils sucked Zoey in like a vortex.

Then Christine dropped onto her chair with a sound that was not quite a sob, more like the drop had knocked a pained little grunt into the room. As though nothing else was left.

"I am very sorry for your loss." The room didn't have another chair. Zoey leaned against the cubicle wall, which thankfully was sturdier than it looked.

Was this a normal situation? She pressed her palms against the prickly fabric of the wall. *Nothing about a cop killing is normal, Zoey.*

Bowman cleared his throat. Christine raised her head, her gaze aimed at him, not back at Zoey.

"This is unorthodox." The detective rubbed the deep groove beside his lip. "But sometimes procedure flies out the window when you have a fallen officer." His eyes met Zoey's. "Mrs. Austin was here when you called," he said, answering Zoey's unasked question. "She has a few questions she'd like to ask you. As the last person to see her husband alive."

Zoey's palms felt damp. Christine kept her eyes averted. Did she really want to ask her questions, or was this some tactical maneuver on the part of Bowman? He may not have pre-planned this encounter, but he was facilitating it. Did he think he'd learn something new this way? She wiped her hands, one at a time, on her sweatpants and replanted them against the wall.

Christine's head swiveled, slowly. She swallowed, loud enough for Zoey to hear. Zoey smelled her now—some sour animal mantle of grief, stale body odor mixed with tears and unwashed hair. "Was Stan happy?" the woman croaked, without raising her eyes. "Was he having a good evening?"

Zoey bobbed her head, even though the woman didn't look up. "I got every sense he was happy to be a police officer."

"Did he suffer?"

Her hands slick, Zoey wanted to slither down the wall and to rest her butt on the floor. She shook her head. Surely Detective Bowman had told this woman how her husband had died, that it had been instantaneous. "He didn't know what hit him." Her voice broke.

Christine's head jerked up, her eyes piercing Zoey. "Why didn't he know?" She rose, using the edge of the desk to steady herself.

"What do you mean?" But Zoey knew what the woman meant. Stan Austin had been a professional law enforcement officer. How had he been caught off guard?

Christine's face flushed. She pointed a finger. Like the rest of her, it was long and skinny. "You can't lie to me. He didn't want to have a ride-along." She stepped toward Zoey, the finger snapping back with the others into a fist.

Zoey crabbed sideways along the wall.

"Why didn't he call for back-up?"

"The license plate." Zoey's voice trailed off as she tried to remember what the dispatcher had said. Something reassuring.

"Stolen," Detective Bowman muttered. "We didn't know at the time." He seemed to be saying this for Christine's benefit.

The info about the plate did nothing to placate Christine. She tensed, wild-eyed, too near Zoey. "I'll tell you why." She raised her fist. "He was distracted."

"Distracted?" Zoey edged to the door. "Not by me."

"How do you know?" Christine said. "You don't know what was going on in his head." The rage in her stare could vaporize stone. "He didn't want a ride-along," she repeated.

Bowman positioned himself one lunge from either of them. But he wasn't stopping the verbal assault. His sympathies lay with the widow. Zoey was alone, the other cubicles quiet. Empty.

The situation was untenable. "All right, your husband did sense the shooter," Zoey snapped. "He assumed a stance to fire." She was not going to let Mrs. Austin pin her husband's death on her. She returned the woman's glare. "But the driver got the jump on him. He knew his target, while your husband had to entertain the idea the driver could be a regular citizen."

Christine took another step, no longer seeming shaky. She towered in Zoey's personal space. "I'm sure some *writer*," she spat the word like a bite of rotten fruit, "ready to criticize his every move, caused Stan to hesitate."

Anger boiled up. Zoey knew her face must be scarlet. "This is not what happened." Her words hissed. "Your husband made a mistake." *Probably more than one.* "He could have used his PA."

Christine crossed fists over her chest, her bottom teeth jutted out to trap her top lip, and she rocked her torso, working mightily to restrain herself. Her mouth opened. "That's the way people are now," she said bitterly. "With their cellphones. Ready to make every cop look like he's some racist or killer."

"That's not me." Zoey shot daggers at Detective Bowman. He'd led her into an ambush. And how could she even mention her notes now? The last thing she needed was for Christine to learn of her new novel with its opening—the killing of an officer named Stan.

Zoey spun out the door into a maze of cubicles. Christine hurled herself after her, a hand clamping Zoey's shoulder. Just as suddenly, it was pulled away. Zoey glanced back. Detective Bowman was restraining Christine by the shoulders.

"This is not over!" Christine thrashed and snarled, looking rabid, capable of anything.

From down the hallway, two officers raced toward the scene. Detective Bowman wrapped Christine in burly arms and shushed her like a child.

"Please escort Ms. Kozinski out," the detective said to the uniforms. *Unnecessary.* There was nowhere she wanted to be more than *out.* She hurried past the filing clerks, who stood and stared, alert to the commotion, and rounded a corner, instinctively finding her way into the civilian safety of the foyer, the officers superfluous in her wake. Outside the building, she paused for a second to huff the fresh Playa Maria air.

That was surreal.

Inside her car, Zoey locked her door and rested her head against the steering wheel to calm down. Then she checked herself in the rearview. A haunted woman stared back, as ashen as Mrs. Austin. She sank back into her seat.

She may not have distracted Stan, but there was no denying he'd gone after that white sedan with the broken taillight for her—to liven up her evening. To impress her. Because in spite of his marriage, there had been a hint of sexual energy percolating in the patrol car. He didn't want to appear weak by calling for back-up on a simple car stop.

She had wanted her Stan character to make a procedural mistake, and the real Stan had obliged. She squeezed shut her eyes.

She was guilty.

Guilty.

Guilty.

Chapter Sixteen

Guilt skewered Zoey to her car seat. This cop killer had to be found before Christine Austin enacted some screwed-up vigilante justice with her as the target.

In the meantime, she needed help. Zoey looked around, making sure Christine was nowhere in the parking lot. Drawing a shaky breath, she checked her phone. No message from the hypnotherapist. Only a text from Camille saying that she was staying at the High Tide with Ryan.

Zoey rolled her eyes at the casually dropped name. *Ryan.* As if she cared about her mom's latest stud muffin.

Her mom and the new boyfriend seemed to be clicking, though. Ryan probably wanted the good life, and Camille wanted eye candy hanging on her arm, a *de rigueur* accessory.

She checked again for any sign of Christine. Nothing. There was a back way out, through the fenced-in patrol cars and racks of stolen bicycles, the way they'd brought her in for questioning. So maybe Christine had left that way.

Her body felt like a bag of lead, like it would be hard to lift her arms to drive. She called Maureen Magill, expecting to leave a message, but the hypnotherapist answered immediately, her voice upbeat. "I was just about to call you."

"You can see me?"

"At two."

That left her with a couple of hours to fill, not enough time to make driving all the way home and back worthwhile, especially with the engine icon lighting up.

Brianna sometimes nipped home for lunch. Nothing sounded better than a dose of her friend's solid, comforting presence. Plus, Brianna kept a serious supply of Tater Tots.

Zoey put on her favorite Sirius XM station, *Little Steven's Underground Garage*, and in five minutes, found herself at Brianna's apartment complex. Only a few blocks from the beach, the neighborhood, to her constant amazement, defied gentrification. The parking area made a U around a communal strip of grass with palm trees swaying at each end—the site of some crazy parties, all of which seemed a lifetime ago.

Damn. An olive-green Jeep sat in the parking lot, making her plan less appealing. The vehicle belonged to Curt. He was a bass player in another band, so he and Brianna shared holding the bottom in common, but other than that, she couldn't understand how Bri could stand him as a housemate. Curt was duller than beige.

She curved around the grass area to the other side of the parking lot. No sign of Brianna's car. She pulled into a space and texted Brianna—which she should have done in the first place.

Climbing out of her SUV, Zoey sat at a picnic table under the gazebo in the middle of the median. A nice place to wait for a response. Gulls squawked overhead, and a breeze off the ocean stirred the smell of freshly cut grass.

In the middle of a workday, the complex was peaceful. The lot almost deserted. A man was sitting in a sedan. *Compact. Gray.*

She'd never seen the car around. It wasn't a large apartment building, but people moved in and out. The man stayed in his car. It was shiny clean. *Chrysler.*

A lost tourist? The summer season had wound down, but smart people knew this was a great time to visit Playa Maria. Fewer crowds, better rates, gorgeous weather.

She glanced at her phone. She'd give Bri one more minute to respond, then she was outta here.

Her neck hairs prickled with the feeling of being watched. She shot a look toward the car.

The man was staring. He didn't turn away. He climbed from the Chrysler. *Tall. Slender. Young.*

"Hey, Zoey."

She reeled around toward the greeting. Curt lumbered toward her, surrounded by a fusty cloud of marijuana fumes. What else was new? When was Curt not herbed up?

"Looking for Brianna?" He gave her a lop-sided grin. His eyelids sagged.

She swung back around on the picnic table bench to see if the tourist would come to her rescue. Ask for directions. But the man hastily retreated to his car.

Odd.

"Bri's at lunch with Sabbie," Curt volunteered.

Jealousy stabbed her even though it made perfect sense. With her usual finesse, Bri had squeezed Sabbie into a lunch date, which put boundaries on the time Sabbie could suck up. Bri had probably turned off her phone to focus on their lead singer because Brianna was a brilliant band manager.

"Thanks, Curt." She rose, but Curt didn't move. Zoey glanced over to the gray car. In spite of her uneasiness, she laughed inside at the idea of the tourist asking for directions and her letting Curt take the lead on giving them.

Curt startled her by asking, "Wanna go to Taco Bell?"

"Nah." She wouldn't eat at Taco Bell in a million years. And wouldn't eat at Taco Bell with Curt in two million. "I've gotta take my car to the dealership. The engine light is on."

He bobbed his head. "Sounds bad."

The guy in the Chrysler was just sitting there. Engine off. Windows up. The reflection off the glass making it hard to get a look at him.

Curt hovered.

Stoned. Apt word, Zoey thought. "Do you know anyone who drives a Chrysler?" she asked.

"Huh?" He tilted his head and squinted. "Nobody in Playa Maria drives a Chrysler. But speaking of rides, could I hitch one?"

She pointedly eyed his Jeep. Curt didn't respond. He waited like a big, shaggy Saint Bernard. The Taco Bell was right on her way, two blocks before the dealership. "How will you get back?"

"No worries," he drawled.

She didn't want to be a dick. "Come on." She stepped off the grass onto the asphalt.

As they headed out of the lot in her Element, the young man ducked in his car like he didn't want to be seen.

Weird.

She checked her rearview. The Chrysler was backing up.

"Hey, Curt."

"Huh?" His head lolled against the back of the passenger seat. He gazed at the blue sky.

"What are the three hardest years in a bass player's life?"

"First grade." He grunted. "Got anything new?"

"Is that Chrysler behind us?"

"Is this another joke?"

"No. The car from your parking lot, is it following us?"

He twisted around, faster than she would have thought possible, and way too obvious. "There's a gray car back a ways behind another car. If it's a Chrysler, must be a rental."

"Hang on," she said.

She hit the gas.

The Element jerked. It didn't have great acceleration on a good day, and this was not a good day. Still, Curt grabbed the oh-shit strap.

The light ahead turned yellow. When they reached it, she swerved right on the red.

Curt blinked at her, eyelids lifting.

"Give me a report," she said. "What's going on?"

"The car that was behind us stopped at the light. Now it's turning behind us. That gray car is turning wide around him—"

She gunned the engine.

Curt snapped upright. "Turn here."

She squealed into what appeared to be a parking lot. The Element chugged.

Threatened to stall. A frisson of fear shot up her spine.

With a buck, the SUV suddenly accelerated.

"Straight through to there."

Curt's finger-point led to a narrow alley that ended at a tee-intersection with another alley.

"Go right."

The alleyway led back to face Curt and Brianna's apartment building across the street. She swung onto the street, her heart beating fast.

"I've always wanted to do that." Curt was grinning like a ten-year-old.

She zoomed straight through the light where they'd turned.

Curt twisted to look out the back window. "Was that car chasing us?"

Good question.

She could think of only one reason for someone to tail her, and that reason seemed crazy. Paranoid. Besides, the cop killer had his own car, and it was white.

She checked the rearview, prompting Curt to crane his neck to the side mirror and then to look back over his shoulder again. He lifted both hands into the air. "I swear to God there's a whole posse of light-colored cars behind us now."

* * *

When she dropped off Curt, no car followed her into the Taco Bell parking lot. And she couldn't think of any rational reason there would be. All she really had was a gray vehicle with the looks of a rental turning out of a parking lot behind her. After that, she had only the word of someone who was clearly stoned and had always wanted to do a car chase.

The driver of the Chrysler, when he'd gotten out at the apartment, had looked barely old enough to shave. How could he be a cold-blooded killer? And she thought of the poor guy in the hypnotherapist's parking lot. He'd only wanted directions.

Regardless, she felt safer when she entered the Honda dealership. The service manager, dressed in khakis and a banlon shirt with nary a drop of grease under his nails, informed her it would be an hour before they could run a diagnostic test on her car, but the test itself wouldn't take long. She made the appointment, her stomach growling in a way that prompted the manager to say, "There's a deli across the street."

She knew the place, a local chain where her sweatpants would fit right in. Scouting for gray cars—which suddenly seemed non-existent—she dodged traffic to cross the four-lane Scenic Drive.

In spite of the temperate weather, she ordered chicken soup. *Comfort food.*

Dallying, she watched people and brooded—about the shooting, about Christine Austin, about Harvey's plans, her stalled book and her mom. Whether she'd been pursued. Even petty worries, like whether Sabbie was griping about her while lunching with Brianna, dropped into the cauldron.

When the hour was up, she hoofed it back to the dealership.

"Your Element has a problem with its air/gas mix. Not an emergency," the service manager said, "but it's going to run ragged. You should get it fixed as soon as possible."

"Can you do it today?"

He made a production of going to his desk, off to the side of the counter, and typing at his computer, making her wait. Letting her know that if it were possible, he'd be bestowing great good fortune. Finally, after a study of the screen and several neck rolls, he returned to the counter. "We're booked until late in the day, but we might be able to squeeze you in before closing. About four."

"Perfect. I have an appointment now anyway."

"Be careful driving that thing."

Now that she knew the problem, the unevenness in the SUV's performance seemed obvious. Why hadn't she noticed? Maybe the fits and jerks were becoming worse? She felt lucky the dealership could work her in; she didn't want to drive into the mountains with her car like this.

When she reached the medical complex, Zoey exhaled in relief.

Maureen Magill waited for her behind the reception desk, her wild hair tamed into a loose knot at the nape of her neck. She came through the door into the waiting area, a denim skirt swishing over black tights.

"Because we've done the initial interview and intake, we can get right to it," Maureen said brightly, wiggling cupped fingers to indicate Zoey should follow her.

The therapist's inner office projected Maureen's aura—professional, but warm and comfortable. Except for the chair. *Too much like a dentist's.* Especially when the therapist made it recline. But then weren't dentist's chairs designed for comfort?

Zoey settled back. Let her flip-flops drop to the floor.

"Would you like a blanket around your legs?"

"Sounds great."

The therapist tucked her in. "How's that?"

Zoey's eyes teared. "I feel like a baby." *Mothered.* Or how she imagined mothered should feel—nurturing, warm, protective.

"Good," the woman purred. "I'm glad you're wearing comfortable clothes."

"Believe me, I didn't choose to go out in the world dressed this way."

"Do you want to talk about that during the session?"

"No. I want to stay focused on the shooting."

"Okay. We went over most of this yesterday." Maureen handed her a headset. "You'll hear soft melodic music—in this case, *Space Serene,* my favorite." Maureen gathered her shawl about her. "Are you warm enough? Because the process will cause your body temperature to drop."

"Yeah. The blanket's great." Zoey positioned the headphones but kept them partially off her ears while the hypnotherapist finished talking.

"Once I start the music, you'll hear binary beeping embedded in it," Maureen explained. "Here are the glasses."

Zoey had expected big, alien-looking things like virtual-reality headsets, but these were much closer to a pair of large sunglasses.

"As we discussed, when you listen to the music, you'll be watching patterns made by LED lights. They are bright enough that some patients like to keep their eyes closed."

Zoey smiled. "A light show." In this safe space, her muscles were relaxing. Her accumulated weariness sank into the chair cushion.

"Yes." Maureen returned the smile. "The lights and sound will keep your mind occupied while you hear the message I've designed for you. It's not exactly subliminal or hidden. You can hear it, but it's not necessary to pay attention to it."

Maureen maintained such intent eye contact that Zoey wondered if it were already part of the hypnotism.

"As a matter of fact," Maureen murmured, "I encourage you to let your mind wander. Usually the music and lights do the trick. The process elevates melatonin and serotonin. Some patients become so relaxed they fall asleep."

"You are getting sleepy—very, very sleepy," Zoey joked, but it sounded perfect. It seemed like a year since she'd had a good night's sleep.

* * *

Zoey blinked awake. The light show and music were gone. The eyeglasses had been removed. The heavy blanket snuggled her.

Maureen padded into the room with a CD in hand. "I'd love to invite you to relax a bit longer, but my next client is here."

Zoey struggled to sit up, like she weighed two hundred pounds instead of one hundred ten.

"This is a CD for you with the music and messages." Maureen slipped the CD into a white sheath. "I recommend finding a place to relax and listen to it daily until we see each other again."

In a daze, Zoey dropped her legs off the side of the comfy chair and slipped into her flip-flops.

"You can rest out here until you feel awake enough to drive." Maureen escorted Zoey to the reception area. Light cut through the opened vertical blinds. An older man in a suit, upright and formal, waited for a session. Maureen opened her box of teas on the counter. "A couple of these are good stimulants." She edged up packets from the local DiviniTea, which happened to be where Brianna worked. Maureen hoisted an Apple tablet from the desk behind the reception counter. "I recommend that you return next week."

Zoey blinked. *What happened? Did anything happen?*

"Give the session a little time to settle," Maureen said and apologized again for rushing her along. "You can call me with questions later."

They set up another date. Then Maureen turned her full attention to the man. "Come on back."

Settling in the reception area, Zoey slid the silver disc from its envelope and stared at it. Who used CDs? Would Best Buy carry a CD player she could hook up to her laptop?

She reviewed her memories of the shooting, from the moment the white sedan pulled over until the parade of law enforcement arrived. Not a single new detail presented itself, and she felt anxious enough to take up nail biting. How long was *a little time to settle*?

The murmur of Maureen Magill and her patient seeped through the cracks around the door. Zoey squirmed. It wouldn't be easy, but a natural-born snoop like herself might be able to overhear bits of their private conversation.

She stood, her body heavy but her head weightless and floaty, like she'd been on a journey through outer space, the blue ball of Earth hanging magically before her, shimmering at its curve. But no profound memory popped over its horizon.

Chapter Seventeen

Outside the therapist's office, Zoey relaxed in the cocoon of her SUV's warmth. She checked her phone. Both her mother and her agent had called while she was in her session. Back in the day, the two women had joined forces to coerce Zoey into a professional photo shoot. It would be interesting to see them locked in a small room together, a sort of psychological MMA cage match.

She'd bet on her mother. Helga was blunt. Her mom was deft. Helga would tap out.

She listened to Helga's message first. "Great press. Front-page sidebar. Better than I hoped." The agent cleared her throat. "Got Cranston to mention your titles." She said this with a pinch of long-suffering, as though Zoey should have worked the information into the interview herself, or at the very least should have called to thank her. After all, Helga was her agent, not her publicist, although you couldn't tell. Then: "I need Chapter One, Kiddo."

She didn't say goodbye. Helga never did, so the curtness didn't necessarily mean anything.

Zoey drew a deep breath before listening to her mother's message. Even on the tinny phone speaker, Camille's voice was as smooth as Al Green's crooning "Let's Stay Together."

"Darling, this must be so hard on you. Let us take you to dinner. Or if you prefer, I could leave Ryan here to entertain himself. We could go for crab."

So like her mother to bribe with something beyond Zoey's budget.

Zoey texted. *Crab's not in season.*

In less than a minute, her phone vibrated.

Fish then. I can pick you up at seven. Just the two of us. Wear something nice.

After a quick body scan to make sure she'd recovered from the therapy drowsiness, Zoey started her car, thankful that the engine turned over.

Traffic clogged Scenic Drive. Zoey composed a message in her head and used Siri to send it. *Pick me up at the Honda dealership on Scenic. 4:30. Early dinner. I'll be wearing what I'm wearing.*

This could work. She'd have a free meal, a ride home if her car had to spend the night at the dealership, and she'd mortify her mom with her outfit, all in one fell swoop.

Threading the car through traffic, she headed to Best Buy to purchase a CD player. Her pink iPhone remained dead; her mom might refuse the counteroffer.

But a couple of minutes later, when she stopped at a light, the response came. *Okay, sweetheart.*

She nibbled a cuticle. That had been too easy.

* * *

Zoey sat rigidly in the Honda dealership's waiting area, a corner of the showroom with two perpendicular couches, magazines spread across a glass coffee table, and a muted TV programmed to CNN. She riffled through the magazines without hope that anything could distract her from the shit storm of Officer Austin's shooting, the YouTube video, the angry Mrs. Austin, somebody chasing her around town, her stalled work-in-progress, and whatever Harvey might be up to.

She thumbed through an article memorializing celebrities who had died, gradually losing herself in the glossy litany of public tragedy.

The automatic doors whooshed open to her mom, ambushing her with Macy's bags swinging from both arms. "Still a size six?"

Zoey slapped the magazine onto the coffee table. Her mom sounded surprisingly chirpy for someone who didn't approve of her figure. Size six would be fine if Zoey were four inches taller.

"I saw the clothes you took this morning." Camille plopped down the shopping bags. Like a magician, she pulled out the first offering and unfurled plush leggings in mossy green, Zoey's favorite color. She tossed them into the lap of Zoey's sweatpants. The fabric rippled, luscious as velvet. It wouldn't chafe her naked bottom.

"They're mid-calf, so they should work perfectly on you as full-length."
So cunning.

"And look at this." Her mom held up a flowing top with an abstract design that included splashes of the same green. "These will look smashing together."

The long blouse would hide any camel toe from the snuggly leggings. Zoey sank into the cushion in defeat.

A saleswoman, cruising by on her way to the coffee machine, halted. "What a gorgeous top!"

Camille draped the garment under Zoey's chin as though she were a seated display mannequin. "Look how it brings out her eyes."

"A perfect pick." This from a saleswoman in a black pencil skirt and shimmering ivory blouse, a person who knew style.

Camille beamed at the woman.

"Your sister?" the saleswoman asked Camille.

"She's my mom," Zoey snapped.

Camille's mouth crimped.

Casting a sideways glance at Zoey, the saleswoman tossed off a joke about Camille starting while in the cradle. She sashayed on toward the coffee pot.

Camille spun toward Zoey. "Why do you have to be like that?" She took a tiny nip at her lip, but caught herself, instantly retracting the tooth, either not wanting to muss her lipstick or not wanting Zoey to know she'd landed a blow—a little too late for that.

"Like what? A truth teller?" Her mom loved to pass for hovering near forty, part of the reason she kept her latest boyfriend, Ryan, around. A personal trainer, if Zoey remembered right. "Oh, come on," Zoey muttered, even as part of her wondered why she was *like that*. Why couldn't she graciously allow things to slide? "That woman butters up people for a living. She probably thought she could sell you a luxury SUV."

Camille rebounded by dumping the contents of the other Macy's bag onto the couch. She'd bought shoes, too. Not just any shoes. Tawny leather ankle boots with two-inch heels that would raise Zoey close to a grand five-foot-four.

"You are going to look stunning."

Zoey had to agree. And it wasn't like she didn't need some new threads. She hadn't bought an article of clothing since before her last book release.

Her mom inclined her head in the direction of the coffee pot. "The restrooms are over there."

Zoey gathered the loot. So much for the plan to embarrass her mom with baggy sweats and exposed, unpedicured feet.

Chapter Eighteen

At the entrance to the Playa Maria wharf restaurant, Zoey stopped cold. Taped to the glass door was a photo of PMPD Officer Stanley Austin. Below, a legal-sized sheet of paper bore the message: SEA CUISINE SUPPORTS OUR POLICE.

Her breath hitched. Stan, serious in his uniform, stared out at her with those piercing green eyes. She thought of Christine—hollowed out and angry in the detective's office, her husband gone in a finger snap. Her three children suddenly without a father.

Camille rested a hand on her shoulder. "Very handsome man," she said.

"Whose wife would like to kill me."

"Don't be silly."

"Silly?" Zoey removed Camille's hand and spun to face her.

"I'm sure she doesn't want to *kill* you."

"And how do you know that?"

Camille sighed and opened the door. Zoey found herself at a window table spread with white linen, not quite sure how she got there. She peered at gulls bobbing on the Pacific and listened to the barks of sea lions. Her mom was flirting with their waitperson. The guy looked early thirties, fully adult but sheathed in youth. "And, young lady," he said to Camille, "what can I bring you to drink?" He had her mom's number and was laying it on thick, the charade too discomfiting to watch.

The waiter flashed his dimples her way. She ordered the Hawaiian Ono.

"And to drink?" he asked.

"Storr's chardonnay."

"A glass?"

Zoey hesitated. She faced at least an hour of this because Camille didn't eat; she dined. Camille was paying. And driving.

"A bottle." That would cost about twenty-two dollars—at BevMo.

"I never knew you to have such good taste," Camille said.

Zoey winced. If she'd wanted fancier clothes, a downtown condo, or a racy car—Camille's idea of *good taste*—her mom would have made them happen; what Camille couldn't grasp was that Zoey preferred what she had, what she'd earned on her own.

Her mom watched the waiter walk away and then kept her head twisted, maybe hoping Millard Cranston would barge into the restaurant to interview them. Now that she'd gotten Zoey dolled up and seated in the restaurant, her mom had obviously achieved as much as she'd thought through.

The soft chatter of other patrons filled their silence. Camille unclasped the purse in her lap and discreetly inspected herself in a pocket mirror. "What about that landlord of yours?"

So her mom had met Harvey. Or, at least, spotted him. "Did you notice his truck?" Zoey asked. "His clothes? The saggy porch?" Good to remind her mom that Harvey had no money. Not, Zoey supposed, that Ryan had any.

Camille's purse snapped shut. "I thought marijuana was the new green."

It was easy to spot the field from Zoey's trailer.

In the nick of time, a female server swept in with their drinks, a dry martini with olives for Camille.

Zoey took a sip of the chardonnay. "Perfect."

As though sensing tension, the server chunked the bottle into its ice bucket and flitted away.

"Why did you really come to Playa Maria, Camille?"

"That's the way you treat your mother?" Camille pursed her lips. "Who bought you a lovely new outfit." Her palm swept over the linen and candle and sparkling silverware. "Who's treating you to this meal?"

Zoey steeled herself. She didn't take the bait.

Her mom turned again, perhaps hoping the waiter would reappear. After a pause, she rotated back to Zoey. "The newspaper article mentioned another book."

Ah, yes, of course. Her mom's little star—her name on marquees and bookstore windows. Camille could tout, "That's my daughter."

Zoey had to work not to succumb to her mother's pride, not to weaken in its Kryptonite glow, to remember it had everything to do with Camille having produced a successful writer and not a jot to do with Zoey's writing. She seriously doubted Camille had read either of her books.

"I haven't even written the first chapter." She sipped her wine.

Her mom, usually so adept at maintaining the face she wanted the world to see, let her mouth turn down. Camille knew that meant the new title might not hit the shelves for a couple of years.

Zoey enjoyed her chardonnay. Writer's block had never given her so much pleasure.

* * *

In the comfy seat of her mom's rental car, Zoey slouched, her head sinking into the leather. She barely lifted her eyelids to guide Camille into the mountains, up to the trailer. She hadn't been this drunk in a long time. She wouldn't have been able to drive even if her car had been ready.

In the daytime and stone-cold sober, a person faced treachery on this twisty, narrow highway, and that was before turning onto the rough mountain roads. Her mom clutched the steering wheel with white knuckles, making her hands look their age.

"That damned driver behind me will not get off my tail."

"People drive like maniacs on this road." Zoey lifted herself. "Why don't you move into the slow lane?"

"Why doesn't he go around?"

That was her mom, expecting the world to adjust to her. Zoey turned to look out the rear window. The driver roared around them, passing on the right. He steered with one hand. His left. His driver's side window glided down.

Was he going to give them a one-fingered salute? She couldn't blame him with her mom putting along in the fast lane. But the driver didn't do anything. The window zipped shut as the car passed. Another nondescript light-colored sedan with muddy license plates. Like the one she'd seen at Brianna's? Zoey shot upright and leaned forward, but too late to see if it bore the winged emblem of a Chrysler. The car curved into the darkness.

Now she was being silly. How could that gray Chrysler be following them now? If they were in her green Honda Element, maybe. That was a distinctive vehicle; her mom's rental car—not so much.

"Oh, no."

"Now what?" her mom asked.

"That's our road."

The tires squealed as her mom veered.

A thought brushed Zoey's brain, delicate as an eyelash kiss. *The car. The white sedan that night.*

Chapter Nineteen

Ray gripped the phone receiver like he could strangle his reality. Outside his office, the Tumoba harvester rumbled by, making it hard to hear. Domingo, the foreman, was pulling it into the shed and shouting at the four fieldworkers who'd spent their day tucked inside the machine, plucking up the cut stalks and tossing them into the bin sorter. Their sorry asses were only now leaving the packing sheds to go home to their families. For a second, Ray allowed himself the fantasy of converting all his fields to sprouts—going completely legit.

Too late for that; he was in up to his eyeballs in this mess. "What are you telling me?" he shouted. At least the cop-killing idiot on the phone didn't have his cell number. "No. Wait a minute. Don't answer that. Are you calling from a secure line?"

"A burner."

"Well don't call me." He dropped his forehead into his bulky palm and massaged it. "Report to Stuart. He'll fill me in. *Capisce?*"

"What does that mean?"

"Jesus H. Christ." Ray's head was as heavy as a bowling ball in his hands. He scrubbed his forehead and skimmed a palm up over his smooth dome, now slick and greasy. A person didn't need an Italian mom to know the word *capisce*.

"I thought you'd want a progress report," the kid said.

"Only one that says, '*Finito.*'" Ray pinched the bridge of his nose. "That means The End."

"I thought you didn't want me telling Stuart this stuff."

Ray heaved a sigh. "That's right. You tell him 'the job's done.' That's all. And he'll tell me."

"So I do need to report this stuff to you," the kid dogged on. "Her name is Zoey Kozinski. She was in the paper. Kind of a big deal."

"*A big deal?*"

"A writer."

"I don't think you can top cop-killer for *a big deal.*"

"I picked up her scent."

"You want a medal?" The muscles around Ray's heart clenched, a painful ache in his chest. Ray pulled a bottle of beta blockers from his top drawer. "Call Stuart when everything is taken care of."

As the phone traveled to its stand, the voice called into the air, "There was two of them."

Ray clamped the receiver to his cauliflower ear. "Say what?" He shook out a pill. "Now there are two witnesses?" He dry swallowed the beta blocker.

"I spent the whole morning staking out her friend's apartment," the kid whined. "Then, like a miracle, this Zoey Kozinski appeared." The idiot had a gift for storytelling. "But this burly ape joined her and rode with her almost to the Honda dealership. There wasn't any opportunity to take care of things." He paused as though catching his breath. "I parked and snuck up though, and the service manager was saying they could work on her car at the end of the day, which was a lucky 'cause my mom called for me to pick her up."

Ray's head throbbed. He pressed two fingers between his eyebrows.

"I came back," the kid said defensively. "But then," he paused dramatically, "out of the dealership walks two short redheads."

"Why is this a fucking problem?"

"What do you want me to do?"

"Don't you know which one is the witness?"

"Seriously, dude, they could pass for sisters."

"*Dude?*" Ray yelped.

"You said not to call you Boss."

"You'd just seen this Zoey character. Didn't you notice how she was dressed?"

"That's the weird thing. Neither was dressed that way—not even close—although one of them must've been her."

Kill 'em both. He didn't say it because he didn't trust phones. And because…well…he couldn't. "Use your judgment." *If you have any.*

At this point, the easier option might be to dispose of this Justin, Jacob, or whatever his name was. But Ray didn't have anyone to do the job. Stuart was his fixer, and had taken care of a lot of shit, but Ray had never asked him to whack anyone.

"Wanna hear something interesting?" The kid piped like a first grader.

"Not unless it's good interesting."

"I think it's *good interesting*, Boss."

Ray squeezed his eyes shut and massaged his forehead. "Just tell me." And here his baby brother Gugli griped about finding good personnel at his restaurant.

"The two redheads drove up in the mountains near where the tow truck took my mom's car, but—"

"How do you know where the tow truck went?"

"Covering my bases, Boss."

"Don't fucking call me that!" This time Ray used the button to end the call rather than waiting for it to click off in its stand. He didn't want to hear more. The kid had acted like he had no way to get around without his mom's car, yet he'd had the wherewithal to follow the tow truck. How, exactly, had he managed that? So far, the only thing that had gone right was the visit from the cops, even more cursory than Ray had expected. As he'd figured, they had an impossible amount of territory to cover.

The kid was resourceful. He'd give him that. Tracking down the witness. And knowing where they'd towed the car—holding evidence of Ray's collusion—that was cunning. Ray rubbed his fingernails.

The beta blocker worked fast, his heart beat already slowing. Seriously, if the idiot couldn't take care of this problem ASAP, their best bet would be to take care of the idiot. Domingo might know someone—a desperate illegal, maybe.

In the meantime, he would pay his old pal Harvey a surprise visit. Have a beer and shoot the shit. Scope out the situation in person.

He laced his thick fingers on top of his head. The idiot's last bit of information was *good interesting*. The road to Harvey's was an in-and-out in a sparsely populated wooded area. People didn't randomly drive it. If the witness lived out there, that narrowed down the possibilities considerably. And it offered a secluded spot for the deed. The mountains had a stellar reputation as a place to dump bodies.

He stood, put on his jacket, and took the gun from the drawer. Tomorrow he'd give his friend a surprise visit. Check out the lay of the land.

Chapter Twenty

The square footage of Zoey's house cramped any serious pacing, eliminating any way to outrun the idea that she was being followed. The gray car at Brianna's apartment. The car tailgating her mom. The whispering of the trees outside her windows, usually comforting, suggested ghosts. Or worse, real people. The cop killer. Or Christine Austin. *Plotting. Stalking.* She regretted not inviting her mother in, which meant, even drunk, she was seriously on edge.

The new boots and the Macy's bags full of her old clothes bulked by the door, limiting her space. She punted the bags to the glass, angry that she'd given in to her mom's bribery.

There was no sense changing into pajamas. Even half-anesthetized with wine, she wasn't going to sleep.

In her mind, Stan Austin's widow, Christine, crept through the trees armed with a weapon. After all, if Christine were a character in one of her books, that's what the character would do. In Detective Bowman's office, the widow's face had been contorted with rage. And, she was good with a gun. Her husband had made a point of that.

It's your fault.

Clearly Christine had latched onto this narrative. Zoey had been with Stan. Zoey had distracted Stan. Stan was dead. And Detective Bowman not only allowed Christine to spin that story, he'd hooked Zoey into it.

She snapped off the lamp on the table—no sense being a target in a light box. She padded to her slider in the shadowy light from the half moon. Angling herself, she peered toward Harvey's house, its whiteness swallowed in ethereal moonlight.

Then it blazed alive. *The motion-sensor light. Triggered by what?*

She shrank back from the glass, a blast of adrenaline clearing the remainder of her wine fuzz. Her skin frizzed with electricity. She peeked out the window. The lights revealed everything—the knots in the fence, the rust on Harvey's truck, the blades of tough grass around their parking areas. All empty.

She waited and watched, frozen against the wall until the outside lights blinked off. The sudden blindness amplified the sound of her rapid breathing.

If a critter was out there, its next movement would reactivate the lights unless it had passed beyond the sensor's reach. *Coming toward her house? Where was Rambo?*

In the dark, she spun and made her way through her furniture. Her imagination outpaced her.

Why had the driver of that passing car on the highway opened his window? Before that, the last time she'd seen a car window open, a gun had whipped out. She pulled down her ladder for an escape into the loft, if necessary.

Her hand froze on one of the pine rungs. The man at Bri's apartment, the slender form—barely more than a kid—had gotten out of that rental and headed toward her across the asphalt. With intention.

She shivered. Could he have been the shooter? Had the appearance of Curt saved her butt?

On full alert, she strained to hear any foreign sound outside the trailer. The fiberglass shell ticked in the cooling of night.

Zoey glanced up the rungs. If she climbed the ladder, she'd be caged with no exit. She couldn't fit through the hopper windows. She yanked open the drawer with her kitchen supplies, her three spoons and three forks, can opener, and cork screw rattling forward. She took out the all-purpose knife.

Girl, you need to get a grip.

Her hand tightened around the hilt.

That is not what I meant.

She sat on an ottoman in the darkest corner of the living area, the knife in her lap. Was the car on the mountain highway the one she'd seen at Bri's apartment? It seemed fancier, somehow. She wished she knew more about makes and models.

How could the shooter have tracked her to Bri's apartment building? If her life were a novel, the idea would strain the reader's suspension of disbelief. She was being paranoid.

She ran her thumb and forefinger along the knife's edge. Dull as a sitcom. It wouldn't pierce an assailant's clothing much less penetrate his dermal layer.

No, in her novel, she'd plot it so Christine convinced someone to whack her, maybe a fellow officer, the thin blue line and all of that—at least as believable as the shooter having tracked her. This effort to distract herself from her situation—sitting in the dark imagining a boogey man outside— was not working.

She texted Helga.

Recent events might provide a better book. Time to renegotiate?

She made her way to the kitchen area and brewed a cup of DiviniTea's SereniTea. Nothing had reactivated the lights. Rambo hadn't barked.

Settling on her cube, she laid the knife on the table and installed her new CD player, her fingers clumsy from a day that seemed impossibly long. Had she really snooped around in Harvey's house that morning? And then there was the confrontation at the police department, the car chase, the hypnotherapy, and dealing with her car—all topped off with the emotional tumult of an evening with her mother and a bottle of wine. Alternately resting her head on her arms and sipping the soothing tea, she listened to the disc from the therapist.

* * *

A crash woke her. Liquid dammed against her foot. Keyboard buttons pressed into her forearm. *Space Serene* swelled into the room.

Blinking, Zoey turned off the CD. Pre-dawn light softened the edges of her table, the cube beside her, the stairs up to the loft.

Her mug rested on the floor, the last of the tea pooling against her toes. Zoey didn't move. She listened to the whishing trees outside and remembered.

The car. The one with the broken taillight. The one driven by the cop killer. It had a decal on the back, a palm tree.

She'd seen the logo before.

Zoey bolted upright, fully awake.

The palm tree. The palm tree decal advertised....

She snapped her fingers, trying to dredge up the connection. *An eatery.*

She Googled Hawaiian food in Playa Maria and scanned the possibilities. *Kamea Bar-B-Q.*

Her heart raced. That was it. She opened the restaurant's home page, and the logo sprang up in the banner. The killer's car bore a decal for Kamea Bar-B-Q!

She'd eaten there a couple of times—a small, hip, downtown joint with loyal customers who relished kalua pork. Maybe on one of those days, she'd walked right by the guy who shot Officer Austin in the face. Her stomach hollowed out. The killer could have been sitting at the next table, munching grilled Spam.

Spinning around to her kitchenette, she tore off a paper towel and mopped up the tea on the floor. Fortunately, none of it had splashed onto her new leggings.

She tapped the computer to wake it. Four o'clock in the morning, but she had to tell someone about this. She couldn't reach Detective Bowman now, and this was not info she wanted to leave in a message. It was too early to call Brianna.

She tugged an earlobe. *Jimmy?* She hadn't heard from him. Maybe the kisses in the brewery parking lot hadn't meant anything, or maybe he was playing it cool—not wanting to seem overeager. She had no use for coyness, no patience with dancing around attraction. If you're interested, you're interested.

She sent him a DM. *I have a lead on the cop killer!*

She stood and stretched, her shoulder muscles aching and her head throbbing from the wine. She drank a large glass of water before pushing balled-up sweatpants, the laptop, and CD player ahead of her up the rungs to her loft. Setting the devices beside her futon, she stripped off the new blouse from her mom. It was wrinkled and smelly and would need dry cleaning. Still, she draped it carefully from a bar of her electric piano's stand.

The plush leggings were comfortable enough to sleep in, but she peeled them off, folded them, and placed them beside her laptop.

Instead of pajamas, Zoey slipped on her sweats in case she needed to spring into action. She nestled under the covers, turning on *Space Serene* again. Maybe another detail would magically present itself.

Chapter Twenty-One

Day 5

No revelation materialized. Maybe because after the snooze on her computer keyboard, she didn't drift into sleep again. She rested on her futon until she gave up. The hypnotherapy had dislodged other memories, though, that followed her as she clambered down the ladder.

Weak sunlight struggled through the trees. So much for their Indian summer. She plugged in her electric water pot and set up her drip cone for coffee while she plucked up the thread of one of the memories. She'd been eight and her mom had gone off on a cruise with some new boyfriend, leaving Zoey with a nanny.

Nothing terrible happened. At first, in fact, it had been fun. The young nanny let her do whatever she wanted—eat Sugar Frosted Flakes every day, watch cartoons, and stay up late so she was droopy-eyed and cranky at school. But after a few days, a sense of abandonment dropped around her like a net. She made up a song about the nanny's boyfriend and danced around singing it.

He's so ugly with elephant ears/he's so ugly he causes tears....

Back then, there weren't cell phones everywhere, and what would the nanny have said anyway? She wasn't supposed to have guests.

Zoey smiled at the cleverness of her little self. *He's so ugly with great big feet/he's so—*

Her phone rang, startling her. Never good. Friends texted.

Helga. What had she expected? It wasn't the crack of dawn in New York.

Zoey added an extra scoop of coffee. "I don't have it," she blurted.

Helga cleared her throat. The click of a cigarette lighter. An exhale. Pause. "Saw your text." More sucking and puffing on her cancer stick.

She pictured Helga frowning and plucking a bit of tobacco from her thick, coral lipstick. The woman expected better than a text. "Your mom tells me you are at the center of the most compelling crime drama in Playa Maria history."

"This is my life, not some storyline." Zoey ended the call.

Not a smart move, girl. She slumped against the counter. What was wrong with her? She had suggested the new writing direction. Was she reacting to her mom's meddling? Or was it that her mom meddled when it pleased her, then vanished as she had in the newly dredged memory? With almost forty years of experience with Camille, how could she let any of this get to her? She was like an egg with a cracked shell.

In fairness, though, she was not yet caffeinated.

She poured the boiling water, sloshing it outside the drip cone.

The phone rang again.

"But it's a good storyline," Helga said. "I'll get an extension, Kiddo."

Helga disconnected.

It *was* a good storyline, but Zoey felt ill at the idea of using the raw pain of the Austin family as material. She would be exactly the cold-hearted bitch Bowman had implied she was.

She wiped up the waterdrops on the counter with the cuff of her nightshirt. She added more water to the cone, her hand steadier, the aroma of coffee perking up her world. She turned to her table.

Jimmy had written. *Wanna meet up? Where do you live?*

The last question made her bristle.

But wouldn't she ask the same, to suss out a good meet-up spot, a midway point. And now that her mom had located her, did she need secrecy about where she lived? Especially if she might leave Harvey's farm, anyway.

She dodged Jimmy's question by suggesting a twelve o'clock lunch at

Kamea Bar-B-Q. *Kill two birds with one stone.*

C ya. A curt response. Maybe he didn't relish a meat-centric venue either. Zoey had eaten there at the insistence of Brianna, who deserved to pick a lunch spot now and then. She'd certainly eaten more than her share of "sprouts and quinoa" to accommodate Zoey.

Splashing a hefty dose of half and half into her coffee, Zoey checked the time again. Detective Bowman had previously called her around eight in the morning, so it didn't seem too ridiculously early to try his number. She seated herself on her cube, speared a pencil through her hair, and hit the call back.

The detective barked his name. He knew she was the caller, but didn't offer one iota of apology for leading her into the ambush with Christine Austin.

"I remembered something." She extracted her pencil and tapped the table. "I decided to try hypno—"

"What?" he growled.

"I tried hypnosis."

The detective groaned. "Not a good idea."

"Why?" She pressed the pencil tip into her notepad.

"Anything you remember that way is inadmissible in court."

The pencil lead snapped. She brushed it onto the floor, heat rising up her neck. As a mystery writer, she should have known. "But you can still investigate based on what I remembered, can't you? If you find something, that's admissible, isn't it?"

"So whatdaya got?" Bowman's voice was taut with tension, the angry sound of Camille's Rich Husband #2, the one she married when Zoey was a little girl. The detective was naturally on edge. He had on his hands a fellow officer murdered, no leads to offer the public, and a widow crazed with grief who had assaulted Zoey in his office.

Still, his tone, so like #2's after his third martini and a line of coke, set off alarm bells. Zoey used to circle her dolls around her body, readying them for defense. She'd been a brave little soul. She marshalled her courage now and told the detective about the decal on the car.

"That's it?" His angry tone shifted to disgust.

"It could help identify the car."

"We haven't located *the car*. Which means unless the shooter suddenly becomes stupid, we are not going to find *the car*."

"Aren't criminals usually stupid?"

He begrudgingly agreed with her, but his voice sagged toward depression. Or exhaustion. Or both.

"Are you going to check out Kamea?" she prodded.

"To what end? Do you think the minimum-wage staff of a place like that know which customers drive white cars? We don't even know if the shooter put that thing on the car," Bowman said. "He could have bought it used. But call me if you have any other memories."

Did she detect sarcasm? "So you aren't going to check it out?"

"Look," he said. "We are doing everything in our power to find the shooter, but at this moment we have another problem."

"Something that trumps a dead officer?" She knew she was stepping in doo-doo, but it was like when she hurled her doll at Rich Husband #2. She couldn't help herself.

"Christine Austin is initiating a civil suit against the department, against the Ride-Along program," he said. "Claims it distracted her husband. And claims the program is responsible for the YouTube video, which caused her 'great psychological distress.'"

The slam of Bowman's phone receiver crashed into her ear.

She sat on her cube, stunned. No wonder Bowman had led with hostility. She'd started the call pumped up with her Big Clue; now she felt gutted.

Maybe she did bear some responsibility for Stan Austin's death. At the very least, there wouldn't be a lawsuit—at least not this one—if she hadn't been in the cruiser.

But the YouTube video? How could anyone pin that on the Ride-Along program? On her? She hadn't posted it.

The memory of hurling the doll at Rich Husband #2 flowed back in its entirety—her favorite doll missing the target and smashing against the wall, its head disconnecting and rolling across polished wood floor. The man, towering over her, screaming, "You spoiled brat!" His heavy hand gripping her shoulder.

She flinched under the memory.

He shook her until her lips burbled. Her brain rattled. She crumpled to the floor.

Zoey rested her memory-battered brain in her hands. Nothing had been accomplished. Not then. Not now.

Tears dampened her palms. Sadness for little Zoey. Sadness for big Zoey. Maybe this hypnotherapy was not such a great idea, the way it loosened all sorts of detritus to float to the surface, not just details from the shooting.

Her mother reattached the doll's head somehow. So, it hadn't been a complete tragedy. The doll survived. And her mom's heart glinted briefly like a gold nugget. The usual Camille would have simply bought her a new doll.

She sipped her coffee and stared out her slider at the worn patch in the grass that served as her parking area, then out to the road and forest beyond. Another memory floated up like a mirage on the glass. *Stan.*

She had not plucked the name of her fictional character out of thin air.

During the ride-along, Officer Austin had told her he'd responded to the baby shooting, one of Playa Maria's most horrific crimes. A photo had filled the front page of the *Playa Maria Reporter*, the father of the shooter on his knees, reaching toward his son, restrained by officers. Only law enforcement were identified in the caption. One of them had been Officer Stan Austin.

Zoey propped her chin in her hands, surprised at its delicacy. Maybe the call to Detective Bowman hadn't been a zilch. If she hadn't pushed at him, if he hadn't snapped, she wouldn't know anything about the civil suit against the Ride-Along program. That was not information a detective would normally divulge.

And examined coldly, she had to agree with him. The decal wasn't much of a clue.

It's nothing at all.

She tapped her temples. *How stupid to set the meet-up with Jimmy at Kamea*

Bar-B-Q. She didn't even like the food. The more practical problem for her attention was how to get to town. Uber drivers didn't exactly circle the mountaintop.

Even with a nine-to-five job, Bri would probably pick her up, but Bri had never been to her place. GPS was useless and explaining the route challenging.

It was too much to impose on a friend.

The only two candidates were Camille and Harvey.

Her phone rang. *Millard Cranston. The curmudgeon.* She let it go to voicemail, but her curiosity got the better of her. She tapped the icon for transcription. "Like the article?" The words paused as though he expected her to pick up. "Yeah, heard about your little encounter with the widow." The statement read like a juicy, squirmy piece of bait.

How does he know about that?

"Care to comment?" The words stopped again like he knew without a doubt she was aware of his message. His self-confidence was galling. And gaffing.

"Yeah, I'd watch out for that Christine Austin," Cranston said. "She's more of a hothead than her husband was." She imagined the words delivered with his sinister chuckle. "And she's a better shot."

Stan had shared this same detail with her, but how did Cranston know it? And why was he repeating it? Was he using scare tactics to flesh out a colorful feature article?

"Call me." Cranston left his number. *Very old school.*

Chapter Twenty-Two

Ray drove into the mountains, glad that his parents and younger sister were all dead. If this shit storm blew up, they wouldn't be around to suffer the humiliation. There was his brother. *Gugli.* An oopsie for their folks. He was a lot younger than Ray, so they weren't tight, but Bill was a good guy.

Dread churned in Ray's belly. Bill knew what he did for a living. Or, at least, the cannabis part. Ray tapped the steering wheel. No one cared about cannabis cultivation. But a cop killing…a cop killing would not only destroy his life, it could destroy his brother's business. His brother's whole life, really. And the life of his kids.

As Ray took a curve, the Colt slid and thumped in the glove compartment. On the other half of the S turn, the gun whacked the other side. The highway didn't offer much in the way of pull-offs. Even if he found one, reentering traffic would be a bitch. The banging felt like it had lodged inside his head.

The tires of the Ram squealed as Ray almost missed the road off the highway. He marveled that Stuart had been able to direct the tow-truck driver to the farm in the dark. Once off the highway, the directions went along the lines of *watch for the yellow mailbox. Take the second nearly invisible hairpin right turn. You will know you've missed it if you dead-end into a goat farm.*

Ray worried now that the cops might have identified the kid's car. His mother's car. How, he had no idea. Street cams? Lack of logic didn't stop the idea from pestering him.

He tapped the brakes as a curve tightened, sharper than he'd anticipated, the gun sliding and whopping. Harvey would have a gun, too, and he'd be much better at using it. The thought carried only a trace of bitterness. They'd been friends since the first day of kindergarten, and Harvey had always been smarter, more athletic, and better looking. The only advantage Ray ever had was people liked him better. He was social. He liked team sports.

But Harvey, Ray silently shook his head as he cranked the wheel to make the hairpin turn onto a dirt road. The gun bashed the side of the glove compartment. Harvey could have excelled at any sport, but chose the isolated trails of cross-country. Some people speculated what happened with Rachelle caused Harvey to withdraw, but Ray knew he'd been a goddamn loner all his life.

Chapter Twenty-Three

Zoey elevated on her toes to get the best possible view, but couldn't spot any vehicle in front of Harvey's farmhouse. So much for a ride from Harvey, although on occasion he parked his truck down by the barn. Out the back window, she couldn't glimpse his hat bobbing among his plants, where he was pretty much every day, all day long, at this time of year, unless he was inside the barn packing product.

She slipped out into the misty morning, crossing the verge in front of the fence, the grass curled and yellow. She didn't need just a ride to town. She felt unnerved. Jittery. The emerging memories, the call with the detective, the reporter's veiled threat. She could use some company. If she had to beg or bribe Harvey to drive her, so be it.

Her shave-and-a-haircut on Harvey's door went unanswered, as expected. No Rambo snuffling around in greeting, either.

At the far corner of Harvey's house, bright orange globes hung in his huge persimmon tree. A dirt road ran down to the barn. She pounded down the dusty track hedged with madrone, wax myrtle, and fragrant bay laurel. No truck in front of the ancient structure, its traditional red paint faded and peeling. If Harvey planned an operation to extract honey oil, this was where he'd set up. Plenty of room. Away from the house.

She listened to the silence. There wouldn't be many opportunities when Harvey was gone. Sometimes you had to carpe the moment.

Sprinting back to her house, she stuffed her phone into the pocket of her sweat pants in case she wanted photos, then stepped back outside. Normally she loved it here. The solitude. The quiet. But with Harvey and Rambo gone, the farm suddenly felt too isolated. She was so completely alone.

The quickest way to the barn was not to circle Harvey's house, but to use the trail running along the rim of the ravine. It was a little tricky. Harvey's fence ran to the edge of the ravine, but she'd stepped around the end of it many times to use the shortcut. Besides, at the end of the fence, the drop was a manageable incline for a few feet before it plunged into wilderness.

She gripped the end post. One foot remained on the trailer side of the path. She lifted the other, straddled the four-by-four, and searched for her usual purchase on the other side.

The ground gave way. Clods tumbled down the slope. Her foot dangled in the air.

She swung back to her side and peeked around the post. A couple of inches below the path, a protruding rock had caught crumbs of the dirt. *Don't be so lazy. Go to the road.*

But this wasn't about lazy. Obstacles brought out her determined streak. Stubborn streak, her mom would say.

Holding onto the post, Zoey extended a toe and pushed down hard on the rock. More clumps of dirt tumbled into the brush, but the rock didn't wiggle. She put more weight on it. Still good.

In one deft move, she pulled herself, pirouetting, to the other side.

Harvey called his grow a field, but it was more like a large backyard garden, a few plants on the side of his house and rows of plants in the back. He'd trimmed the outer growth, and the marijuana looked denuded, except for the floral stuff in the back, which peaked later. She followed the narrow path to the last two rows, then tunneled between them. The unharvested plants loomed over her, the bouquet intoxicating like the overpowering scent of narcissus.

A crow cawed and flew up from the ground so close the flutter of its wings fanned her face. She put a hand over her thudding heart.

The marijuana passageway ended near the barn. Harvey was definitely gone. If he'd pulled his truck as far to the back of his house as he could—where she might, conceivably, have not seen it from the road—she'd see it now. Definitely no ride into town from Harvey.

Time to investigate.

She hoped not to find more evidence that Harvey was expanding his business. She really, really wanted him to stick to growing marijuana.

A padlock hung on the hasp of the bat-wing doors. Harvey couldn't afford vandals getting into the barn. She yanked on the lock to be sure. No luck.

On the near side of the barn, there was an aluminum-framed window, a modernization of the original barn. Rust pockmarked the frame. Black cardboard covered the inside. She put her palms to the glass to see if she could make the window slide, another ridiculous endeavor. She banged on the window to try to dislodge the cardboard. It stayed in place, wedged tight or maybe taped.

She squinted along the bottom to see if there might be a gap, but Harvey had thoroughly blocked the view. *No surprise.*

When she had been researching *Cannabis Cutter*, he'd escorted her through this barn, the back strung with wires from wall to wall. Clothespins pegged clothes hangers along the wires. Suspended by stem notches, marijuana had dangled from every inch of space. Below the drying cannabis, clean sheets of plastic stretched to catch stems and curled leaves.

"I sell the litter to a guy who makes hemp products." Harvey had been puffed up and proud.

She couldn't square that Harvey with a guy who'd produce honey oil.

The sun had burned away the morning dampness. Above her, the sky spread a guileless blue. She shouldn't be snooping.

If Harvey caught her here, he'd probably accept whatever excuse she offered. But what about Rambo? Her heartbeat sped up. The dog tolerated her as long as she acted in her customary way, but change one little thing, like when she'd confronted Harvey about the persimmon bread, and the dog had nearly snapped her hand off. How would it react to arriving home and detecting someone by the barn? The Doberman wouldn't wait for excuses.

Next time she was in town, she'd buy some dog treats and try to bribe the dog into liking her better.

For now, Rambo would be with Harvey, and Harvey could call a command before Rambo's fangs latched onto her leg, provided Harvey could see it was her, which he couldn't if she was on this side of the barn.

Keeping an eye out for any chink in the siding, she turned the corner to the back. On this north-facing end, the weathered boards were tighter and in better condition, except for mold growing up near the eaves. No way to look inside.

Harvey might be engaged in an illegal enterprise with his grow, but he'd always seemed so...*ethical?... principled?...innocent?*

When she rounded to the far side of the barn, a truck rumbled in the distance, growing nearer—too big and powerful to be Harvey's.

Police? Christine Austin? Panic shot through her. People did not drop by to visit.

The vehicle didn't stop in the front yard. The growl of its engine continued toward the side road down to the barn.

Zoey tore off around the barn and into the cover of the marijuana plants.

The vehicle stopped at the barn entrance. A black Ram truck. Double cab. Long bed. A behemoth.

She gulped. If she could see the driver down the field row, he could see her. She scrambled from the plants, across the path, and onto the ledge of the ravine. She dropped to her knees. Two yards behind her, the incline took a sheer plunge, the redwoods marching steeply downward. Far below, their tops wove a dark green carpet. Vertigo spun through her.

She shrank even lower. From this position, she couldn't see the truck without lifting, so she figured the driver couldn't see her.

Redwood duff and laurel leaves spread over silty dust slick as a bobsled track. Crawling, Zoey moved sideways through scrub, brambles scratching her arms. She stopped. Two feet ahead of her, a plant with three-leaf prongs, the green tinged with yellow and red, covered the ground. The poison oak tangled through the scrub, all the way up to the lip of the ravine and down to the drop-off.

She itched just looking at it. Pulling into a squat, she tested her ability to stand. Her Keds slid on the powdery dirt and duff. Grit filled her shoes. She lowered back to a squat before she'd determined whether the driver of the Ram could see her if she stood.

With her tender skin, she'd be better off contracting herpes than crawling through poison oak.

The narrowest part of the poison-oak patch was near the path. At that point, she might be able to step over it, but she'd be visible to the man. If he walked to the front of the field. If he looked.

Zoey crabbed sideways up the incline and tried standing again. Her footing held. She stepped over the growth. Her foot took off sledding. She landed on her side, her right hand smacking into the poison oak.

Tears of frustration stung her eyes. Making certain not to touch herself, she moved toward her house. Near the faux fence, she clawed her way to safety. Standing, she grasped the fence post and tested the stepping stone.

It held. She whipped around the fence to the other side, hurried to the trailer, and used an elbow to open her front door. Mixing a scrub of vinegar and salt, she coated the hand that had planted in the poison oak, massaged the skin, and rinsed it with cold water. She glanced at the time on her phone. She was never going to make it to lunch with Jimmy. But she couldn't deal with that now.

As she poured the dirt from inside her shoes, the truck tore back up from the barn area and skidded to a stop, pluming dust, in front of the farmhouse. She pulled back into her trailer and locked the slider. Had the driver spotted her when she stood upright on the path?

He climbed from his truck and slammed the door. As he approached the farmhouse, he emerged into her sightline—a stocky, paunchy guy in slacks and windbreaker. At the door, he got the same lack of response she had. He spun toward her tiny house and tilted back his hat. She ducked away from her door, then glanced out the corner of the glass.

The older guy, about Harvey's age, stared in her direction as though he could see through the fiberglass. He studied her place, each second of his study elevating her heart rate.

She'd never seen this truck or this man.

He stalked along the fence, coming toward her trailer.

She scampered up to her loft and squatted in the corner by her electric piano, where he wouldn't be able to see her from the door. Lifting a hand, she cranked open a loft window. Ears perked, she strained to hear. No footsteps. If he wasn't coming to her house, where had he gone? He certainly hadn't driven away.

She wished she had a window in the loft that faced the field.

The field!

The man didn't fit her idea of a field thief. Harvey said most pot bandits were lowlife scum. This guy had a new shiny truck and a confident swagger. And he hadn't been carrying any garbage bag to haul off loot. On the other hand, how hard would it be for a bulky guy to conceal folded garbage bags inside his jacket? And in spite of his attire, there was something about him that reminded her of fieldworkers.

When the man had found Harvey's place deserted—the ideal time for a thief to strike—he'd driven back to the house and headed along the fence. *If he wasn't coming to her trailer, why follow the fence? Why hadn't he harvested plants when he was in the back, hidden from sight?*

Had he surveilled Harvey's set-up? Did he know there was no side fence?

Still, even if the answers were yes, he'd make the theft in the back. It would be senseless to haul product down the trail and around the fence.

Zoey tapped out Harvey's telephone number with little hope he would answer. His cell phone was the begrudging acknowledgement of the Twenty-first Century by a man who prided himself on living off the grid, who didn't even own a television.

He kept his mobile phone on Do Not Disturb, checked it when the spirit moved him, and her call depended on reception—not guaranteed in the mountains. With Harvey, a person might as well be operating in the world of You've Got Mail.

She left a voice message and then sent a text: *Old white male in black Ram snooping around your place.*

"Have you heard from the idiot?"

Zoey almost dropped her phone. The man sounded like he was in her house. He must be right below her open window. For a split second, she thought he'd seen her and was talking to her. Did he mean Harvey?

"No one seems to be around, but do you know what kind of car we're watching for?"

The voice moved away, then tinder-dry twigs snapped as he came back toward the trailer. The feet stomped by, heading back along the fence toward Harvey's house.

Phone in hand, she clambered down her ladder and changed into rust-colored pants and a flannel shirt of green and brown plaid, almost camouflage. She put on socks and hiking shoes and checked out her window. The truck was still there. The stranger was nowhere in sight.

She eased open the sliding door. Slipping out, she walked around the high end of her trailer, farthest from the farmhouse. Rather than clear the short distance to the fence in the wide open, she headed directly into the trees, the incline here slick with bay laurel leaves.

What am I doing?

The man hadn't looked dangerous. Her whole reaction reeked of leftover paranoia—her off-kilter state since the shooting. But he was on the alert for someone unknown in an unknown type of vehicle. Could it be her? If so, she didn't want to be corralled in her trailer.

Latching onto weeds, she edged past the end of the fence. Grabbing the rock she used as a foothold, she hauled herself up to the path to clear the poison oak. Then she dropped back where she'd be out of sight. At the last rows of marijuana, she grasped a sapling to hoist herself. Sweat trickled down the nape of her neck. Hiding behind the trunk of a redwood, she listened, hoping to hear the truck leaving.

A blue jay spotted her and scolded as though to proclaim, "Hey, she's over her!" It would not shut up.

The man appeared around the corner of the barn, the last rows of marijuana telescoping her view of him. Even with his hat, the man didn't top five foot seven.

Hat? Her heart fluttered. That was it. His was tipped back at a cocky angle, but if he were to plant it atop his head, where it would actually do some good, it reminded her of something a fieldworker would wear.

The man's head swiveled toward the blue jay racket. Her heart jumped as she realized, too late, that her sight line down the rows of plants led right back to her.

She shrank against the bark, glad to be small.

But the man strutted down the rows of floral plants, coming at her, one hand in a heavy-hanging pocket of his windbreaker.

Chapter Twenty-Four

Zoey ran along the incline. Her shoes slipped on the duff and her body skated, her hands flailing. Her hipbone smacked a rock. The same side she'd fallen on earlier. Pain shot through her. Her body continued to slide toward the drop.

Eyes full of grit, she grabbed blindly at foliage, grasping a small trunk. She hung, feet suspended above air, the perilous plunge below them. The weight of her body yanked at her rotators.

The man shimmered through her tears, peering over the rise above her. She scissored her legs, searching for a place to secure her feet. Her shoulders screamed.

She blinked, but no gun pointed at her. Not that it mattered if the alternative was falling to her death.

"Who the hell are you?" the man bellowed.

She opened her mouth to answer and coughed. Her left foot found purchase on a rock. Her other foot found solid ground a little higher up. Arms relieved of her dangling weight, she lay spread-eagled, panting. She could probably pull herself onto all fours, now, but she stayed flat. She released one hand to wipe some of the dust away from her mouth. Her fingers reeked of vinegar. "I live here." She spat dirt from her mouth. "That's my trailer."

"So why are you running away?"

"I don't know who you are."

"Usually works the other way. People run when they know who I am." He chuckled, then swiped off his hat and scratched a bald head. He continued to peer down at her. "Harvey didn't tell me he had someone living up here."

He knows Harvey's name. Zoey lifted her head a little.

"Oh, geez, a redhead," the man said. "That explains everything."

She worked saliva into her mouth. "So who are you?"

"Old friend of Harvey's."

She decided against asking why she'd never seen him before. Or why he'd been snooping around Harvey's property, returning to the barn when he knew Harvey wasn't there.

He planted his hat back on his head.

"Where's The Man?" he asked.

"No idea." She added quickly, "But he should be back any minute."

He looked at his watch. "Are you okay to get up out of there?"

She wormed forward a bit. "I'm fine. Everything moves." Her right shoulder hurt, but only a little. Through the trees, the sun blazed overhead, meaning the day was speeding toward noon. She was going to be late, late, late to meet Jimmy.

"If you work your way up here, I'll give you a hand," the man said.

"That's okay."

He frowned down at her. *"That's okay?"* the man parodied. "What the fuck do you mean by that?"

"I'll crawl up when you're gone."

He glanced at his watch again. "Whatever floats your boat, sweetheart."

He spun on his heels and disappeared from view, muttering "crazy gingers."

She waited, listening. The man wasn't exactly physically fit, and it took a few minutes before the slam of his truck door echoed in the trees. She pushed onto all fours and crawled through the undergrowth.

But the truck didn't roar to life and drive away.

Above her, the stupid blue jay jabbered like he was following her with some personal beef.

Why wasn't the guy leaving?

Pulling out her phone, she texted Jimmy. *Running late.* That was an understatement. Dirt caked her palms. She didn't even have a ride yet.

His response arrived immediately. *How late?*

Very, she wrote.

Cancel?

She should. She had a thousand other things to do. But the urge to continue consumed her. *Continue what, Zoey...investigating?*

Why not ask Jimmy to come get her? Give him directions. Tell him there was a strange man lurking on the premises.

Harvey's friend, she corrected herself.

And, she wasn't entirely sure about Jimmy. The shooter had been a man, sitting tall in a white sedan. Jimmy was a tall man in a white car who appeared at the scene of the crime. Until she knew him better, she didn't want him to know where she lived.

She responded. *Two hours?*

See if I can rearrange lunch breaks.

Brushing dirt from her pants, Zoey clambered to the path, thinking about Jimmy's response. She didn't even know what he did for work, but at least he had a job, one with enough power to determine when people took breaks. That was good. She peeped around the end of the fence.

The man was sitting in his Ram truck. Waiting.

Chapter Twenty-Five

Ray sweltered in the cab of his truck. He pitched his hat onto the passenger seat and wiggled out of his windbreaker, draping it carefully over the hat. Turning on the power, he lowered his window, the breeze refreshing. He twined his hands over his head. *What to do?*

This girl had to be the one. *The witness.* How many red-haired females could there be on this mountain road?

He could have shot her.

Should have shot her?

Should shoot her? Roll her down the mountainside?

His eyes turned toward the end of the fence where he expected her to appear. At some point. She was taking her sweet time.

There were issues with shooting her. Starting with the pang in his heart. He thought he was past that—finally. But the moment he'd seen that red hair, the old familiar grief had ambushed him.

He gripped the steering wheel and drew a deep breath.

With a stubby thumb, he ticked off the first real problem with killing the girl.

In Vietnam, his only bullets were of sweat as he sat in a Quonset hut, banging out requisition forms. He hadn't killed a single gook, so he didn't even know if he could pull the trigger. When he'd looked down the drop, at that girl lying there flattened on the ground, maybe he could have done it then, but she'd lifted her head, the curly hair spilling around her, and he'd snapped back to age twenty-one. An unbearable sadness had poured into him, a feeling worse than any of the racking fear in Vietnam.

That was the first problem. His forefinger drummed the leather. Second. Even if the mountains were famous for body dumps, if she was found, it would attract police to the place they'd stashed the car.

What were the odds? He wished he could make book with them.

This point reminded him to tell the idiot not to dispatch her here on Harvey's property. But even if the body disappeared elsewhere, Harvey would miss her. The moment Ray had laid eyes on the girl, he understood Harvey's attachment. This was a matter of the heart. Not something you could argue about.

He rested his head back against the warm black leather seat of his truck.

So they'd have to wait until they really destroyed the car. Then it wouldn't matter if the cops came around Harvey's property.

He dropped his middle finger against the steering wheel and sighed. The third thing. *Harvey's property*. He and Harvey shared a lot of history.

Guys born on May 31, 1952, had drawn the lottery number 018. So after high school, Harvey was going to Vietnam. His own number hadn't been great, but he might have escaped the draft. It was just with Harvey leaving….

The assault of memories—this whole situation—gave him a headache. He squinted back toward the end of the fence, waiting for the little ginger to emerge. The girl with spunk and attitude like Rachelle.

Not a girl. A woman. You weren't supposed to say *girl*, anymore. His daughter lectured him about stuff like that. But he still thought of his daughter as a *girl*, and she was older than the little redhead, who was a good deal older than Rachelle had been.

The redhead's resemblance to Rachelle spelled some deep psychological hoo-ha going on in Harvey's relationship with her. What happened with Rachelle had affected Harvey as badly as it had him, even though he'd assured Harvey a thousand times that it wasn't his fault.

It was the fault of some overzealous pigs.

He whapped the steering wheel. Why wasn't the girl coming around the fence? Why had she rabbited away from him in the first place? Harvey attracted crazies, but this one took the cake.

And where was Harvey? The guy lived like a hermit. He should be here. *Out delivering product, most likely.* Harvey should hire help. 'Course, with the hot water Ray was in, he had to admit Harvey might have the right idea. It was like that old saying about two people could keep a secret if one was dead.

He straightened in the seat. Was that a hiking boot sticking around the fence? The girl acted like she was afraid of him. *Why?* Did she suspect him? *How?* The possibility only made her more dangerous.

He bent toward his jacket and eased his Colt .45 from the pocket, his hand curled. The safety depressed under his grip.

She'd said Harvey was coming home soon. Harvey wouldn't be into killing her. Obviously, he was smitten with the girl or he'd never let her live here. Shit, the girl had stirred his own memories of Rachelle. The pang in his chest had been undeniable, and he was not given to pangs.

The girl was lying, of course; she was as clueless as he was about Harvey's whereabouts. She didn't have any idea when he'd be home.

He jetted air through his nostrils. On the other hand, Harvey probably was coming back soon. It wouldn't be like him to be gone long during prime season.

He pressed the power button to open the passenger-side window.

The girl poked her head around the fence and gave a tentative wave.

Chapter Twenty-six

The man in the truck had his head turned toward Zoey, as though his vision had been trained on the fence post, where she would appear. His passenger window, facing her, zipped open.

Heart banging, she snapped her head back behind planks, not that they could stop a bullet. She hunkered down.

The engine roared to life. The tires crunched in a three-point turn. Stopped.

Her heart stopped, too. What was he doing?

After a few seconds, the growl of the engine faded down the road. Why had the driver been sitting there in his truck? Was he waiting for Harvey? Waiting for her? She swung around the fence and raced to her trailer, locking the door behind her. She brushed dirt from her clothes to the floor, keeping an eye out, her ears alert. It would be good to get out of here. To have someone near her.

She called her mom.

"Sweetheart," her mom said, "why are you panting? Are you working out?" she added hopefully.

"Yes, Mom. I've been running."

* * *

As soon as she spotted the rental car, Zoey flounced out the door. She'd be damned if Camille received another chance to set foot in her sanctuary. Not that it felt like a sanctuary at the moment.

While she buckled up in the passenger seat, her mom's head retracted to survey her. "What about those nice clothes I bought you?" She reached over and flicked a curly bit of foliage from Zoey's hair. "What have you been doing? Communing with the forest?"

She inspected her mom in turn. The woman wore a draping pale pink cashmere sweater over leggings with a multi-colored design and pink—*pink!*—high-heeled, tooled leather boots. Camille's idea of casual wear.

"After you take me to my car," Zoey said, "I'm headed to a barbecue joint."

Camille's nose twitched like a rabbit's, as though picking up traces of eau de vinegar. "That's why you're dressed like a lumberjack?"

Anxiety welled in Zoey. She'd washed up at the sink but had felt too vulnerable to strip off her clothes and climb into the confined space of her shower. "Do you think you could drive?"

Her mom *tsk*ed at her rudeness but pressed the ignition with a pink fingernail. "I named you Perfect because you were. Right out the chute. You were the cutest baby. Little bowed lips. A perfect doll."

"Mom," Zoey moaned.

Camille smiled faintly at the word and turned the car to head down the dirt road. She drove like an old person, fingers wrapped firmly at 10 and 2. An opal ring glinted its iridescence.

"Barbeque?" Camille lifted a brow. "Not a good choice. I assume you're eating with someone?"

"Yes," she hissed, wanting to push her mom's leg down on the gas pedal.

"At least earthy hues suit your coloring."

* * *

From the car dealership, Zoey drove like a wild woman to downtown. She squeezed her car into a free parking spot and race-walked down El Mar, a leafy street lined with Victorians. In another block, El Mar intersected the main downtown avenue, but Kamea's sat on the corner across from her. Jimmy was leaning near the entrance, a bicycle helmet dangling from his fingertips and resting against green skinny jeans.

She puffed up to him. "Been waiting long?"

He shoved himself off the side of the building. "Long enough to contemplate leaving."

"Sorry."

He stretched a hand to her hair, plucked something, and held up a pine needle.

Her cheeks heated. She was a mess while Jimmy was decked out in a checked, button-down shirt. "It would have taken longer if I washed my hair."

"How about combing it?"

Her mild blush turned into an inferno. Her ears flamed. "You sound like my mother."

He gave her a crooked smile. "My hair takes like a year to dry, and it's not even as thick as yours." He unlocked a black townie bike chained to the pole of a No Parking sign. Threading the chain through the straps of his helmet, he relocked it.

"Where's your car?"

"I prefer to bike."

Zoey turned to the entrance of the barbeque joint. The window displayed a neon yellow poster board with the black magic-marker message: WE ♥ OUR POLICE OFFICERS.

She swallowed. The whole community was aligning with the police department. Expressing its sympathy for the fallen officer. As it should.

But the gathering sentiment felt threatening, like a lynch mob. If Christine Austin rallied the troops and convinced them she was to blame for her husband's death, would she become the pariah of Playa Maria? Would the community want to string her up? She shuddered.

Behind her, Jimmy said, "It's been a tough few days."

She looked up at him. The eyepatch had distracted her from the weariness etched on his face. "Have you been able to sleep?"

He shook his head.

She yanked open the light wooden door. The screened top rattled as it slammed behind them. A heavy inner door sagged into a single room, dark after the outside sunshine. Smoke from the barbeque in the back blurred outlines; chatter and clanking silverware filled the air. The scent of grilled pineapple mixed with the heady sauce. Even though she avoided meat, drool pooled in her mouth.

"I hope they have a good special," she said over her shoulder, trying to sound upbeat. "I'm starving." Her stomach rumbled, affirming the veracity of her tossed-off statement.

Crawling through the woods worked up an appetite. And she hadn't eaten well in days.

"I've never been here." Jimmy matched her new tone. "But my mom loves this place."

She didn't respond. Jimmy fell silent. In spite of their efforts to reclaim normalcy, the window sign had caused Officer Austin's murder to bloom fresh in Zoey's mind. She imagined the same image filled Jimmy's—Austin's sprawled body strobing in the lights of the cruisers.

She bellied up to the counter. A girl appeared at the cash register, flashed them blue braces, and waited. Zoey tried to concentrate on the chalkboard menu.

Another couple banged through the flimsy outside door and stood behind them, waiting to order. The counter girl leaned her weight onto one leg.

"Do you have any car decals?" Zoey asked.

Jimmy nudged her shoulder. His one eye widened, questioning.

The teenager wrinkled her smooth forehead, turned, and called into the kitchen, "Chuck, do we have car decals?"

Over the sizzle of a grill and a burst of Spam aroma, a drawling deep voice said, "Not no more."

"*Not no more*," the girl relayed.

Jimmy edged forward. "I'll have the chicken and slaw plate."

Eyes bluer than the braces moved from Jimmy to Zoey and back. "Is this together or separate?"

"On me," Zoey said. "Since I suggested this place."

"Okay," he said. "Thanks."

Zoey liked that he accepted without protest. No machismo. No wasting time with an unnecessary dance. She turned her attention back to the girl. "When did you stop giving out decals?"

The counter girl sighed, spun toward the kitchen, and shouted the question, in an aggrieved voice. This service clearly exceeded her job description.

"Maybe two, three years ago," the manly voice replied.

Zoey ordered the special and a beer. The girl quirked a brow at Jimmy.

"Just water."

Most of the squeezed-together tables were occupied, the room full of conversation and clatter. Not a great place to talk. But then, she didn't plan to tell Jimmy about her morning.

Two guys got up from a corner table. She torpedoed to the prime spot, sliding into a bench seat under a waxy checkered tablecloth.

A busboy hustled from the other side of the room and cleared the dishes. Jimmy scooted into the bench against the other wall. "So, what's all this about decals?"

"Nothing."

"*Nothing?* Why do I feel you are being less than forthcoming?"

Forthcoming. The word pinged. *Educated. A little stilted.* And why *was* she withholding? Why wasn't she spilling her guts about the bald guy with the gun?

The busboy breezed back to drop off Jimmy's glass of water and two bundles of silverware wrapped in paper napkins. Jimmy unfurled his and tapped the red-checked tablecloth, his uncovered eye inspecting her. "And what about this big clue?" He bent toward her ear. "On the cop killer?"

She shivered at the words *cop killer*. Reticence gripped her. What did she really know about the man beside her? *Good Samaritan. Good kisser.* "I don't even know who you are." The words tumbled out of her mouth.

Swiping a strand of blond hair behind his ear, Jimmy leaned back into red vinyl cushion. He draped his long arms along the top. "Anybody ever tell you you're kind of blunt?"

"My mom." According to her mom, it was one of the qualities that would keep her single. *Maybe true.*

"Your mom sounds blunt, too. Are you alike?"

"We look alike. But it's easy to tell us apart. She's stylish."

Jimmy's head bobbed like he was absorbing this information, really thinking about it. He sipped his water. "You're stylish."

She smiled wryly. She was currently dressed, according to her mom, like a lumberjack. The night of the shooting, she'd been wearing ripped jeans. Jimmy must be thinking of her She Cats outfit. Or more likely, the She Cats uniform as strutted by Sabbie.

"The way you're holding back," Jimmy said, "hardly saying anything, makes me feel like you don't trust me." His one eye narrowed. "Like you think *I* could be the cop killer."

"You think I ask cop killers to lunch?"

They stopped talking as the counter girl swooped over with their plates. Speedy service had catapulted Kamea's into a popular lunch spot—crowded with hipsters who had to return to work. As he lowered his arms to the table, Jimmy checked his retro Shinola watch.

Now that was stylish.

Zoey looked down at her steaming meal. A sticky-looking red-brown sauce smothered the chicken breast. Her mom was right...again. Barbeque was a terrible meal to eat with someone you barely knew. She spooned up a few black beans, catching a tantalizing morsel of the smoky, slightly sweet sauce.

Jimmy picked up the base of a drumstick and chomped into it—comfortable and down home. Not like her mom, who'd use a fork and knife. Like anybody ever ate drumsticks that way.

He twitched his fingers on his napkin. "So what do you want to know about me?"

The girl came by with the beer. Zoey took a swig. Ice-cold. Perfect. Except for the shooting pain of brain freeze. Palm to forehead, she curled her tongue to the roof of her mouth. After a moment, she asked, "Where do you work?"

"I manage the downtown record store." Watching her, he resumed gnawing the drumstick.

"I love that place." Playa Maria Records, known as PMR, was a landmark, a long, low-slung, funky building wall-papered with concert posters. She admired it as a smart business, too, that had made the transition from vinyl to CDs at the right time and then had pivoted back to vinyl.

Jimmy forked up slaw, eating hurriedly.

She'd been late. The poor guy had rearranged his schedule to meet with her and now didn't have time to chew. She sliced off a bit of chicken breast. "I'm sorry I've been such a dick. Thanks for taking the time to meet me."

"Does that mean you're going to tell me what you found out?" He wiped his mouth. "The big clue?"

"No. The more I think about it, the dumber it gets."

Jimmy checked the time on his yellow-faced watch. They ate intently in silence.

"How do you feel about guns?" she asked.

Jimmy's fork clattered against his plate. "You sound like the police."

Eyes trained on him, she tried to decipher every nuance of his reaction.

He balled up his napkin and threw it on the table. "So you do think I might be a psycho killer?" He stood, arms flying out, palms up. "I shot a cop, drove away, and then returned to the scene of the crime?"

He hadn't whispered. Other patrons gawked at them. A brawny diner in cargo shorts shifted in his chair.

"Of course not," she said. "Calm down." But she wished he'd responded differently, maybe said something like 'I hate guns.'

Slapping tip money on the table, Jimmy strode across the room, followed by stares. The brawny man rose to his feet. Fear shot through her.

The flimsy door of Kamea's smacked shut behind Jimmy. The brawny man remained at his table, patting the many pockets of his shorts as if he'd forgotten where he'd stashed his phone.

Zoey scurried across the floor and out the door.

Jimmy was opening his bike lock. He strapped on his helmet, moving brusquely, ignoring her.

She knew the record store was at the end of Playa Maria's main drag, no more than a half mile away, but even if he was the manager, he was late. And he was pissed.

"Hey," she said, "the way I'm acting is not about you."

"It's not you, it's me." Jimmy parroted the old line with only a trace of snark, like he was disappointed, not disgusted.

She pushed her hair back, feeling less than desirable but wanting to reassure him. "Wanna get together later?"

Jimmy swung a long leg over the bike frame and rode off the curb. His words bounced away. Something about seeing her.

Before she could fret about Jimmy's anger, up the street, a tall blonde woman wearing gray sweatpants steamed around the corner. A stack of fliers flapped in the crook of her arm.

Christine Austin.

Chapter Twenty-Seven

Zoey's body trembled as though an earthquake shook the sidewalk. Christine Austin was on the opposite side of the street, but Zoey still considered hightailing it to her car. Instead, she flanked the storefronts of El Mar Street, staying in their shadows, edging in the direction of the woman until she passed her.

Christine trooped along, a woman on a mission, leaving one store to pop into the next.

At the intersection with La Oceana, the main downtown drag, Zoey crossed El Mar and backtracked. Now tailing Christine, she entered the first store, a surfer shop.

Behind a glass counter stood a redhead like herself, although he was tall, tanned, and buff, with a nose that looked perpetually peeled. His sea-green tee advertised the business: All a Board.

"Did a woman just come in here handing out fliers?"

The redhead whipped his head toward her—startled. A surfer dude sliding flannel shirts along a display bar turned to look, too. Downtown businesses were subject to aggro street people wandering in on a daily basis. As the clerk took her in, his shoulders relaxed. "Yeah."

"I'm curious," she said. "Could I see the flier?"

"Sure." He bent down and retrieved a sheet of legal-sized typing paper from under the register. "I have to check with the manager before I put anything in the window," he explained.

She reached for the paper.

The sales clerk pulled it back. He stooped and returned the flier to under the counter. "I don't know," he said. "Maybe come back later and read it in the window."

Zoey felt like winging over the display of keychains and lip balms to throttle him. He didn't look like a teen; he must be pushing thirty. Why was he timid about making such an unimportant decision?

"I'm not trying to give you a hard time," he said. "Maybe some other store already has the poster in its window."

She took a deep breath. He was right. She thanked him and stepped back to the sidewalk.

Three doors down, Christine exited an olive oil store. Mouth agape, Christine froze and stared at Zoey.

Zoey's heartbeat thundered in her ears. As much as she sympathized with the widow, it pissed her off that Christine blamed her for Stan's death.

The widow strode toward her, ponytail switching like the tail of an angry cat.

Behind Christine, two women left the olive oil store, gabbling to one another under the awning. They seemed blissfully unaware of the drama playing out and walked off in the opposite direction. Behind Zoey, on La Oceana, passersby conversed, their voices like a garbled foreign language, unintelligible to her ears. The people around offered no reassurance. All of Christine's rage lasered in on her. She was not safe.

Christine stuck her finger out like the barrel of a gun. It took all of Zoey's willpower not to step back. The woman towered over her. The papers in her arm vibrated with her rage. Her face mottled red. "You have a lot of nerve."

Zoey forced herself to stand straight, to look up into the woman's blazing eyes. "For what?"

"Showing up here."

"I live here."

Christine jabbed her clavicle with the gun finger. "Not if I have anything to say about it."

Zoey latched onto the finger and bent it back. "I didn't kill your husband."

"You little cunt! That fucking hurt." Christine clenched her hand into a fist, whether to punch her or to relieve the pain, Zoey wasn't sure. "That's assault," Christine snarled.

"You jabbed me first." *Oh my God, we sound like children amping up for a playground fight.* She had to switch tactics fast. "What does your flier say?"

Christine unclenched her hand to slap a paper against Zoey's chest. "Read it and weep." The woman spun and hustled toward her next store.

Hands trembling, Zoey tilted the paper into reading position.

IN LOVING MEMORY OF OFFICER STAN AUSTIN.

Under the text was a photocopied picture of Officer Austin in uniform. The same one she'd seen in the window of the Sea Cuisine.

But below this one, it said: BAN THE RIDE-ALONG PROGRAM!

Beneath the screaming headline was a paragraph of normal text:

Officer Stan Austin was murdered by a deranged shooter—and the PMPD Ride-Along Program. Without an assigned passenger to distract him, Stan Austin would be alive.

She couldn't breathe. The conjecture was ridiculous, but what did that matter? Witch hunts started that way. Over the course of history, people had been stoned and burned because of whispered rumor. She leaned against the surf store, the stucco prickling her back.

Christine's accusations were unfounded.

The flier shook so much, Zoey could barely read the rest of the paragraph. Christine had not named her, but anyone who'd read *The Reporter's* coverage would know she was *the passenger*. Christine was out to crush her.

Damn Helga for siccing the reporter Millard Cranston on her.

The paragraph ended with a call to action, to contact the PMPD to protest the program and to visit a GoFundMe site to finance the legal battle.

The clerk leaned out the doorway. "You okay?"

She sucked in a ragged breath. "Not really."

He stepped out to the sidewalk. "Are you going to faint?"

She righted herself. Chugged another breath. "No, I'm going to fight." She wheeled around and strode down El Mar.

The flier was already taped in the window of the olive oil store. Zoey glanced into the next store as she passed. Racks of dresses surrounded

Christine. Jaw jutted and index finger stabbing the air, Christine leaned aggressively toward a cowed employee.

The woman was on a warpath.

Chapter Twenty-Eight

The sight of Harvey's rusty GMC truck calmed Zoey. As she climbed from her SUV, the fragrance of the woods embraced her. A crow cawed. She turned her head toward the bird, perched at the end of the fence. Images of the stocky man rushed her, knocking away the momentary sense of tranquility.

She crossed dry grass, the blades sharp enough to slash skin. The memory of the man nudged in beside her worries about Christine. The widow had channeled her grief into an outlet, and as Zoey slid open her door, she felt the bull's eye on her back.

In her living area, she turned in a circle as though being spun by her thoughts. Now she had two tangible people to worry about—Stocky Man and Christine. Maybe three: *The young man who followed her.*

And Jimmy. And Camille. And Helga.

At least if the stocky man came around again, Harvey would be home, along with Rambo. And her car was working now. She wouldn't be stranded on the farm.

To settle her heart rate, she scrambled to the loft, towing her laptop and the new CD player. She stripped and tossed the camouflage clothes over the edge, sprinkling dirt.

A Google search of Christine Austin Playa Maria yielded pages of links. She had expected the wife of a law enforcement officer to be more circumspect, but Christine Austin was a proud Mama Bear. She touted her kids' athletic and academic achievements, and they'd earned a fair number.

It didn't take long to track down a Pinterest photo, the son Robert—tall and too handsome for his own good—mortarboard mounted on thick, wavy hair, graduation gown billowing from broad shoulders. She smiled. The kid was standing on the front doorsteps, a bouquet of balloons flying into him, revealing the house's number, 5124.

She typed 5124 and Playa Maria into a search, received a small array of house photos attached to that number on various streets, and quickly found the one with a matching red door. *Booyah.* With ten minutes of work, she knew where Christine Austin lived. Not that she had any idea what she'd do with the info. But it empowered. Like she had ammunition. Two could play at this game. She had options.

Zoey pulled the pillowcase off one of her pillows. Stretching on her futon mattress, she covered her naked body with a throw and draped the pillowcase over her eyes to block the afternoon sun streaming through the three open windows. Outside, the trees susurrated, sighing peace. Cool forest-fresh air breezed over her. She traced the bumps of the CD buttons and pushed play. *Space Serene* floated into her ears.

* * *

Zoey blinked awake in surprise. How had she managed to fall asleep? She stretched. Groaned. Scampered in nothing but her socks down from her bedroom.

Eventually she'd need a shower, but for now, since she was dirty anyway, she tugged on the rust-colored pants and plaid shirt. She was groggy, as though the *Space Serene* nap had exacerbated the usual late afternoon torpor. She hadn't eaten enough of her lunch for the barbecue to be the culprit. She plugged in her electric kettle and scooped coffee into the single-serving filter.

Setting her laptop on the table, she opened her work in progress, bending over to reread the beginning while the water heated.

...Finally, the designated intersection. He's late to the party. Officers lined up in formation, handguns and rifles at the ready, are inching down a cul-de-sac toward The House.

His friend Stan is set up across the street from the target, his red thatch of hair poking up behind a fence. The name Stan would have to go with a find and replace.

Without sitting down, she typed *Stan's crazy hat bobbed above the planks.*

Behind her, the water roiled to a boil. She ignored it. Stared at the screen. If Stan had on a hat, how would her protagonist see the red hair? That made no sense. Why had she written it?

A cold steel claw gripped her gut. She knew why. The hypnotherapy had dredged another detail up from the murk of her subconscious. Not the hat. She'd already told Detective Bowman that the cop killer had been wearing a hat.

But when Officer Austin had pulled up behind the white car, the driver had been silhouetted in the cruiser's lights. She'd seen the *shape* of the hat. A peculiar hat. The same kind as Stocky Man with the gun.

Christ! Was he the cop killer? Snooping around, carrying a weapon, staring her right in the face? Had he come here to eliminate the witness? At minimum, the idea provided a rational explanation for why he'd been at the farm.

Another thought rode the coattails of the first. What if she shared this discovery with Christine Austin? Tried to convince the woman to turn her rage toward a different target—the real villain. They both wanted the scumbag killer to be caught. What a waste of energy to battle each other.

They should join forces. Christine possessed useful qualities—determination and fearlessness—and she was, according to two sources, good with a gun.

But Stocky Man was not the shooter. Certainty moved over Zoey like a cloud. He was too short and squat and old.

How did she know all that? The shooter had not even gotten out of his car.

Yet, maybe because of *Space Serene* or because of the hypnotherapy, she knew the shooter was younger, taller, leaner than the man who'd shown up this morning. The shooter had been more like the driver of the rental car. The guy who'd followed her.

The hat clue lost its luster, but didn't disappear. Why would the two men wear similar hats?

She turned and slowly poured hot water over the dark French roast, the fragrance unfurling, encouraging her to inhale. She sat, sipped, and reflected. Maureen Magill, her hypnotherapist, had said traumatic memory was stored differently. In that deep storage, her mind could have tucked away the image of a body sitting taller in the seat. Broader shoulders? A longer neck? Little details that had bubbled to the surface.

She finished her coffee. It was time to have a conversation with Harvey.

Moving to her back window, she spotted his head among the farthest plants, the ones with the floral bouquet. Even though her trailer was elevated, Zoey couldn't usually see him there unless he was on a ladder. He was slaving away late into the afternoon. What was he going to do when he couldn't handle the physical labor anymore?

Slipping on her Keds, Zoey hurried to the edge of the fence, wanting to catch Harvey before he retreated to the barn. She hollered to alert him. And Rambo.

The Doberman padded up the path to Zoey's crossing point. He panted and snuffled.

"Hey, there, Rambo."

She poked a shoe around the end of the fence.

"Rambo!" Harvey shouted, followed by a shrill fingers-in-the-mouth whistle.

The dog hurled away down the path and then swished through the plants. Zoey swung around the fence.

She found Harvey up two steps on a small ladder, tenderly holding some of the top buds and sniffing them. Rambo sat on his haunches, peering reverently up at him.

"What's up, Red?" He stepped down, tugging off his gloves. The raffia brim of his hat hid his eyes.

On the surface, his hat was nothing like Stocky Man's. Harvey's brim was frayed from use. A tie-dyed band, faded from the sun, clamped a hawk feather. Buttons of all sorts armored the crown. A marijuana leaf. *Shop locally. Don't believe everything you think.*

If she erased the symbols of Harvey's personality and refurbished the brim....

As though he could feel her scrutiny, Harvey swiped off the hat. He wiped his forehead. "Did you want to ask me something?" He resituated his hat, slapped his gloves against his thigh, and frowned at her.

The hat was the same type as Stocky Man's, the kind a lifeguard wore, providing good sun protection. *Not peculiar exactly*—the hat made perfect sense atop Harvey's head—just peculiar on Stocky Man. It didn't go with his clean slacks and light-weight jacket, which were not the attire of someone who worked in the sun. Why did Stocky Man wear a hat like that?

And more to the point, why would a guy driving a car at night be wearing such a hat?

Since she kept staring at Harvey, he stared back, waiting.

"Did you get my messages? About the guy in the Ram?"

"That was Ray." He stuffed the gloves into a pocket of worn jeans.

"He came back here into your grow." She studied Harvey's face.

He looked away toward the barn, then bent to scratch behind Rambo's ears. The dog regarded him with worshipful eyes.

"You ever have one of those friends who only shows up when he wants something?" Harvey asked. "But who you have a long history with?" His eyes remained on the dog, his voice distant. "Maybe are even indebted to? But would rather not see?"

"My mom," she said.

Harvey chuckled grimly. He straightened, rubbed the side of his face, and yanked the gloves from his pocket, signaling he needed to get back to work.

"So why was he snooping around?"

He turned away from her and folded the small ladder. "You know how you don't want me asking about your mom?"

"Yeah." She bit her lip. "But my mom's not dangerous."

Harvey spun, almost whacking Rambo with the ladder leg. The dog jumped back with a shocked whimper. Harvey narrowed his eyes. "Why do you think Ray's dangerous?"

"He was carrying a gun."

"You saw it?"

She bristled. "I saw his sagging pocket."

"You write too much crime stuff, Red."

Her weight rolled to the balls of her feet, and she straightened to her full height. "That's right, Harvey. I do. That's how I know when someone's packing heat."

"*Packing heat.*" Harvey laughed and turned away. "I need to get to work." He trundled off, ladder under his arm, Rambo at his heels.

"I know something's going on here," Zoey called after him.

Without glancing back, Harvey started singing the Buffalo Springfield's song *For What It's Worth.*

Infuriated, she chased after him. Rambo swung around and growled a warning. Harvey sauntered toward the barn without calling him off.

She backed slowly away, but shouted, "Where'd you get that hat, Harvey?"

Chapter Twenty-Nine

Ray stood in the doorway of his processing shed. It was plopped down in a field of Brussels sprouts—one of three long, run-down, inconspicuous-looking farm buildings. His foreman, Domingo, took care of the sprouts, actually made a little money, and didn't ask questions.

If Ray had to say so himself, it was pretty brilliant processing here, hiding in plain sight. The marijuana grow tucked in back of the hills behind the fields of vegetables.

Plant litter and dust floated in the air of the packing shed. In the corner where two long sterile counters joined, a small Bose speaker cranked out hip-hop, which he detested. Stuart picked the music to keep the young workers motivated. They'd just unloaded a fifty-kilogram mass from the hydraulic press. The first worker was cutting bricks, the second was swathing them in plastic, and Stuart was taping the bundles and labeling them with destinations.

Ray didn't trust many people—certainly not his ex-wives or his two worthless kids, who disapproved of his enterprise but were happy to leech the money. He could count on one hand the people he'd trusted in his life— Stuart (first and foremost), Harvey (most of the time), his first wife Suzette (for three years or so), his baby brother Bill, and his sister, at least the way he remembered Rachelle. Who knew what she'd be like if she'd lived?

His heart clenched up. Pushing fifty years, and her death could still do that to him. He pulled a bottle of beta blockers from his pocket and swallowed one. Damn it all to hell that the witness resembled her.

Stuart swung around as though some spider sense had alerted him to Ray's presence. Lowering his face mask and sliding up goggles, Stuart hustled toward him, then wheeled abruptly and went back to lower the music. Two young bucks at the counter turned to see what was going on. Spotting Ray, they snapped back to their work.

Because of legalization, only outlaws like himself bothered with old-fashioned brick weed, meant to package the product to move it to "dry" areas. Trichomes were lost in the process, no doubt, but his brick was decent—relatively free of stems, and no rot.

Resentment surged in him toward the legal growers. They pretended to be so goody-goody when half of them sold out the back door, forcing the little guys like Ray into more extreme measures to stay in business.

Stuart arrived into Ray's shadow, cast long across the concrete floor from his stance in the doorway. He leaned toward Stuart. "On that car? You removed the VIN?"

His right-hand man scratched his forehead, the raised googles wiggling. "Of course." He was the most forgettable guy you'd pass on the street—middle-aged, average-height, a good build but not buff. He looked like a dad in the bleachers at Little League games, which on any given weekend, he might be—all things Ray liked about him. "What's wrong, Boss?"

Behind Stuart, the gloved workers continued to pack units, their backs stiff. *Boss man in the house.* He gestured for Stuart to follow him to the opposite corner, where the shelves of a former industrial bakery held neat rows of bricks from the last batch out of the press.

"The missing VIN makes the vehicle *more* suspicious," he whispered.

"Well, sure." Stuart brushed at his San Francisco Giants sweatshirt, sprinkled with sticky marijuana bits. "But who's going to stumble across the car up there?" Stuart rubbed the edge of an eye, the irritating plant dust an occupational hazard. "And if someone did stumble on it, why would they check the VIN?"

Ray didn't want to frighten Stuart with the extent of their troubles—that the witness, a person who'd know what the car meant, lived on Harvey's farm and was already sniffing around the barn area.

"Harvey's not going to want to store the car forever." He fought to keep his voice neutral, but he was exhausted, having spent the better half of the day trying to work out what to do. He'd called the idiot to "abort the mission for now," but the burner phone was already out of commission.

Stuart ran a finger over his lips. "What do you propose?"

"Burning it?"

Stuart frowned, glancing behind him as if to make sure everything on the assembly line was running smoothly. "Could be problematic. That area is dry as dust." Stuart shifted his weight. "We'd have to make sure the fire stays contained, which means sticking around."

A bad idea. Everyone was on edge about fires. Smoke would draw attention, even in that remote area.

"And if we stick around to control the blaze," Stuart continued, "car fires are toxic." His expression didn't reveal a thing. It took someone who really knew the guy to sense the question in the word "if," the almost lascivious thrum of hopefulness. Stuart reached into his pocket and pulled out a tiny plastic bottle. "'Scuse me, Boss." He tilted back his head and administered drops. Blinking, he said, "We're talking carbon monoxide. Off gassing that can kill you."

Ray swept off his hat and tapped it against the leg of his pants, sprinkling sweat onto the concrete. "Suggestions?"

With the tip of a finger, Stuart wiped away the drizzle on his cheeks. "Push it down the ravine?"

"I was just up there scoping out that idea," he said. "Too many trees. We don't want the car getting snagged twenty feet down."

The idea of burning it—destroying it—seemed better, but Ray wasn't prepared to go for the argument Stuart was constructing in his careful, roundabout way—bringing up issues, so they could be knocked down—clearing the way so he could do what he wanted—to let the whole mountain catch on fire.

Ray jiggled the bottle of beta-blockers in his pocket. No matter which option he chose, he'd have to get Harvey and the girl off the property to dispose of the evidence, so the idiot could then dispose of the girl.

He didn't share the last part with Stuart. Money sailed Stuart along as a loyal assistant; it was expensive to buy a house and raise three offspring in Playa Maria. But in spite of the way Stuart jonesed for flames, he could be prone to scruples. He'd gone along with covering their tracks after a horrible, stupid mistake by an employee, but might draw the line at killing the witness. It didn't help that the witness was young and female, Stuart being the father of three girls.

Ray put his hat back on. Truth be told, the whole thing gnawed at him, too, especially now that he'd seen her, the ginger hair and the wide eyes stirring up memories of Rachelle. Felt like he'd have a heart attack.

And he didn't have any brilliant idea for how to make sure both Harvey and the girl were off the property. It really might be better to get rid of the idiot cop killer and forget about the girl. But either way, they had to do something about the car.

In front of him, Stuart waited for a decision, seemingly patient, but his stance was rigid, like that of a child not wanting to commit any error that might jeopardize a reward.

"I'm not sure we can trust Harvey in this," Ray said. Harvey clearly had a thing for the girl or he wouldn't let her live next to his grow. Ray smashed his hat and moved it back and forth to scratch his itchy scalp. He'd ordered dozens of them for his fieldworkers, but they seemed popular with the other workers, too. A whole stack of them had gone missing. "It's a tricky ball of wax."

Ray could lure Harvey from the house with the offer of a memento from Rachelle, but once Harvey returned and saw the burned car, he'd put two and two together and be pissed as hell, more about the deceit than the fire. He was touchy as all get out about things related to Rachelle. And wanting to talk business wouldn't work. He'd offered to buy out Harvey in the past, and it had only royally ticked him off.

"So whatdaya think, Boss?"

He handed Stuart a scrap of paper with the make/model/and license of the girl's car. Below, he'd scribbled a description of Harvey's truck.

"These belong to the people who live up there. Put someone to watch the place." He shook his head. "If both these vehicles are gone, burn the car."

A smile flicked across Stuart's face. Before they'd hidden the car, Stuart had suggested setting it ablaze. Ray had argued the cops would peg the remains as The Car, adding weight to the theory that the shooter hadn't fled the area, which would only intensify the local manhunt. But here he was, back to Stuart's original idea.

Stuart's leer, though, was about more than having the boss come around to his thinking. His "concerns" about burning the car had been part of a dance.

"A controlled burn," Ray growled, not about to give permission for Stuart to set fire to Harvey's whole place. And God knows what else.

Stuart's smile tightened but didn't disappear. Ray knew he'd still get his rocks off with a good blaze. A fetish that came in handy now and then.

"And I need contact info for the idiot," Ray said. "He's already tossed the burner."

"The less contact we have with him, the better."

Ray felt himself coming unglued, losing control, his face engorging with blood. "I'd be happy if he disappeared."

Stuart didn't flinch. "I deleted everything from my phone, but I may be able to scrounge something up." He crossed the room and talked to the two workers. One of them checked his phone. Stuart said something. The worker thumbed his screen, spoke, and returned to work.

Stuart came back and rattled off a phone number.

"That was easy."

"And that's the problem with him *disappearing*," Stuart said. "He's too easily traced to us."

Ray blinked. "What did you think I was suggesting?"

Stuart tilted his head and squinted. "You tell me."

Ray didn't wait to psychoanalyze what he might have meant. Instead, he drove the three miles into Playa Maria to Bill's Place, his brother Gugli's establishment. Nine years separated him and Gugli—Bill to most people— but the older they got, the less the age difference mattered.

Like the name, Bill's Place lacked imagination. It was a diner with booths along the sides and heavy, lacquered, wobbly wood tables in the middle. For reasons neither Ray nor Bill understood, in the last fifteen years, it had become The Place to eat variations on eggs, potatoes, and bread.

The place closed at three in the afternoon, but Angelo, Bill's oldest, saw him peer through the window. Angelo stopped filling a sugar container and crossed the wood floor to let him in.

The door opened to the smells of greasy grill and strong, fresh coffee.

"Uncle Raimondo," Angelo boomed. "How's it hanging?" Angelo was a stocky guy in his thirties with all the best Italian features, including a thick mass of curly dark hair. "Want some java?"

He shook his head. What did it say, Ray wondered, that he liked all of Bill's four kids better than his own?

"Just want to use the phone."

"Sure thing." Angelo jerked his thumb, unnecessarily, toward the office, but Ray moved to the actual phone booth tucked in the back corner. It was part of the restaurant's retro charm.

Angelo returned to the big bag of sugar on the counter, bordered by a gallon container of catsup and napkins fanning from a ripped-open package.

Wedged in the cubicle, Ray dropped coins into the slot and dialed. After three rings, he received a recorded message in a woman's voice. She didn't sound young like a possible girlfriend. *The idiot's mom?*

What the fuck was he supposed to do? He should have asked Stuart to remind him of the kid's name.

"This message is for your son. Don't do anything until we take care of the car." Sweat popped on his forehead. Should he tell the idiot to confirm receipt of the message? Stuart had said the less contact, the better.

But if the idiot didn't contact him, how could he be sure the message had been received?

"Call work. ASAP." He slammed down the receiver so hard Angelo frowned at him as he passed by the counter.

"Everything okay?"

"Just ducky."

He would have banged out the door, but he had to wait for Angelo to unlock it. "We have some chicken noodle soup left. Want some to take home?"

"Nah. Thanks. Tell that lovely wife of yours I said hello." He scooted out the door before he had to engage in more pleasantries. Even if the idiot shooter got the message, he couldn't trust him. The kid had already demonstrated he was a loose cannon. Who knew what he might do?

Ray's head felt like it might explode.

* * *

Jared listened without picking up, enjoying the panic in The Boss's voice. The guy was such a blowhard.

He crossed the room and deleted the message from their landline phone. What an idiot to mention "the car." He'd told The Boss the car belonged to his mom. What if his mom had heard the message?

Jared flopped on the couch and finished his bag of Flamin' Hot Cheetos.

The Boss wanted to get rid of the car before he did anything up at the farm. That was understandable, he supposed. But—thanks to his brilliance—he knew where Zoey Kozinski's friend lived. He sucked the red powder from each fingertip before wiping his hands on his jeans. They didn't have to worry about the evidence of the car if he took out the target at the apartment building.

Chapter Thirty

On the futon mattress, devices surrounded Zoey—laptop, phone, CD player. She sat cross-legged like a yogi, but couldn't concentrate worth a damn. After the epic bomb of the decal memory, she refused to get excited about the new clue dislodged by the hypnotherapy. So what if the shooter's hat resembled Harvey's?

Still, Harvey's reaction when she'd asked him about it—that was something. It unnerved her enough to pick up the phone.

"DiviniTea," Brianna answered brightly, even though Zoey had called her cell number.

Maybe Brianna wasn't supposed to accept personal calls at work.

"Can I go to your place and take a shower?"

"Sure," Bri said. "Plumbing problems?"

"Way more complicated than that."

"Let's talk when I get off work."

"Sounds good," Zoey said. Brianna could hardly converse about a guy walking around a marijuana farm with a gun while she designed advertisements for the local herbal tea company. And Zoey didn't want to chat on the phone about Harvey's friend Ray or about Christine Austin, anyway.

"Do you still have a key?" Bri asked.

"Yeah."

"I'll pick up some pizza on my way home."

Keyboard clacking came over the phone.

"How about Curt?" Zoey asked.

"He'd get off on you taking a shower at our place."

"Eeww."

"No worries. He has a gig."

* * *

Curt might have a gig, but his dirt-streaked Jeep didn't look like it had moved from the apartment's parking lot. Zoey groaned. Maybe she wasn't the only one with car problems. Well, she wasn't going to let him manipulate her into giving him a lift again. If he tried to bum a ride, she'd tell him to call an Uber.

As she climbed from the Element, fear crept up her spine. She'd tried to convince herself that the young man in the rental had not chased her, but she felt sure he had. She glanced nervously around, but the lot was nearly empty. She was pretty sure she'd seen the two other cars on previous visits. Neither looked like a rental.

A change of clothes clutched in one hand, she hurried toward the apartment complex. With its palm trees and location near the beach, the building must have aspired to be more than it was now: a two-story, tan block in need of paint.

She bounded up the steps, the cheap, free-standing concrete vibrating under her. A shower was going to be delicious. In spite of her wiping and slapping, a patina of dust coated the "camouflage" clothes she'd put on that morning, and it had sifted back through the fabric onto her skin.

She rapped on the door in case the Jeep meant Curt was at home. When no one answered, she unlocked the door and opened it into a plume of ganja and jasmine. Two figures loomed in the dim corners.

Her heart jumped.

Sheesh. Two stand-up bass. Instruments that were always there unless Curt or Bri had a performance. Clearly, her nerves were shot. She draped her clean clothes over the back of the couch and called out for Curt.

No response. She tapped on his bedroom door. No answer. He must have caught a ride and be using his electric bass for the gig.

Moving to the kitchen area, Zoey slid open the window to air the place.

Brianna smoked occasionally, but Curt was a bona fide pothead. On their burl coffee table sat a hardback copy of Zoey's *Cannabis Cutter*, white dust jacket with a big shiny marijuana leaf embossed on the front. *Nice of Bri to keep the book on display.*

Brushing aside fake sheets of music, Zoey plopped onto the couch's squishy cushions. A plane flew overhead, and then an uneasy silence returned. In front of her, a small flat-screened television stood on a brick and board shelf, surrounded by an array of dusty ceramic pieces and small instruments— maracas, bongos, a soprano ukulele, even a triangle.

A creak. She reeled around at the sound, catching a movement in the corner of her eye. Nothing behind her. She spun back, heart racing, her ghostly reflection flashing across the black face of the television.

She'd seen herself move.

But what had she heard? She called out to Curt one more time.

Nothing.

A chill drafted over her. She crossed the room to the kitchen window, stood on tiptoes, and stretched over the sink to peek out to the walkway. Dusk was settling. Everything was still.

She took deep breaths, shut the window, and turned on the outside light before resettling on the couch. With one finger, she spun her book, the paper jacket slick against the burl. *Would she write again?* A band of pain tightened around her head.

Her marijuana research had been years ago. *Cannabis Cutter* had flown out of her. She massaged her temples.

Nothing was the same now. Not her writing. Not the pot industry. Legalization of recreational use for one thing. Once she'd finished her book tour, she'd been so burnt out on the topic, she'd paid only marginal attention to the trends. Where were things now in the world of cannabis?

Harvey griped that the state had promised to license farms of no more than five acres so as not to drive out the little guys. But then they had proceeded not to restrict how many licenses any given entity could receive. One rich grower could buy a lot of five-acre farms.

Bureaucracy at its finest. Certain to rub at Harvey's libertarian streak. Enough to drive him into honey oil production? Justify it in his mind?

She twirled her book some more as though it were a wheel of fortune that could point to an answer. Maybe Harvey felt screwed over enough to throw in his hat with the armed man prowling around the farm that morning.

Hat!

Why did that guy—*Ray*—and Harvey—and the cop killer—all have the same kind of hat?

Her stomach turned at the idea Harvey could be connected to Officer Austin's killer, even by a taste in headwear. Her finger trembled against the marijuana-leaf image.

Using the arm of the couch, she leveraged herself from the spongy cushions, picked up her clothing, and headed to the bathroom. She locked the door behind her.

The bathroom was kitschy with old pink fixtures, the shower inside the bathtub.

She tucked her clean clothes and her cell phone beside a ceramic pink-spotted pig by the sink.

Sitting on the toilet seat, she took off her shoes and socks, which left a rime of dirt on her calf. It was embarrassing to think she'd been out in public—had met with Jimmy—this way. But she'd been sooooo late.

Beside a rack holding fresh towels hung a watercolor of a piglet standing on two legs and wearing a flower-covered straw hat. Zoey had been with Brianna when she'd snatched up the artwork at the flea market.

Pigs were Brianna's *thing*.

"So cuuuute," Bri had said.

"Piglets grow up to be hairy sows."

Bri had been indignant. "They are super intelligent."

"And dirty."

As she peeled off the rest of her clothes, the waistband of her pants sprinkled the tile with dirt. *Pigs had nothing over her.*

At the flea market, Bri had clasped the bamboo-framed watercolor. "Did you know their organs are more like a human's than any other animal's are?"

Bri's eyes had glittered. "They've contributed a lot to science." Bri shelled out two dollars to the vendor. "Pigs are underappreciated."

As Zoey examined the painting now, it struck her that Bri could just as well have been defending bass players. *Underappreciated.* Especially Bri as a bass player. She provided the steady beat of the She Cats in more ways than one. She kept the band functioning. Yet everyone cracked jokes about bass players.

Did you hear about the drummer who locked his keys in the car?

It took him four hours to get the bass player out.

Bri was smart. And beautiful. Zoey bit her lip, wondering if there were something personal in Bri's affinity for pigs. She regretted her remark about *hairy sows.*

Stripping her underwear, Zoey climbed into the tub and drew the curtain—covered with pigs, of course. Even as the hot spray hit her back, her heartbeat accelerated. She was naked and compromised.

Ray, the stocky man with the gun. Then Christine, on a mission to bring down the Ride-Along Program, and Zoey in the process. Even Jimmy, who drove a white car and had been Johnny-on-the-Spot at the scene of the crime. She couldn't trust any of them.

It didn't seem possible all three people had crossed her path today. Time felt lengthened, stretched like taffy.

The hot water worked its magic, unknotting her muscles. She relished the water pressure. In her trailer, she washed under a dribble. She helped herself to Bri's body wash, a soothing, tingly mint.

Something was up with Harvey. Was it just expanding his business? Was Ray—Harvey's "friend"—related to a possible new venture? And, back to the hat. Why was he wearing a raffia hat like Harvey's?

On Harvey the hat crowned his character. Frayed, functional, blocking the sun. But the stocky guy in slacks didn't belong in that kind of hat.

Why were either of them wearing a hat like the killer's? Or, more to the point of her investigation, why was the killer wearing a hat like theirs?

Investigation. She scoffed at the word in her head.

If her agent Helga recommended giving a psychopathic character a hat,

Zoey wouldn't pick that one. What kind of killer went around in a straw lifeguard hat?

A bang on the bathroom door sailed her heart into her throat.

"Bri!"

Zoey turned off the water. Dripped into the tub.

"No, Curt. It's me. Zoey."

"I've gotta get in here," he hollered.

Dripping in the tub, Zoey reached for a towel. "I'll be out in a couple of minutes."

"I need in now." He hammered on the door again. "I'm late to my gig. Way late."

"Coming." She coiled the towel around her, grabbed another for her hair, and unlocked the door.

Curt didn't even bother to ogle her. He unzipped his jeans as she passed, muttering, "What are you doing here?"

Urine gushed before the door clicked into place.

She hadn't grabbed her clothes, so she stood, dripping, on the carpet, the whole experience reminding her of the shower at Harvey's. Curt didn't seem concerned about an answer to his question. She moved into Bri's bedroom to towel off.

A white terry robe dangled from a hook on the back of the door. She slipped into it—almost full length on her. She sat on the bed and waited for Curt to leave.

Chapter Thirty-One

Jared's nerves frizzed with excitement. The Element, the distinctive boxy crossover SUV in puke green, was right here in the apartment parking lot! *Too easy.*

He backed the rental into a slot near the lot's entrance for a clear view of the building.

How to proceed? He had no idea which apartment belonged to Zoey Kozinski's friend, the bass player. *Brianna.*

A group mailbox stood at the street. He got out and sauntered to the large silver rectangle atop a pole. There was only one address on the outside, and you needed a key to open the door. Inside he imagined rows of neat cubicles with numbers and names, all the information he needed. He hammered the metal with his fist before ducking back into his car.

The end of a workday sucked as a time to explore. People were arriving and returning to their apartments, a much busier scene than midday yesterday.

And it was time for dinner. He was hungry.

He pulled out the car rental agreement and, on the back, drew a rough sketch. The side of the building faced the lot, but it was easy to tell the back was sheer and boring, and the front—two stories, nine doors each. He drew little rectangles to represent them.

He put an X on the rough drawing, eliminating the lowest and closest apartment. It was possible that Brianna lived with the mother, trailing three pre-school-age kids who'd gone to that door, but he doubted it.

Another car trickled into the lot—a Subaru that had seen a lot of use.

The silver-haired driver threw a look back at Jared's car like there was some law against parking near the entrance. He shrank down. He should have gotten as close to the building as possible like everyone else so he didn't stick out.

The woman retrieved two bags of groceries from the back of her Subaru and headed to her apartment.

Jared Xed out the door on the far end of the bottom floor. It was guesswork, but he didn't imagine the bass player living with her mother or having this older woman as a roommate.

This process of elimination would make his job easier once darkness provided cover. There sure weren't many trees or bushes to help him out. All landscaping efforts had been put into the area running down the middle of the parking lot.

He hoped the bass player, Brianna, lived on the lower floor. Going up to the walkway along the top floor would leave him exposed. He'd have to get all the way down the steps to make his getaway.

Two men arrived in a Prius. They got out, dressed in khakis and tucked in polo shirts. Top floor. He added an X.

A group of three rowdy people about his age emerged from an upstairs door. Jared sat up and pulled his pistol from the glove compartment, peering through the gathering dusk. The trio jostled and joked as they descended and walked along the green strip, and Jared felt a familiar, unnamed hollowness.

All guys. Not Zoey Kozinski. Not her friend. The group continued past his car, out of the lot, and down the street on foot, probably headed to the popular pizza parlor a couple of blocks away. The thought made his mouth water.

He eliminated their apartment.

A door banged open. On the second floor, the big guy he'd seen with Zoey Kozinski crashed onto the walkway. A huge black case banged against the railing. He took the steps two at a time, the case whapping the concrete steps.

A bass player. A musician who had chatted with Zoey Kozinski and had driven away with her. It wasn't her friend Brianna, but that must be the apartment.

He ducked down as the bass player roared by in his Jeep. He was glad the guy had left. A man that size, you'd need a good shot to bring down. And he'd been lucky—or unlucky—to take out that cop. Ghost guns didn't exactly come with warranties.

Jared toyed with the pistol—loaded and ready to go. He'd thought the aqua color was cool, but maybe it was stupid.

The location of the apartment was the worst. Upstairs and in the middle of the walkway. He swallowed.

Why do this? he asked himself. He could take this car right now and head south to Mexico.

And do what? He'd been so busy antagonizing Mrs. Godinez back in high school that his Spanish had barely progressed beyond, *"¿Cómo está usted?"*

But if he stayed and didn't do this, The Boss and Stuart would be coming for him.

He regretted that he'd parked so far from the building and allowed the near spaces to fill. He started the car, drove forward, and backed into the space the Jeep had vacated, four slots from the front.

Slipping the gun into his jacket pocket, he got out of the car. The ocean misted the air, softening the edges of everything. The lights of the parking lot snapped on from poles snuggled up to the palms at each end of the green.

Shit.

He lowered back into the Chrysler and slouched in the seat. Five minutes later, another vehicle entered the lot, an old model Bronco that reversed parked like he did, directly across the green from him.

Even in the shimmer of the ocean mist, he recognized the bass player—the woman named Brianna—so tall with those big bazookas.

She was bending back into the cab and came out trawling a paper bag and a pizza box. The sight sent him salivating. His stomach growled.

Hip shutting her door, she spotted him across the asphalt. Too late for him to do anything but look back.

She started toward the walkway. His heart rate stampeded. Now there would be two people to contend with. And this woman was large. He'd need to kill her first.

She stopped, turned his direction, and squinted.

His heart stopped.

She walked toward him. He slid the gun under his thigh.

She made a motion for him to open his window. He should have gone to do the deed ten minutes ago, before the parking lot lights came on. He couldn't do anything here. Or now. If he did, he'd alert the whole building. He'd never make it up the steps to take out the target and get back to the car.

He opened the window.

"Waiting for someone?" she asked cheerfully.

"Yeah."

"That can be a drag. Would you like a slice of pizza?"

The spicy fragrance wormed its way right through the cardboard. Pepperoni, his favorite.

She lifted the lid. Her eyes were big and warm.

"You're a lifesaver," he said.

* * *

"Feel free to dig in." Bri air-kissed Zoey, kicked off her professional shoes, and placed the pizza on the counter. "Don't wait for me. I've gotta get out of these clothes." Her blouse was over her head before she reached her bedroom door.

Zoey lifted the lid and smiled to see her friend had already consumed a huge slice. She unloaded salads and napkins from the paper bag and transported them to the coffee table.

When she returned for the pizza, footsteps sounded on the walkway. Zoey squatted alongside the cabinets below the sink, feeling stupid.

Brianna returned, wearing sweats. "What are you doing?"

"Who's walking by outside?"

Brianna cocked a brow, but leaned over the sink.

"Just my neighbor." Pizza box in hand, Brianna crossed the room, curled against the arm of the couch, and tucked her legs under her. "So what's up, Zoe?"

Zoey plopped against the other arm of the couch and pushed up frayed cuffs of a long-sleeved Yosemite tee, the fabric worn to rag status, but she didn't want to stain it with marinara sauce.

"I still have my shirt from that trip, too," Bri said, showing patience and restraint. As always.

"One of the highlights of my life." She and Bri had wrangled reservations for a tent cabin in the park's valley. They'd hiked up the Mist Trail of Vernal Falls and splurged for dinner at the Ahwahnee Hotel. "I wish I could be teleported back there right now."

She eased into things by telling Bri about the incident with Curt.

Bri laughed. "He must have been super zonked." She crunched a crust edge and frowned. "Being late to a gig is radical, even for Curt. But why is that making you act paranoid?"

Zoey continued with an edited version of events, focusing on the arrival of her mom, her doubts about Jimmy, the wild accusations of Officer Austin's widow, and her fear of the stocky guy with a gun prowling around Harvey's farm.

"A gun! Holy shit."

"That's why I couldn't shower at home. You might as well cue up the *Psycho* music."

More footsteps. Zoey swung her body toward the window behind the television. But it was a bunch of footsteps like a small stampede, accompanied with loud voices, not someone sneaking up on them.

Brianna sighed. "Other neighbors. Wish they'd move already. If you can sleep through a party, you're welcome to spend the night."

"Would Curt be okay with me spending the night?"

"Move in with me. I'll get rid of Curt." Brianna picked up a piece of Zoey's discarded crust and nibbled it.

When Zoey smiled, her face muscles felt like they were flexing for the first time in a year. Brianna's suggestion was offered in the spirit of friendship, but reality made it way too complicated to take seriously. "I might take advantage of that offer if I need to move my house." She stirred the remains in the pizza box.

"Move your house? Because of the guy with the gun?"

She hadn't shared her suspicions about Harvey and found herself hesitant to do so. "Where does Curt get his weed these days?"

"Do you want some?" Brianna's eyes moved toward a small ceramic pot on the television shelf. "I thought even indica made you paranoid."

"It does." She had excised the marinoia incident from her story, too. *And the therapist.* Quite a bit of stuff, she realized.

"From his dealer," Brianna said.

With a napkin, Zoey wiped up crumbs from the coffee table. "Still? Why?" She dumped the napkin into the pizza box.

"Cheaper." Brianna languidly rose, plucking up plastic clamshells oily with salad dressing and putting them inside the pizza box. "Inertia, I suppose, with Curt. He's been buying from the same guy for twenty years." She wiped up the rings on the burl table and cleared the mess into the kitchenette. "There's no risk to the customer," she said over her shoulder. "Long as he keeps the purchase under an ounce."

Zoey pulled her phone from the pocket of her sweatpants and searched for articles about legalized marijuana in California.

It had not raised the expected revenue for the state. Purveyors of cannabis blamed high prices and shortages—the results of regulation, licensing fees, taxes, and strict rules on distribution. Sales were depressed.

"Texting Jimmy?" Brianna teased. "Putting your doubts to rest?"

"Nah. I'm trying to make some of the pieces in my puzzle fit together." She tapped another link. "Curt's weed might not stay cheaper," she said. "This article says the legal growers are pushing for a crackdown on illegal growers."

"No surprise. Big guys pushing out the little guys. Story of our whole economy."

Brianna resettled in the nook of the couch and ran a hand over the soft brown material. She went silent.

Zoey looked up.

"She Cats has been invited to perform at the spring street faire."

"Geez, I didn't even ask about your day. I'm getting as bad as my mom."

Bri snorted a laugh. "You have a ways to go."

The faire, with closed-off streets and a number of bands, was a big Playa Maria event. "Paying gig?" she asked.

"Only if you count exposure."

"A person can die of exposure." She stretched on the couch, resting her feet in Bri's lap, relieved to be talking about the kind of dilemma that last week might have risen to a top priority. "What do the others think?"

"There's always a big crowd, so Sabbie—"

"Wants to be in front of it," she finished.

Bri peeled off Zoey's socks, pinched her nose, and tossed them onto the carpet.

"Hey, now, I just showered."

"Your socks didn't." Brianna sang "Stinky Feet."

It was true. She'd forgotten to bring fresh socks. "My feet were freezing."

"You could have used some of mine." Bri smoothed her hands over the tops of Zoey's feet. "Sabbie's such an attention whore. Have you ever met anyone as bad?"

"This girl—Mary Alice. In third grade." The warm hands brushing over Zoey's feet were pure bliss. If she were a cat, she'd be purring. "Mary Alice. Such a trip. Always waving her hand. Always wanting to answer." And there was her mother, of course.

"Maybe we should start a new band," Bri murmured.

Zoey's eyes drooped. "Yeah? You, me, and who?"

"Curt? He plays guitar, too. He's pretty good, actually."

"The guy who was so stoned he was late to his gig?"

Bri pulled Zoey's pinky toe. "Like Andrea's not a stoner?"

She opened her eyes to gauge Bri's level of seriousness. "So we swap one stoner guitarist for another?"

"Yeah. And Kath would be happy to drum for us. She's in her 'living-by-my-art' phase." Bri stopped the foot massage to make air quotes.

Zoey wiggled her toes against Bri's belly, a signal to please continue rubbing. "No wonder there's tension in that relationship. Kath's partner doesn't strike me as the kind who wants to live in poverty."

"She's a lawyer, remember? Makes super money. It's more about equity."

Bri maintained a studious profile dipped toward her feet, as though mulling over possibilities for the band, so Zoey continued the thread. "How about lead vocals?"

"Curt's got a great voice."

"True," Zoey mused, "but he's not a performer." She added reluctantly, "No one performs like Sabbie."

"True," Bri conceded.

They both fell silent. They weren't disbanding She Cats. Sabbie possessed the ability to lose herself to adulation, to interact with the audience like metal rubbing metal, producing heat and magnetism. That kind of charisma was a rare commodity. For a second, Zoey appreciated the quality, even in her mother's showy persona—a magnanimous warmth dug up by Bri's thumbs pressing into the arches of her feet.

Bri yanked Zoey's big toe with a note of finality. "The offer stands if you want to spend the night."

So tempting.

Zoey retracted her feet and sat up. "Thanks, Bri. A huge part of me would love to, but at some point, I've got to face the music—so to speak. Get back to my life."

To punctuate the point, she pulled on her socks, the grit from her morning caught in the fabric.

"I'll walk you," Bri said. "There was a guy hanging out in the parking lot earlier."

Zoey froze, her shoe half-tied. "What kind of guy?"

Bri wrinkled her forehead. "A young guy. I gave him a slice to check him out and figured he was waiting for my neighbors to come home." She shrugged. "But you never know."

Zoey jammed her foot into the other shoe. "In a gray rental?"

"What's up, Zoey?"

"I think he's following me."

"Following you?"

How could she explain to Brianna all the stuff she'd excised from her account? "Is there someone who could check if he's still there?"

Brianna strode to the door. "I can look."

"No!"

Brianna stopped and turned. "Seriously, Zoey. What's going on?"

"That guy could be the cop killer."

"That kid?" Her voice was the equivalent of an eyeroll.

"Do you have another neighbor who could check out the parking lot?"

"Why not me?" Brianna asked.

"Because I don't want you to die."

"Die?"

"Yes," Zoey said, her eyes hot and damp. "If he tracked me here, he must have figured out we're connected."

Brianna placed a hand on each of Zoey's shoulders and pressed her down onto the arm of the couch. "Let's say all of that is true. Why would he want to kill me?"

Zoey squeezed her eyes shut. Heat crept up her neck at Bri's condescending tone. Her face flushed with fear and sadness and anger. Using her wrists, she whacked both of Brianna's hands from her shoulders.

"Whoa, girl." Brianna backed away, throwing her hands in the air. "I don't appreciate that."

"I'm sorry."

Without responding, Brianna picked up her cell and made a call. "Hey, Peanut, could you do me a favor and take a look in the parking lot to see if a guy's hanging out there in a gray sedan. I'll explain later."

Silent, eyes averted, Brianna waited for a response. After a couple of minutes, she looked at her vibrating phone and said to Zoey, "All clear," but she didn't look at her.

Chapter Thirty-Two

The Element bounced over the mountain road. Zoey felt low—worse than she had at any moment since this nightmare had started. Her evening had shifted with disconcerting speed—like a corkscrew on a rollercoaster—from the contented bliss of a foot massage to Bri being pissed at her in a way that a simple apology wasn't going to fix.

Zoey sniffed. A toxic-smelling smoke whispered into the SUV's cab. Could it be the car? The light on the dash had not come back on, but maybe the dealership had missed the real problem. She needed to pull over.

The narrow road plunged into a ravine on her side. She parked as far to the right as she dared and put on her emergency flashers.

Outside, the stink whiffed in the air—distant and faint—definitely not from her engine. Panic nibbled at her nerves. She turned in a circle, snuffling, but she couldn't tell the direction from which the smell came.

Continuing up the road, she scanned the forest for flames. She slowed and studied the rearview. A person didn't want to get trapped on this in-and-out road with a fire cutting off the escape route.

The stench didn't smell like a forest fire, though. Anxiety churned in her. She turned onto their entrance road and drove as quickly as she dared.

Had Harvey started his stupid enterprise? Was she too late? Was he burning the place down already? That could account for the noxious underpinning to the smell. It was getting stronger as she approached the farm.

She tried to rationalize that mountain people were a crazy bunch, renegades, a lot of them with contrarian streaks bigger than Harvey's. One of them could be doing an illegal burn that included plastics.

At night?

Plus, the nearest neighbor was a mile on the other side of Harvey's.

Harvey's house blocked any view of flames, but eerie light in the night sky silhouetted the redwood trees behind it. She shook all over. Was Harvey there? Was the fire in the barn?

Rocking to a stop in front of her trailer, she sprinted to Harvey's house, screaming his name, even though his truck was gone. Silence pervaded the night except for the guttering of fire.

Her Keds whapped the dirt as she ran to the barn road.

Where's Rambo? Where's Harvey?

Outside the open barn door, a car was ablaze, the stench overwhelming. The heat intense.

What the fuck! Whose car is this? It wasn't Harvey's truck.

Flames licked toward the marijuana field, scorching the nearest plant. Her head spun with dizziness.

Heart banging, she hurried to the sliding glass door into Harvey's bedroom. It opened, unlocked. She screamed Harvey's name.

Nothing.

She snatched up the fire extinguisher she'd seen earlier. Did she even know how to operate one of these things?

The directions were in capital letters on the side:

1. PULL PIN. HOLD UNIT UPRIGHT.
2. AIM AT BASE OF FIRE. STAND BACK 6 FEET.
3. PRESS BUTTON, SWEEP SIDE TO SIDE.

Her hands were slick with sweat and the heavy canister slipped. Panting, panicked, she set it down. She'd need something to protect herself from the toxic smell. She tugged on a dresser drawer. It stuck.

She tried the next one, almost falling back with the force of her pull. The photo on the dresser crashed to the floor, glass splintering over the wood. As she grabbed a tee-shirt from the drawer, a handgun skittered to the front.

A Glock semi-automatic. Not surprising. Everyone up here was armed.

Tying one of Harvey's tee-shirts around her nose and mouth, she hoisted the extinguisher and hobbled with its weight toward the fire.

Stay back, she remembered.

She pulled the pin. Heat scorched her eyes. Sparks shot up, the inferno intent on consuming the car.

This extinguisher would be useless against it. She pivoted away from the car, toward Harvey's field. She pressed the button.

She felt like she was operating a machine gun. She sprayed foam, back and forth as the directions said, first on the smoldering plant. Then she circled the car, making a ring of foam, protecting the barn. Protecting the house. Praying the car fire would feed on itself and burn out.

Whoozy. She was dizzy. Maybe from the fumes.

She staggered toward the farmhouse, the canister slipping from her hands.

Chapter Thirty-Three

Wetness nuzzled Zoey's face. A whimper like a baby's cry tunneled into her ear canal. Her eyelashes fluttered. In the dark, a presence loomed right above her. A face so close its breath puffed on her face. It stank.

Another form, smelling of beer, bent toward her and tore away a cloth from her mouth. Had she been gagged? He slapped her face.

She was lying on a floor. The forceful hand landed on her chest. Was she being raped? But the hand rested there, didn't grope her breasts or tear at her shirt.

Her eyes adjusted to the dimness. A face came into focus. Old, wrinkled, bushy mustache.

Her nose was pinched shut. She couldn't breathe. A strong hand tipped her head back uncomfortably. She grunted, squirmed in terror, kicking her legs.

The image reared away. "Well I guess you're resuscitated."

Harvey! Confusion filled her.

"What are you doing?" she muttered. Her words slurred. She wasn't sure the question came out intelligibly.

"I should ask you that question," Harvey said. "Thank God, you're awake. I was about to start mouth-to-mouth."

She turned her head. Rambo licked her face. *The floor of Harvey's room?* Her head throbbed. She tried to push up onto her elbows.

"Don't move," Harvey growled.

"What's going on?" A gauzy memory of the fire fogged her brain. She must have been overcome by the smoke. The gasses. Her hair reeked like an ashtray.

"Stay where you are."

She lay there, her body not so hot on the idea of moving, anyway. She twisted her head away from the dog's tongue. Shards of glass sparkled in moonlight streaming through the sliding glass door. "Why don't you turn on the lights?"

"Shhhhhhh."

"What's going on?" she asked again, her voice hoarse, her throat parched.

Harvey crunched over broken glass, took the pistol from his dresser drawer, and chambered a round—slap of magazine, rack of the slide. Zoey scooted back against Harvey's bed, ready to roll under it.

Rambo's nails clicked across the floor. He faced the door, body tense.

"Anybody out there, Rambo?" Harvey stood to the side of the glass.

His stance, his grip on the gun, the way he took up position, were the moves of someone comfortable with a firearm—a former soldier. The fluidity reminded her of the shooter, the steady turn, and the gun—in a nanosecond of flashing top lights.

Cold sliced through her.

Rambo didn't growl. He looked up at Harvey and whimpered like maybe he was bad for not detecting an enemy.

Harvey changed his grip to one hand and pointed the barrel at the floor. He patted the Doberman's sleek head. "That's a good boy." He nudged the animal. "Go guard Red."

As though he could understand English, Rambo trotted to her side and sat on his haunches, facing the sliding glass door, ears pricked. Beyond the glass, the burned frame of the car bulked, stark in the moonlight. A sedan. The barn, a dark outline behind it, stood completely intact. The redwoods beyond that bore silent witness to the craziness.

"Are you going to tell me what's going on?" Her voice rasped, as scabrous as her agent Helga's, as if she were a chain smoker.

"You go first," Harvey said.

"Whose car is that?"

"Wish I knew."

She squinted at him but then recounted arriving home. The smell. The fire.

"Good work on saving my plants," Harvey said. "How'd you know there was a fire extinguisher in my room?"

She swallowed. And coughed. "I must have seen it."

"Yeah," Harvey said. "And when was that? I don't recall us ever coming back to my bedroom." He added drily, "I think I'd remember that." He kept the Glock down but remained beside the door.

"I snooped."

"Never trust a redhead." He shook his head. "You'd think I'd know."

His voice strained to be light and teasing, but it failed. A razor's edge of bitterness cut through.

"I thought you might be considering honey oil," she said, ashamed of her betrayal of his trust. "I wanted to know if I had to worry about being blown up. That's all. So the day I showered here, I looked around."

"Why didn't you just ask me?"

She met Harvey's hard stare. "Okay. Are you?" Rambo's head dropped a fraction, as if he were fatigued, or maybe the tone of the conversation made him wonder if he was still supposed to guard her.

"I might change my operation." He edged away from the glass and bent down to retrieve the framed photo from the floor. He laid it face down on the dresser.

Queasiness fluttered in Zoey's stomach. The photo had looked weirdly familiar because the woman's long, untamable hair defied any time-telling style. The picture might be old, but the hair looked like her own. "Who is that?"

"Gal named Rachelle."

"You're not answering my questions," she said. "About the honey oil. Or the woman."

Harvey squatted on the other side of Rambo, facing the slider, pistol dangling between his knees. "That's because my business is not your business. The less you know, the better."

"Honey oil production could jeopardize my safety, too."

"Red." Disappointment weighed his voice. "I can't believe you think I'd make BHO—contaminate my product with butane. Or some other flammable shit." He sighed. "I've always been about natural and organic."

Relieved, she drew a breath, stirring the crap in her lungs and sending her into a paroxysm of coughing.

Harvey pounded her back.

She flailed her arms. "That's not helping, Harvey. I'm not choking."

"Sounds like you are."

She hacked up a ball of dusty, acrid phlegm and spat it into the tail of her Yosemite tee.

Harvey didn't comment.

"So why do you have a tank for butane or propane or whatever in your closet?"

"Wow, Red, is there any place you didn't poke your nose?"

"I needed a towel."

"That tank's for my welder."

"Why was it in the closet?"

"Did you see all those face masks, too?"

She nodded.

"I bought the wrong ones. I needed to return them and fill the tank. When I heard knocking at my door, I stashed them in the closet—as a precaution. Didn't want anyone getting the wrong idea," he said pointedly. "Just because it was only you, didn't mean I'd go and pull everything out."

"Bad timing," she muttered. "I didn't know you wore a mask when you worked."

"The stuff you don't know about me could fill a universe."

"Enlighten me. What about the woman—Rachelle?"

"Truly none of your business." He lifted up an arm and tugged the dog bed to the floor. He curled up on it, facing the outdoors.

"What are you doing?"

"I'm gonna sleep here," Harvey said. "You can have the bed."

She readied herself to protest, but her fears rushed back at her. She hadn't even been able to shower in her own house. And that was before the fire—an intentionally set fire. Right here. Close to her home. A fire that could have consumed Harvey's field and licked up the parched undergrowth right to her trailer. A fire that could have set the mountain ablaze.

Could she trust what Harvey had said? The fire seemed like it could be a message of some sort—maybe for him not to expand his business.

Or to pressure him to change it?

And why had the car been facing out from the barn? Some people, like Brianna, always reverse-parked, but why bother with a car you planned to torch? She worked off her shoes, flopped down, and flipped the top quilt over her body. Rambo clambered up where his bed would normally be, his weight and warmth against her feet. Her head pounded. "Did your *friend* Ray do this?" she asked.

"Why do you think that, Red?" The comforting voice drifted up from the floor.

"He appears one day out of nowhere. Then there's a fire." The tension drained from her body into the dog cuddled against her calves. "Mighty coincidental."

"Have to be careful of false cause and effect," Harvey said. "Learned that in the army. Just because one thing follows another, doesn't mean the two are connected."

"Yeah," Zoey muttered. Logically, he was right.

Chapter Thirty-Four

Day 6

Zoey slipped into sleep thinking about the burnt car. Why was it here? Where had it come from? Was the fire a threat?

But why would anyone care if Harvey was going to make a little something on the side, which Harvey claimed he wasn't? And why bring a car all the way up here to make a point when they could just burn down Harvey's grow?

Unless the car was already here.

She started awake. Rambo was gone. Harvey was gone. Light slanted through the slider onto the floor, highlighting the marks of broom sweeps through the dust. The broken glass from the photo was gone. The picture frame had disappeared from the dresser.

How had she slept through all of that?

Outside, a mockingbird ran through a repertoire that included a shrill sound like a fire alarm.

"Little late for that."

The aroma of coffee tickled her nose, motivating her to sit up. She tipped her head, and pain stabbed the side of her skull. She stank of smoke.

Lifting slowly, she dropped her legs over the side of the mattress. She crossed the room and pressed her palms to the cold glass of the door. The charred car hulked in the clearing.

The idea arrived to her in full flower. *That car was here. It was driven out of the barn. That's why it's facing me.*

She sucked in her breath. *It was burned because it's the shooter's car.*

How did she know that?

For starters, she told herself, it's a sedan. And what car in the area needed to be destroyed?

Pretty thin, Zoey.

She leaned her forehead against the soothing, cool pane. Sometimes when she wrote, her subconscious chewed away at a knot in her narrative, and in the morning, the solution presented itself like a cartoon lightbulb.

But logically, Zoey?

She tapped her forehead against the glass as if she could pound coherence into her brain. Each gentle tap rattled the pain in her head like a tray of disorganized silverware. The idea the car belonged to the shooter made no sense whatsoever. Why would it be here?

If the idea didn't make sense even to herself, how would she convince anyone else to consider it?

She could start by determining if the car had been white. She stared, skeptically, at the black skeletal remains.

In the shock of the fire, she couldn't truthfully say she'd noticed the car's color. It hadn't seemed light. But eye witnesses were unreliable in the best of circumstances, and she'd been in a full-fledged panic.

She stood at the door, studying the charred carcass. There was no color left.

Nothing obvious, anyway.

If the car had been here, why had Harvey hidden it in the barn?

Footsteps made her whirl. Her heart raced even though it had to be Harvey.

He entered the room, holding one ceramic mug close to his blue shirt and extending another. The mugs looked like they'd been crafted in a junior-high art class. Rambo heeled.

"Thanks."

In spite of sleeping on the floor, Harvey looked showered and fresh. His chambray shirt reminded Zoey of prisoners on the Main Line at San Quentin. His wet hair was tied back with a strip of leather into a ponytail. She'd never seen him without his heavy work boots, and his bare feet seemed shockingly intimate.

"How you feeling?" he asked.

"Achy." She set the mug on the bureau. Without his hat shading his face, Harvey appeared older, his crow's feet deeply etched. The edges of his mustache pointed to the marionette lines running to his chin. His eyes seemed sad. She suddenly felt a little awkward being in his bedroom and asked to use his bathroom.

"You know the way."

Gaze averted, she crossed the room, ashamed of how she'd snooped the last time she'd used his facilities. Of course, if she hadn't, she wouldn't have known about the fire extinguisher.

She rinsed her parched mouth, cupping water from the faucet. Soot smeared the shoulder of her shirt, and the tips of her eyelashes were singed.

She used her pee time to sort through an overload of information. *If this is THE car, why is it at Harvey's?*

Harvey has a hat like the shooter's. Harvey is tall like the shooter. Harvey owns a gun and knows how to use it.

Her fingers trembled on the doorknob. Maybe she should turn the other direction down the hall, flee in her bare feet to her car, and get the hell out of Dodge. *But Harvey? Seriously?*

He peeked from his bedroom. "You okay, Red?"

He came toward her.

Her head spun, thoughts ricocheting like a pinball. Harvey didn't shoot Stan Austin. He wouldn't shoot anyone, she thought.

Don't be naïve. He was standing at his door, ready to shoot someone last night. He shot people during the war.

He was protecting you, she argued with herself.

He was protecting himself.

The struggle continued inside her head. *Harvey wouldn't endanger his farm by burning evidence here.*

Everything about the fire says controlled burn, and Harvey has been very secretive.

Harvey's always secretive. He doesn't trust anyone. That's why he lives like a hermit.

Harvey clutched her elbow. Zoey gasped.

"You don't look so hot," he said.

"I feel faint."

Rambo's toenails clicked over the floor. Harvey guided her toward his room. Whimpering, the dog followed. Harvey lowered her to the edge of the bed. He retrieved her coffee. "Drink."

To avoid sloshing onto the blankets, she clamped the rough earthenware with both hands and bent forward to sip.

Harvey rested back against the dresser, gulped his own coffee, and regarded her. "Do you need to go to Urgent Care?"

She blinked, her eyes too dry to cry. How could this kind man be a killer? And the sedan? She'd never seen him driving anything but his old GMC.

If she deciphered this wild fantasy with Harvey as the shooter, wouldn't he know she was the witness? The ride-along in the cop car? If he was worried about evidence, why didn't he get rid of her, too?

But if there was anyone who didn't follow the news, who might not know she'd been in the cop car, who wouldn't be eating up every detail of the cop killing, it was Harvey. He was the most unplugged, off-the-grid person she knew.

And she hadn't enlightened him about her experience.

Which meant if someone asked him to store a car, he might not have been suspicious.

But why had Harvey been mysteriously absent last night?

"Why are you staring like that, Red?" Harvey crossed to her with two long steps and slipped the mug from her hands. "You need to lie down?"

When she shook her head, a twirling sparkler shot flecks of fire through her brain. "I have to go home." She leaned over to put on her shoes.

"Are you sure you want to hurry over there?" he asked.

She squinted up at him, uncertain. "Why not?"

"The Wicked Witch of the West has flown in."

Chapter Thirty-Five

Zoey peered from the farmhouse door. The boxy outline of her Element sat alone in front of her house, a film of dust muting its shine in the morning sun. "If my mother's here, where's her car?"

Her stomach tightened. Had Harvey seen someone else entering her house, not her mother? She backed into his living room.

He frowned. "Maybe she left?"

"You met my mom, didn't you?" she asked. "The other day?"

"Yii-up."

"And?"

"And nothing, Red." He studied her, shaking his head slightly. "Your mom's a looker, I suppose, but artificial sweetener, if you know what I mean."

"I don't."

"Not like you," he said. "You're real sugar."

Heat crawled up her neck. She'd always known Harvey had some sort of feelings for her, but he'd never tried anything, and this was the closest he'd ever come to saying anything.

He busied himself by putting on the socks and work boots parked by the door. She stood stiffly in his spartan living room, her brain parsing the comment—a little sexist and totally inaccurate. She was a lot of things; sweet was not one of them.

She dumped herself into one of two big plush chairs by the window, angled so Harvey could keep watch over his yard. On a table between the chairs, a lamp stood over a small stack of mail, an empty glass ashtray, and a hardcover copy of *Willie Nelson: American Icon*. A package of Zig-Zag rolling papers, although weirdly, she'd never seen Harvey roll a joint, or smoke.

She kept her eyes fixed on her trailer, watching for any sign of movement.

Her face still warm, she risked a quick glance at Harvey. "Look, I need to ask you a question."

He rested on the arm of the other chair, not committing to being seated or to conversation. But the position enabled her to view him and her trailer at the same time.

"That guy in the cowboy boots who came to see you about a week ago, does he have a hat like yours?"

"That's a peculiar question."

"Well?"

"No. Not at all. He's a cowboy. Wears a cowboy hat."

"But he was the one talking to you about 'expanding your business'?"

"Yii-up." Harvey stood.

She let her gaze follow him. If someone other than her mother had entered her home, it should have taken the intruder all of a minute to ascertain no one was there.

"Is that cowboy a friend of Ray's?"

Harvey paced the room. "That's a lot more than one question, Sugar Pops." Rambo emerged from the kitchen, as though he were restless, too.

"Is he?" she pressed.

"Look," Harvey sighed. "I don't do business with Ray."

She searched his worn face. Harvey was looking down the hallway to some place far away. "Why not?"

"We had a falling out."

"Over business?" She twisted in her seat for a quick look back at her place—no sign of anyone, diminishing the idea of a stalker and strengthening the idea her mom was there, settling in, heating water in her electric pot, sitting on Zoey's cube, thumbing through her mail. Since her mom knew the way to her house, she could have used Uber. Part of her wanted to dart to her trailer and defend her space.

"No," Harvey finally answered, turning back to her, his face contemplative and hangdog. "Well, that, too. But no. Over a woman."

He perched on the arm of the chair again, sadness pouring out of him and filling her. There was heartbreak here, a spot so tender that even her writerly-self hesitated to probe.

"The girl in the photo?" she asked. "Rachelle?"

"Yii-up."

"Did you both like her?"

"You might say that." He made a small, wry smile. "She was Ray's sister."

"Oh."

"She's dead," he added.

Zoey fixed Harvey with her eyes, trying to keep him tethered to her. "What happened?"

"It's the classic story of the buddy's little sister. Ray never liked the idea of me with Rachelle. But Rachelle and I...."

He stooped and plucked up a chew toy for Rambo from the lower shelf of the table. The dog barked and leapt. Harvey chucked the toy across the room and up the hallway.

"Well," Harvey settled back on the chair arm but fell silent.

She wasn't sure he'd continue. Rambo returned with the toy. It might have once resembled a plush stuffed rat. Harvey tugged on it. Rambo playfully growled and resisted. As soon as Harvey stopped pulling, Rambo dropped the toy and looked beseechingly at his person. Harvey bent, plucked up the toy, and Rambo zipped down the hallway as it left his hand.

"Rachelle and I had a whole vision for our lives." Harvey's voice sounded distant, like a cave echo. "I had a bad draft number, but we looked at the bright side. When I got back, I'd get the GI bill, have money for college. We'd get married. I'd find a decent job. We'd start our family." He chuckled mirthlessly at the false hope of youth.

Taking a quick look at her trailer, Zoey waited.

Harvey tussled with Rambo, needing the distraction to tell this story.

"You know that saying. 'Man plans and God laughs'?"

"What happened?"

"Ray's number wasn't too bad, 152, or something like that. But he's never been good at making decisions on his own. He's a joiner, likes being part of a team. He joined up with me." Harvey blinked slowly, as though closing one chapter of his life and opening his eyes to a new one. "Vietnam changed us."

He leaned sideways so his grizzled head rested against the wall, letting the chew toy drop to the floor. "Changed Rachelle, too."

Zoey tried not to display her eagerness for the story. Rambo lay down at Harvey's feet, rolling his eyes expectantly. The dog was much more forthright about what he wanted.

"In Vietnam, I drew what they call a million-dollar wound." Bitterness laced his voice. "Not enough to maim me, just enough to send me home. With Ray handling the paperwork for our unit, I've often wondered if he didn't expedite my return somehow."

Rambo rested his head on his paws as if sensing the play-gig was up.

Harvey pushed from the wall, bounded up, and stepped away from her. "That's enough."

She sprang from her chair. "You can't stop there. What about Rachelle?"

He didn't even turn to face her. With a hand behind his back, he waved her off. "It's time for you to go on home." His voice cracked.

She opened Harvey's door into a day already warm and electric with dryness. She scurried toward her trailer, her head on swivel for evidence of her mom. It had to have been her that Harvey had seen. He knew what her mom looked like, and he didn't seem worried. Heat rose up her neck again as she remembered Harvey's flirtatious comment.

In spite of Harvey's assurance, Zoey pressed against the thermoplastic framing at the back of her trailer, out of sight from the windows, and called, "Mom!" She peeked around the corner.

Camille opened the sliding glass door and leaned out, red hair falling forward to conceal her face. She looked both ways. "Baby Doll?"

Zoey rounded the trailer and climbed the step. "What are you doing here?"

Her mother backed up. "Darling, you look a fright."

Camille, on the other hand, wore Capris so white they hurt Zoey's eyes.

"And why does your voice sound like Darth Vader's? Are you sick?" Camille reached both arms out and seized her shoulders. "What happened to you?" She sniffed. "You smell like smoke." She released Zoey and stepped back to inspect her. "Your hair is singed!"

"How did you get here?" Zoey asked.

"Darling, you always complain that I make everything about me. Here I am showing my concern, and all you want to do is change the subject—to me."

"Mom." Zoey moved around her and sank onto the cube by the table. Fresh coffee steamed from her Sisters in Crime mug. Her mom had indeed made herself at home.

"Taxi." Camille folded freckled arms over a navy-and-white striped top that matched navy-and-white sandals. "I used a taxi service."

Zoey pressed a hand to her throbbing temple. "Why didn't you use your rental car?"

"I would have used Uber, but that's not possible when your daughter doesn't even have an address."

"Mom?"

"Ryan took it," Camille said, aggrieved.

The much younger, personal trainer boyfriend. Why was she not surprised?

Camille pursed her lips. "We had a row."

A row. Who used that word? Her mom must envision herself as a 1930s actress. All she needed was to put the back of her hand to her forehead and swoon. Instead, Camille picked up the mug of coffee and took a dainty sip.

"How do you expect to get back?" Zoey's voice rasped. "This private drive doesn't show up on GPS." She cleared her throat, stretched for a paper towel, and spat into it.

Her mother's face screwed into a moue of revulsion.

I should have used my shirt.

"After all my chauffeuring the other day," Camille said, "you might consider reciprocating."

Zoey leaned into the edge of her table, bent her arms, and propped her head. Her hands shook. She could barely manage her mom when she felt well. "How'd you get in?"

Camille lifted her chin. "The door was unlocked."

Fear shot through Zoey. With the events of the last few days, she couldn't imagine leaving her door unlocked. "That doesn't mean you can barge in." She walked to the slider, opened it, and inspected the strike plate.

"Oh my god," her mother said. "You think I broke in? This is the limit, Zoey Perfect Kozinski."

There were no scratches or evidence the lock had been tampered with—and Camille had waltzed right in—so she must have left it unlocked. With the stress she was under, she couldn't even trust herself to be reliable.

"Well, it's a good thing I'm here." Her mom set down the mug on the kitchen counter. "Clearly, you are not okay. Did you do one of those crazy fire-walking rituals? Just the kind of thing I'd expect in Playa Maria."

Zoey gritted her teeth. "Why are you here?"

"I thought you might be able to help me."

"Help you?" Zoey said. "Me? How?"

"You've done investigative work for your books."

"Research, Mom. Not investigations. I'm not a PI."

Camille perched on the other cube, the one containing dirty clothes. "Ryan's been taking my money."

Zoey covered her ears. Shook her head. "Mom, I can't absorb another single thing. In case you've forgotten, I'm a witness in a cop-killing case. The widow thinks it's my fault her husband is dead. I can't write. I can't think. And last night someone set a car on fire in Harvey's back yard."

"So that's why you look like a butch firefighter."

"You have to go." Zoey tried to pierce Camille with a cockatrice stare, but her eyes wouldn't focus.

Plucking up a navy-and-white beach bag from the floor, her mom lurched up, ramrod straight. "Are you ready to drive me to town then?" Her voice was biting.

"I have to do something first."

"Take a shower?" Camille asked.

Mustering willpower, Zoey walked to the door.

"There's a limit to my influence with Helga," Camille said to her back.

Zoey swung around. "What?"

Her mom flashed a bright, bitter smile. "You think you're such a self-made woman, don't you? So independent."

A cold lump congealed in her stomach. How much credence should she give her mom's insinuation? "You've been talking to Helga?"

Her mom gave that tight, sardonic smile again and then looked at the bright toenails in her wedge sandals. "Self-made is an illusion, Dear Heart. No one gets ahead on his own."

Was she being manipulated? Or had her mom, with her connections, influenced Helga? Is that why Helga acted like a publicist? "Are you implying you arranged for Helga to take me on?"

Her mom remained mum. Controlled. Letting the silence speak.

Zoey slammed out the door, relieved to step into fresh air. Her mom's revelation made her stomach fluttery. Had Camille meant to tell her or had it honestly slipped out in a moment of frustration?

She parked Camille's intimation in the back of her brain to examine when calmer, when her mother was not around.

The sun had cleared the trees, and the day promised to be hot. Rambo didn't pounce in greeting against the opposite side of the fence, so he and Harvey apparently weren't in the field. She passed by Harvey's house and turned down the road to the barn, glad to be on a mission rather than mulling over whether her mother had been responsible for her landing an agent.

Not just any agent. One of the best.

Her shoes stirred up powdery dirt. No music thrummed toward her. A road flare lay extinguished on the ground, a clear burn trail leading to the skeleton of the car, the front facing her. A toxic, smoky stench hung about the remains.

One of the barn doors cracked open. Arms extended from behind it and swung toward her. The hands clutched a gun, ready to blow up her life.

Zoey ducked.

Chapter Thirty-Six

"Oh, it's you." Harvey slid the semi-automatic into a hip holster and lowered his face mask. Beside him, Rambo relaxed. Harvey scraped open both barn doors, their arcs missing the burned car by only a foot.

"What are you doing, Red?" His jaw looked hard, all trace of vulnerability gone from his face. "You should be resting." He tucked back a strand of hair that had escaped the leather tie around his ponytail. "And don't you have company?"

Zoey popped up from the cover of the car, such as it were. "How'd you know someone was out here?"

"For me to know, and you to find out." His lanky frame, usually as loose as his plants, pivoted stiffly, his gaze sweeping his property. He motioned toward the interior of the barn. "I can't afford to stop production. But you—." He pointed a stern finger at her. "You should stay out of sight."

She didn't budge. "How convenient that you and I and Rambo were all gone last night. How often does that happen? Then, supposedly, at just that time, someone drove this car up here and torched it?" She watched his face, but it remained impassive, his attention not even on her. She moved to the side of the car and swept her hands like Vanna White. "Look at this frame. It's banged and dented like the car was in a wreck. Maybe not even operable."

The scenario she'd laid out didn't make sense. What did make sense was that the car had already been at the farm. It was parked face out from the barn because it had been pushed from there to just beyond the sweep of the doors. And it had been backed into the barn because it had been rolled from a car-carrying vehicle.

But that version of events meant Harvey was involved. He would never have carelessly left his place unlocked or even have trusted the combination to anyone. This scenario meant he had allowed someone to stash the car in his barn.

Harvey's arms crossed his chest, reminding Zoey of her mother only minutes ago. "Well?" he asked. "Are you just going to stand there? Or are you going somewhere with this idea?"

A thought froze her. "Did someone break in here?" she asked.

Harvey glanced into the interior of the barn where drying, redolent stems of marijuana covered the lines strung across the back. "All my product is intact."

She noted the non-answer. "I want to examine the car."

He spread his arms wide, gesturing grandly at the black hulk. "There it is."

She stepped back and studied the front of the burned frame. "It doesn't have any plate." Plenty of people ignored the front-plate law, but usually they owned fancy cars. She looked to Harvey.

He glanced down, where the rear plate should be. His focus snapped back to her, his expression neutral.

"So no plate over there, either?" she asked.

He didn't answer. Shading his eyes with a hand, he peered up the road. He swept his inspection in the other direction, squinting at the trail along the ravine. "Where's your mom?"

"My mom?" she asked indignantly. "Tell me, Harvey, was this car white? You must know. You were hiding it in the barn."

Harvey stepped around the back of the car. Rambo lurched to all fours. She backed around to the other side of the burnt metal frame.

"Look, Red, stop sticking your nose where it don't belong."

Rambo, who last night had snuggled at her feet, circled to her side of the charred metal, pulled back his lips, and snarled, a mimic of his master.

Zoey elevated onto tiptoes and spoke across the top of the blackened car frame. "You look, Harvey. Do you know about the cop killing? Six days ago?" Rambo growled low in his throat, waiting for permission to act, his single loyalty to the hand that fed him.

"I saw a poster at the hardware store," Harvey said. "Suddenly everybody loves a pig."

A frisson of disgust shivered through her. "An officer was killed, Harvey." Her voice was husky.

He made explosions with his hands. "And poof. Trayvon Martin and everybody else—wiped out?"

Why bother countering that Trayvon Martin had been killed by a wanna-be cop, a neighborhood-watch volunteer, not a policeman. Harvey's point remained. *Diante Yarber. Michael Brown. Antwon Rose.* All shot by law enforcement officers. All the shootings colored by what it meant to be young and black in America. All of them riveting the nation's attention on policing—on bias and excessive force. But Harvey wasn't a news junkie, or left-leaning. The animosity in his voice flowed from another wellspring. Who had he meant by *everybody else?*

She lowered back to flat feet, trembling, on the brink of exhaustion, held up by adrenaline alone. Whatever he meant, Harvey had a point. Before the shooting, she'd sensed tension in Stan Austin. He was a man who'd been dissatisfied with the restraints of his teaching career. A man who wanted to deal with *punks* more aggressively. A man who wanted to show off his power to her.

Rambo snarled.

"Oh, be quiet," she snapped.

The Doberman stopped rumbling, with a flick of his head toward Harvey.

Harvey did not order the dog to stand down.

Baring his fangs, Rambo tensed forward, eager for a command. Harvey had told her a dozen times that he wasn't an attack dog, but you could have fooled her.

She gripped the frame of the car and studied Harvey. For all his dismissal of Officer Austin's death, for all his impatience with her now, he'd consistently cared for her, from the day he'd let her move to the farm to last night after the fire. His soft spot for her seemed steadfast and real. Even now, he seemed to be watching out for her.

"That police shooting," she said, "I was there." She coughed, her throat still parched. "I was doing a ride-along, Harvey. I saw that officer get his head blown apart. The killer was driving a white sedan."

Harvey strode to Rambo and seized his collar. "Sit."

Rambo obeyed with only a tiny whimper of protest.

Harvey rested his hands on the roof of the car, then lifted them and inspected his blackened palms. He wiped them down his worn jeans. He shook his head. "And you think *this* vehicle was used in *that* shooting?"

"Was it white?"

"I think it was black."

"So it *was* in the barn?" She croaked in frustration. "How could you not know its color?"

"I only agreed to store it for a friend." A note of worry infected his voice.

"Ray?" she asked.

Harvey shook his head. It was a I'm-not-going-to-tell-you waggle rather than a denial.

"So your *friend* broke in?"

"I never said anyone broke in. I left the lock off the door," he said, "and they put the car in the barn and covered it with tarps. I've been too damn busy with harvest to give it a second thought."

She weighed the evidence before her. Or lack thereof. Would the cops be interested in a burned car—*possibly black*? Certainly Harvey wouldn't want her to call in the police.

She returned to the spent flare lying in the dust of the road. It had lit the path to the hood. Zoey circled back toward Harvey. Rambo whimpered, unhappy to be relegated to sitting instead of ripping out a tasty hunk of rump. She stopped at the driver's side door. The blaze had melted off the handles. The windows had either been broken out beforehand or shattered by the flames. She poked her head into the gutted interior, her cheek brushing the window frame.

Past the burned-out back seat in a corner of the trunk area, a black rectangle indicated the remains of a metal box with burned material on top of it.

If she hoisted herself, she could crawl through the window space. Instead, she withdrew her head and edged toward Harvey. Rambo rose to his feet.

"Sit," Harvey commanded.

The dog returned to his haunches but trained cold eyes on her arms. In a single bound, he could tear her open. She forced herself to look at Harvey. "Do you have a crowbar?"

"Does a bear shit in the woods?" He gestured toward a pegboard of hammers, saws, wrenches, and pliers near the front of the barn. Below it squatted an industrial-sized toolbox, the kind seen in contractors' truck beds. "What do you figure to do, Red? This thing is burnt to a crisp."

"Maybe something survived in the trunk."

"Not a chance in hell." Harvey flicked a speck of dirt from his cheekbone, smearing his face with soot. "Only for you, Kid." He tugged at the trunk latch once just to make sure a crowbar would be necessary and then trudged to the toolbox.

His crowbar looked hefty. Zoey reached for it. Harvey pulled it possessively against his body.

Sometimes he could be maddeningly chauvinistic, although he probably thought he was being a gentleman.

He wedged the prybar under a lip of metal and popped the trunk. The ash on top of the metal box vaguely suggested a stack of hats. When she touched it, the mass collapsed into a feathery pile.

With that evidence gone, she extracted the burned box and dumped the ashes to the side. Metal objects clanked inside. *A small jack?* Beneath where the box had been was more blackness. *Nothing.*

She turned the box over. Ash blackened her palms and smudged the underside of her forearms. She lifted the box into the sunlight. There, stuck to the corner, was a sliver of paint, so tiny a person would need tweezers to grab it.

Harvey hovered, peering over her shoulder. "You got your answer."

"Hold this."

He released the crowbar to grab the box. She intended to get her phone to take a picture, but when Harvey grasped the box, the flake of white crumbled. She blinked, tears of frustration sprouting in her eyes. He hadn't even touched the fragment. It had simply disintegrated.

"You need to get out of sight," Harvey said, more emphatic than he'd been before. He returned the box to the trunk and snapped up the crowbar. He nudged her toward his marijuana plants. "Take the back way to your trailer."

Fear shot up her spine. "Let me have that."

He relinquished his crowbar and whipped out his pistol. Rambo swished ahead of them, his ears standing sharp as arrowheads.

Her throat tightened. "What are you thinking, Harvey?"

"Let's say this car *was* used in the officer shooting," he said. "It was safely hidden. Why burn it?"

The scent of the marijuana plants engulfed her. She tightened her grip on the heavy bar of metal. "Destroy evidence."

"Right. But why now?" Harvey pressed. "You said the shooting happened six days ago. Something's changed. A plan is in motion."

"Eliminate the car," he said, "before the cops come here. But why would the cops come here?"

Well, she thought, there was Harvey's illegal grow, and in spite of his denial, possibly a worse enterprise in which he'd entangled himself. And, the cops had indicated an interest in questioning Zoey at her home.

But she knew these were not the answer to Harvey's rhetorical question.

"Eliminate the car," she whispered, "then eliminate the rest of the evidence. The witness. Me."

Chapter Thirty-Seven

Zoey, Harvey, and Rambo piled into her tiny house. Camille gasped and jumped up from her seat. "What is this?" She stared at the crowbar in Zoey's hand and then at Harvey, gun in hand.

"Harvey, my mom," Zoey said. "But I think you've met."

Harvey holstered his weapon. Camille drew back her shoulders and offered an elegant hand with a French-tipped manicure. "Camille," she said, her eyes absorbing Harvey and brightening, seemingly unperturbed that Harvey was a rootin' tootin' gun-toting long-hair with soot on his face.

Harvey reached for the proffered hand and then pulled back. "Sorry. My hands are dirty."

The two stood, examining each other. Camille's smoldering eyes made Zoey blush. But, to be fair, Harvey looked equally transfixed in spite of what he'd said earlier about her mom being artificial. She wondered if the two had actually met or just spotted one another from a distance.

"The dog," Zoey said crisply, "is Rambo."

Her mom detested big dogs, and this one pointed its snout at her, ready to slobber on her sandals. Camille barely glanced. "Darling, now you look like a chimney sweep."

Her mom, by herself, had made her feel claustrophobic in the tiny home. Now three people and a Doberman crammed her space.

Her mom sank onto one of the two cubes at the table, taking an upright, chin-on-fingers pose.

Zoey scooted toward the living room area.

Harvey wheeled toward her. "Not over there," he barked. "Clear shot through the door."

"What?" Camille yelped. "Shooting? Who's shooting?"

Zoey had already reached the living room, so pressing her feet, she pushed her seat against the corner nearest the slider, a tough angle if someone decided to take a shot. She let the crowbar thud to the floor. "So what's the plan?" she asked. "We can't all just hole up here." Getting shot might be preferable. "It's time to call the police, Harvey."

"Police?" Camille directed her question to Harvey. "What's going on?"

When he didn't answer, Camille stood, stepped around Harvey and the dog, and with a cupped hand, motioned for Zoey to join them. "Come over here, darling. Don't be so stubborn."

She didn't budge.

Camille stepped forward.

A crack split the peace of the woods. Glass shattered. Sparkling confetti sprinkled the room.

Springing forward, Harvey grabbed at Camille's shoulder. Her body twisted away from him, her striped shirt torn at the top.

Pop. Another gunshot.

Camille collapsed, her neck blooming red. Her white Capris speckled with blood.

"Mom!" Zoey slithered to her. She tugged her mom's striped shirt up, stuffing fabric into the neck wound. Her mom's turquoise eyes were wide and full of terror. She gurgled something. Zoey was afraid to lift the material to see the damage, afraid it might be arterial and spurt into the room, draining her mother's life.

Harvey flattened, weapon drawn. Rambo barked crazily.

"Down," Harvey commanded.

The dog hunkered beside him.

"Let Rambo get the fucker!" she screamed.

Scuttling to the side of the door, Harvey rose enough to grasp the handle. But the door didn't slide.

"Glass in the track." He pulled off his shirt and whisked away bits. He tried the door again. It slid open. "Get him, boy!"

The dog launched through the opening like a juggernaut. Silently, he disappeared into the forest.

Harvey snaked to Zoey and her mother, his shoulders and chest bare.

Under Zoey's hands, Camille's striped shirt turned wet and red. Her eyelids drooped.

"Mom!"

Harvey's face was so close to hers she could smell the coffee lingering on his breath. Tears streaked down the man's worn face. "Not fucking again."

Zoey's heart fluttered with fear. Was Harvey experiencing a PTSD flashback? He seemed to be functioning, but would he be able to help her? "We have to go—get Mom help," she said. "We know the road. It'll be faster than an ambulance."

Harvey swiped at his eyes, holstered his Glock, and wrestled his shirt on. "The guy must have gotten in close. He used a handgun. If he'd used a rifle..."

He didn't finish the thought. He didn't have to. She knew a rifle shot would have blown her mother apart. But it wouldn't take a rifle to stop Rambo. Her gut twisted with added worry.

Camille's breathing was ragged.

"Tip her head back more. Make sure her tongue doesn't fall into her throat." Harvey stuck his fingers into her mom's mouth. Her mom gurgled. It was unintelligible, but Zoey knew what she was saying. *Don't let me die.*

"Keys?"

"Hold this." Zoey grabbed his free hand and clamped it over the bloody shirt. Crawling to the table, she periscoped a hand and retrieved her keys. Her car was closer, roomier, and in better shape than Harvey's truck. She dug into her stash of clothing and yanked out two cotton tees, one of them her red She Cats shirt.

She tossed the shirts to Harvey. He expertly slid the She Cats shirt over the wound and tugged her mom's bloody shirt down around her spattered, milky skin.

"How are we going to keep the compression while we move her?"

"Got tape?" he asked.

Without answering, she took a roll of duct tape from a kitchen drawer.

The tape whirred as Harvey wrapped it tightly around the tee-shirt, not stopping until he reached the cardboard roll.

"I'll take the shoulders. You grab her feet. As soon as we load her, get pressure back on the shirt. Use whatever you need. Forearm. Knee."

"Won't that strangle her?"

"We're out of options."

"What about the shooter?"

"He's long gone," Harvey said. "He thinks he hit his target."

She felt sick with realization. The shooter had not seen her and Harvey and Rambo enter the house. No foreign car tipped off the assassin that another person might be around. Instead, the shooter had picked out a small, red-headed woman traipsing around in Zoey's trailer. And he'd put a bullet in her neck. A bullet meant for her.

Chapter Thirty-Eight

arvey drove faster than Zoey would have dared, the small SUV jolting over the ruts in the mountain road. Her mother's body, stretched flat, bounced beneath her hands. She fought to maintain pressure against the tee duct-taped around the wound. Back here in the cargo hold, she had no seatbelt. The ride swung her away from her mother and then pitched her forward.

"It won't do any good if we all die on the way," she hollered over the engine roar.

Harvey hit a rut. She bounced up, her tailbone slamming down. Adrenaline had wiped away all her drowsiness, but not the nausea from the toxic fumes of the fire. It took sheer willpower not to puke on top of the wet stripes of her mother's shirt. The first bullet had torn through the fabric and grazed her mom's shoulder, the flesh wound soaking the sleeve of her mom's shirt. Blood dripped onto the metal floor.

The top-heavy Element careened around a corner. "Slow down," Zoey screamed. "This isn't your truck." The SUV tipped to prove her point. She swayed with the curve.

Harvey slowed marginally.

With the back seats folded forward, the Element provided enough space for her mom to lie flat. Her face was white—bloodless.

Zoey's thoughts jarred loose with the bumps. Mostly a mantra of *don't die, don't die, don't die.*

Camille. Zoey couldn't imagine life without her. At heart, her family consisted of just Camille and her—a see-saw of emotions, going way back to when Camille vacillated between abandoning her to a carousel of nannies or dressing her up to parade around as her pride.

She remembered Camille, decked out in a de la Renta, a creamy yellow floor-length froth, and her in a similar, small rendition, specially tailored, silky smooth under her nine-year-old fingers. In a vast marble vestibule, people circled and cooed while her mother's cool fingers pressed her back, urging her forward into the limelight. Then Camille had taken her hand and led her into a majestic auditorium, the walls painted with figures. Huge wine-colored curtains, tall as a building, drew back. A woman swept onto the stage. A complete hush fell, followed by a voice piercing the air, stabbing through Zoey like a lightning bolt.

Harvey turned onto the smoother highway. "How you doing back there?"

Tears coursed down Zoey's cheeks. Her mother had loved her the best she could.

The shirt under Zoey's fingers had grown spongy, and pink oozed from between the strips of duct tape.

Harvey glanced into the cargo hold.

"Just drive," she croaked.

For all the bad stuff, like knowing her biological father only through photos, there'd been the other stuff, being dragged to art gallery openings and soirees. In spite of Rich Husband #2, the abusive prick, and Rich Husband #3, the unfaithful lout, in spite of the weeks she'd been left with strangers as her mom trotted the globe, Zoey had been introduced to writing by Camille. In a literal sense. Because of her mom, Zoey's little hands had shaken those of Toni Morrison, an author who evolved into a personal hero.

And her mom showed up beaming at her book launches, even if it was mainly to claim credit. *"I'm* her mother. *I* sent her to the writing program in San Francisco." Camille could never bring herself to say San Francisco State University. She'd wanted Zoey to end up at Stanford.

On the asphalt road, Harvey picked up speed. "Rachelle was a beautiful redhead," he said. "Like the two of you." He sounded cloggy, like maybe he was crying, too.

Zoey leaned forward to look. A tear drizzled down Harvey's worn cheek.

Harvey's *not fucking again* now made sense. It wasn't about people getting killed in battle. "Was Rachelle shot?"

"When I came home. She'd turned into a peacenik."

Zoey could barely hear him. Harvey kept his eyes on the curving mountain highway. He raced past other cars. She held her breath, hoping he would continue to talk, despite the distraction to his driving. His story lifted her away from the tragedy sprawled before her, from the stickiness under her fingers, the barely audible wheeze of her mom's breath.

"She was shot by pigs."

"Like at Kent State?" Her body rocked as Harvey made an abrupt lane change.

"They launched tear gas. Meant to go over the protestors."

Zoey couldn't tell if he was still crying because she, herself, had started to emit strange sounds that seemed disconnected from her body.

They swerved. The mountain highway dumped onto the freeway at Playa Maria.

She pressed harder against the improvised bandage on her mom's neck. Her mom looked dead—no movement, not a gurgle of breath. They were too late.

"The canister wouldn't have hit her," Harvey muttered, "except she was riding someone's shoulders."

"Your shoulders?"

Harvey veered onto rumble strips, then overcorrected to make their exit. Zoey pitched across her mom's torso, before righting herself.

"I wasn't there. I was in rehab for my leg wound." He added the last bit glumly, as though he'd failed Rachelle. "The canister hit her in the fucking head."

His pain sounded raw, near the surface, even though the event must have happened fifty years ago. Zoey bent her ear to her mother's nose. *Nothing.*

To quell the panic rising in her, she needed to talk. *About anything.* Her voice was tremulous when she asked, "What's going to happen with Rambo?"

"If the shooter had a good escape hatch," Harvey said, gruff, but more like his regular self, "nothing." He paused. "Or maybe right now he has a champion clamped on his arm."

Or, Zoey thought, swallowing hard, there was a third possibility, one that Harvey didn't want to speak. *More pain and sorrow.*

As Harvey ran the stop signs in the hospital parking lot, he honked the horn, over and over. He circled to the Emergency Room in the back.

A sheriff's cruiser sat at the red curb. Two orderlies were rolling a gurney up a ramp. Two deputies, in animated conversation, swung around as Harvey skidded to a halt and jumped from the car, his door gaping open. Harvey dashed past them, toward the orderlies. "We have a gunshot victim here!"

One deputy hurried after Harvey while the other hustled toward the car.

The deputy swung open the back suicide-doors. He seemed more surprised to find her, squatted there, than her mom. Her hands were smeared with blood, and she knew her face was streaked with black soot like a wild Raiders fan. The deputy widened his eyes and then dropped his gaze to her mom. "Gunshot to the neck?"

"Yes."

He craned into the car. His tag said Hashimoto.

"My mom's bleeding to death."

"You need help with the pressure on that?"

"I got it."

"And you?" Hashimoto asked calmly.

"I'm okay."

"Accident?" He stared at her. "Was there a fire, too?"

Before she could scream at the deputy, the automatic doors at the top of the ramp slid open. An orderly pushed out a gurney. It rattled loudly over the concrete, serrated to protect against the slickness of rain or blood. Another orderly and Harvey hustled after him, followed by the second deputy.

Hashimoto backed away to allow the gurney to roll up. The orderlies took a second to absorb the situation.

The deputies conferred, edging close. In some cosmic joke, while Hashimoto had no eyebrows to speak of, the other deputy had eyebrows like caterpillars, Martin Scorsese eyebrows.

Keeping the tee-shirt pressed firmly to her mom's neck, Zoey stepped over the body, away from the doors, wishing the hospital personnel were faster.

"Is that the only wound?" one orderly asked.

"No," she snapped. "She has a flesh wound on her shoulder."

"Good job applying pressure," the first orderly said. "I'll take over as we make the transfer."

There was no time to argue. She let the orderly's hand replace hers. The two men expertly slung her mom onto the gurney.

"Trauma Center," the first orderly commanded, and they were off. The deputy with the eyebrows asked if there were any weapon on the body and then took off.

Body. She shivered.

Like a Russian dancer, she squat-walked across the Element's cargo hold and hopped to the ground. She shot forward, but one of the orderlies shouted at her. "Not here! There!" He jabbed a finger toward an entrance about sixty feet away, Deputy Eyebrows already on his way.

She passed Harvey's long limbs. Hashimoto's tall, slender form shadowed her.

The first deputy had reached the ramp to Admissions and spun back toward them. He commanded Harvey to stop, turn, and spread 'em.

That's not going to go over well. She was a lot less resistant to law enforcement, and she wasn't going to stop. Thankfully, Hashimoto didn't ask her to.

As the doors slid open, she heard Harvey saying, "I don't have to give you my name. California doesn't have a stop-and-identify law. I want a lawyer."

Sticking by her side, Hashimoto let her approach an ER intake window. The woman there looked barely out of high school, her smooth face fresh and unfazed by the churn of tragedy. Glossy hair pulled back from red-framed glasses, her dark lipstick perfect.

Zoey wasn't even forty yet, but the young woman made her feel saggy and old.

"Are you with the gunshot victim?" she asked, almost brightly, a reasonable assumption given the timing and the condition of Zoey's shirt and hands.

"Yes."

The counter separated two realities—on one side, an intact world of people going about their everyday jobs, drinking their cups of coffee, and tapping info into computers, and on the other side, her side, shattered worlds where nothing would be the same again.

The intake clerk peeked at Hashimoto, then informed Zoey, "We have mandatory reporting of gunshot wounds. That probably seems like a moot point, but I'm obligated to tell you." She pushed up her glasses and briskly launched into questions.

Zoey gave her name and her mom's name, but as the questions progressed to medical coverage, medications, allergies, she realized how little she knew about her mother. Notebook in hand, Hashimoto hovered to catch every detail, close enough that she caught a whiff of his aftershave, a subtle, musky smell. He jotted down information.

"And how about you, Miss Kozinski? Are you okay?" the intake woman cocked a brow at her. "Were you near an explosion?"

"I'm fine." A complete lie. She looked over her shoulder, out the door. The other deputy had bagged Harvey's hands. *Ah, shit.*

"Can he do that?" she asked Hashimoto. "Harvey asked for a lawyer." Was it possible to test positive for gunshot residue simply from handling one's own gun?

"An unstoppable force has met an immovable object," Hashimoto said.

She turned from the counter, her body limp as a cooked noodle, ready to collapse. Hashimoto aimed a meaningful look out the door as his fellow deputy nudged Harvey toward his cruiser. "I'm sure you are not holding any weapons," he said, almost apologetically, "but I need to do a pat down, too."

Beyond the ability to resist, she raised her hands. Hashimoto tucked away his notepad to give her a cursory frisk that seemed true to his words, that he knew she wasn't carrying. Or maybe in the MeToo era, he worried about being a male deputy searching a woman's body.

She sank onto a bench built out from the wall. The ER was not a place designed for comfort, at least not on this side of the barrier. This side was nothing more than a wide hallway that curved around the intake cubicles and disappeared into swinging doors at either end.

Overhead lights buzzed inside her head. The blood on her Yosemite shirt was congealing into crusty patches. To think just last night she'd been concerned about a little marinara sauce.

Hashimoto took out the notepad from his pocket. "Did the shooting occur at the address you provided?"

"No. That's my mom's address. The shooting happened at my house."

"Who was there?"

"Me, my mom, and Harvey."

"Harvey?" He glanced out the door. "What's his last name?"

She hesitated. "I'd be more comfortable if Harvey provided that."

For the moment, Hashimoto let that slide. He continued by peppering Zoey with questions to elicit what happened: When did the shooting occur? What did she see? A part of her welcomed the distraction from what was happening beyond the swinging doors, the hidden part of the ER where the gurney with her mother must have rolled.

"We need to visit the crime scene—the sooner the better."

"There's not an address." She cocked her head toward Harvey. "My landlord and I live on a private road. We use P.O. boxes."

"Can you provide directions?"

"Not really."

The bench seat felt as though it were shaking, as if they were having an earthquake. "I need to stay with my mom. Harvey will have to direct you."

"He's not being cooperative."

She lowered her head, feeling woozy. "He's not big on authority," she mumbled into her hands. "Law enforcement killed his girlfriend." *His first love. His only love?* "By mistake," she added quickly.

Hashimoto squatted down to Zoey's eye level. "Are you going to faint?" He didn't wait for an answer. He spun and asked the intake clerk to bring water. "And coffee."

The young woman with the red glasses sprang out of her chair to get the drinks.

"You don't have to go to the scene in person," Hashimoto said. "If we have your permission, all we need is some idea how to get there."

"It's not like that up there."

"The mountains?"

"Yes. His road doesn't even have a name."

Hashimoto knitted his almost invisible brows. "We have to process the crime scene."

"There's other stuff you should know." Raising her head, she managed a jumbled account of her connection to the shooting of Officer Austin and her sense that someone wanted to eliminate her as a potential witness. How her mom resembled her and was in Zoey's house. "The shooter meant to kill me."

"If you're so in the boonies," Hashimoto asked, "how did this shooter find you?"

"He figured it out *somehow*." She drew a shaky breath. "My name was released to the public, thanks to the *Reporter*." Her sense of fairness made her kick in, "And my agent."

"Agent?" he asked.

"I'm a crime writer. That's why I was doing the ride-along." Another idea burst into her head. It spilled from her, uncontrolled. "His wife threatened me, too."

"Officer Austin's wife?"

"Maybe a cop found out where I lived and told her. Officer Austin told me she was a hell of a shot."

Hashimoto didn't make a face so much as freeze his expression in place. Hoping she hadn't permanently lost him, Zoey drew a deep breath to steer the conversation back to her main theme—to tell Hashimoto about Ray— when a mother in sweatpants gusted into the emergency room with a blast of wailing. She lugged a boy, way past carrying age, his feet bare and one pant leg hitched up to reveal fierce bites. The mother dumped the crying boy onto the counter in front of a window. A male clerk started the intake process.

The young woman with the red glasses bustled up beside Hashimoto.

Thanking her, he tucked away his notepad to accept a cafeteria tray. The clerk briskly returned to her station. On her own volition, she'd added a coffee for Hashimoto and creamers, stir sticks, and napkins.

The deputy placed the tray on the nearest available surface, the top of a garbage can. "Water or coffee?"

"Coffee."

Zoey held the cup with both hands, noting the streaks of grime running down the white paint from the swinging mouth of the garbage can. Hospitals were one of the germiest places on earth, with the ER at the pinnacle. And her mother was here, with her neck opened up by a bullet. If that didn't kill her, the surgery might. Infection might. *If she isn't already dead.*

Hashimoto ripped open a sugar packet, dumped it into his cup, and skipped the stirring. He took the time to drink a bit of coffee and to let Zoey sip hers before forging on. "Let's go back to how the shooter found you."

"Maybe I was being followed." She said it even though the first instance of the feeling had occurred during a marijuana-induced paranoia, and the second time, when Curt was with her, no gray car had trailed her into the Honda dealership.

And the driver on the mountain highway? He could have been anyone pissed off at her mom driving forty miles per hour in the left lane.

Still, she persevered. "The shooter may have linked my name to my vehicle. The green Honda Element."

"A distinctive car," Hashimoto said.

Could the shooter have access to DMV records? Her thoughts slid back to Christine Austin.

Zoey shook her head, heavy and sloshing as a pail of water. The night the asshole on the hill seemed to be tailing her and her mom, they'd been in her mom's rental, not her Element.

Another niggling idea fluttered at the edges of her brain.

Chapter Thirty-Nine

Before Zoey could marshal the niggly feeling into a thought, a man in green scrubs swung through the doors at the end of the hallway. He was tall and lean with short-cropped gray hair peeking below his surgical cap. His scrubs were clean, so it didn't seem like the man could be associated with the bloody mess that had been her mother. But then he looked at them and approached slowly.

He telegraphed the news before he opened his mouth.

"Ma'am, could you please follow me?" he said.

She didn't respond. Couldn't respond. She couldn't breathe.

Above Zoey, the doctor—*surgeon?*—wavered in the harsh light like an hallucination. Hashimoto's hand on her elbow hoisted her, guided her after the doctor into a small, private room. Neither she nor the doctor protested his presence.

She sank into a chair. The doctor remained standing, taking a stance in front of her. Long, elegant hands pressed together in front of his stomach. "I'm sorry," he said.

Her head was spinning. A stone blocked her throat.

The doctor remained glued to the glossy tiles as though his position of authority required him to say more. He cleared his throat. "A lot of people talk about the Golden Hour, but with ballistic trauma, we talk about a Platinum Ten Minutes." He looked down. He had the slightly wide stance of a confident man. *A cocky man.*

"You did everything you could," he said. "And so did we."

He waited a beat, said that he was very sorry for her loss, and asked if she'd like to see her mother.

The body he meant.

"No."

Her knot of emotions was hard to untangle, but one thread was *unworthy.* How could she lay claim to wanting to see her mother? She'd never wanted to see her mother when she was alive. It seemed hypocritical to invade her space when her mom could no longer extend her claws, when her body was lying there defenseless.

"The authorities will be taking her clothing and personal effects into evidence." He glanced toward Hashimoto. "I signed and bagged the bullet."

"The bullet was in her?"

The surgeon regarded her. "Bullets can do strange things inside a body. I once operated on a man shot in the shoulder. The bullet was in his hip."

He waited to see if Zoey asked anything more. He said again that he was sorry for her loss, and departed, still debonair, returning to the bowels of the place, where her mother stretched, stripped of the clothing and style that defined her.

She rose on shaky legs. "What next?"

"The Medical Examiner will need to do an autopsy," Hashimoto said.

That was only a tiny fraction of what she'd meant—the rest of it, Hashimoto couldn't possibly answer. As alienated as she'd been from Camille, as the next of kin, did she now need to notify people? Write an obit? Plan a funeral? She felt dizzy with the immensity of the situation. She floated back towards the intake area with the deputy behind her.

The automatic doors slid open. No one entered, only a burst of cold air, as though the doors had been triggered by a phantom weight. Perhaps, Zoey thought, the twenty-one grams of her mom's soul, escaping the hospital, shifting the situation from a dime-a-dozen shooting to a homicide.

The drama would suit Camille.

Zoey stood in shock. The door closed, then opened again as Hashimoto stepped outside, keying his shoulder radio. Time was distorted. The events in the private room had been momentous, yet the male clerk was still gathering information from the mother while her boy sobbed on the counter.

And the woman with the red glasses was engaged in an intent conversation on the phone, which included the question, "Is he breathing?"

Just a typical day in the ER?

Time inexorably marched on like a grandfather clock in a silent room—undisturbed by the happenings in her world and unconcerned with whether a person might be drawing a last breath on the other end of a phone line.

Hashimoto walked back through the doors and to her side. "Why don't you sit back down?" he asked.

She sat. She didn't know whether Hashimoto's words were an order or a kindness.

The ER's mandatory reporting of the gunshot wound had no doubt been updated to a gunshot death—one that didn't look like suicide or an accident. How long before a homicide detective showed?

A male ER nurse squatted by the boy's leg. The child clutched at his mom and nearly fell off the counter.

Zoey averted her gaze to the entrance and tried to order her thoughts. Her mother had been killed outside the city limits—county jurisdiction. Maybe normally someone from the Sheriff's Office would show up, but she'd shared her backstory with Hashimoto, had linked her mom's death and the death of Officer Austin, and had named Bowman as the lead detective.

Hashimoto, trim and unreadable, positioned his body so it blocked her line of vision to the door. Before the surgeon had pronounced her mother dead, the deputy had seemed confident and professional. Now he kept glancing toward the door like he wanted help.

The other deputy no longer seemed to be around. Was he with Harvey? Had he transported Harvey to the station? What did he hope to accomplish when Harvey had already asked for a lawyer? Did Harvey have a lawyer? If the lawyer had appeared—or even if he hadn't—was Harvey released and on his way to the farm?

She wondered if the fact she'd lost her mother and didn't seem to be the shooter made Hashimoto uncomfortable. He peeked at her and then looked away. Whether he'd called Bowman or someone else, it couldn't be too long, Zoey figured, before the dots connected, and Bowman showed up. Suddenly it seemed less like the deputy was concerned for her well-being and more like he was detaining her.

She stared at him until he met her eyes.

"I want a lawyer."

"I haven't even Mirandized you." Hashimoto's tone carried a soupçon of indignation.

She pulled out her cell phone and called Kath, the drummer for She Cats, trying to conjure her wife's name. *Lisa?* She practiced family law, not criminal law, but family law was full of gnarly situations. She'd know what to do.

"Whadzup?" The sudden response from Kath startled her. Edging away from Hashimoto, Zoey huddled in a corner and asked for Lisa.

"Lizzy, you mean?"

"Yeah, sorry."

"We've separated."

"I'm sorry, Kath."

"Me, too."

The automatic doors slid open, and cold night air blasted in. When she turned to look, her dread turned to reality. Detective Bowman strode toward Hashimoto, but the tired eyes in the wrinkled face locked on her.

Given Kath's situation, she felt like a bitch to soldier forward. She kept her voice steady but couldn't hide her urgency. "The thing is, I need a lawyer."

"Lizzy does Family Law," Kath snapped. "Why would you want her? You don't even have a family."

The unsheathed words stabbed her. They were so true. She didn't have anyone. No dad, really. No brothers or sisters. And now, no mom.

"It's too much to explain," her voice cracked. "Do you think Lizzy would help me?"

"Sure," Kath said. "She loves the She Cats. Just not me. But when you contact her, don't call her Lizzy. Use Lisandra."

Bowman remained a respectful distance away, arms crossed over his bulky torso, swaddled now in a light jacket. He listened to Hashimoto but watched her.

The phone number Kath had given her yielded a solemn response. Zoey identified herself.

"You know Kath and I have separated, don't you?"

"Yes. I was sorry to hear that, but this isn't a social call. I'm calling because I need a lawyer. I'm about to be arrested for impeding a murder investigation."

"Did you lie to a police officer?" Lisandra's voice changed from that of an acquaintance to that of a lawyer, brisk and business-like, unrattled by the words *murder investigation.*

"No." *My mother was shot. Killed.* The words threatened to tumble out. But she didn't want the conversation to veer into condolences and sorrow.

"Bribe anyone?" Lisandra asked. "Threaten anyone?"

"No, of course not."

"You're just not being cooperative?"

"Yes."

"Stay calm. There's very little one has to tell a police officer. It's unlikely you can be charged with obstruction." Lisandra paused a beat. "Are they taking you to the downtown station?"

Zoey looked back at the two law enforcement officers, discussing the situation in low voices.

"Are you taking me downtown?" she asked.

Bowman nodded curtly.

"Yes."

"Waste of the taxpayer's money," Lisandra muttered. "Don't say another word. I'll be at the station in a half hour."

When Zoey disconnected and turned, Bowman stepped toward her, doing a visual inspection. She knew what he was seeing—the burnt tips of her hair, the smears of soot, the spatter of dried blood on her shirt. "Hope that lawyer costs a pretty penny." He sounded most unfriendly. "We're already working on a search warrant."

Working on a search warrant—not *have* a search warrant. Harvey wouldn't have said a word. She suspected they had no idea where to search, and for now she was going to follow Lisandra's advice.

"You want to save us some time here, Kozinski?" Bowman asked. "Tell us what's going on?"

She shook her head, not quite understanding herself. Why was she being obstinate? Was she retaliating for the way Bowman had treated her? Was she worried about betraying Harvey, jeopardizing his farm and her place to live? Why risk those things when the shooter was long gone from the mountaintop?

Or was he? How had the person reached her trailer? If he'd parked down on the road, it was a strenuous hike, especially cutting through the woods rather than following their drive. She and Harvey hadn't seen any vehicle on their way to the hospital. The idea the shooter could have reached a car parked along the roads before they'd driven by seemed improbable. Unless the person had been ballsy enough to park close by below the rise.

Maybe the shooter had an accomplice to drop him off.

And, finally, maybe it wasn't a *he.*

If Christine Austin had decided to take a shot at her, could she trust the police? Christine was still the wife of a fallen officer, even if she was suing the department.

Chapter Forty

Lisandra had been right—a total waste of taxpayer money. Bowman had escorted Zoey to an interview room. When she remained mum, he'd left her there, without even an offer of a glass of water, until he'd walked back in with Lisandra and said, "You can go."

The detective ushered them, their footsteps clacking the tiled hallways, an overall sense of emptiness in the station with the nine-to-five staff gone for the day. Lisandra bustled ahead of Bowman like she knew her way, her lawyerly blazer swishing and her leather satchel swinging. At the foyer, the lawyer turned to Bowman, offered her business card, and wished him a good evening.

Zoey was impressed. Lisandra had arrived in short order, as promised, wearing neatly-pressed slacks, a hint of shine on her lips, and her shoulder-length hair impeccable and glossy.

On the station's steps, she and Lisandra stopped as if in synch. The night air was nippy. Zoey blinked. Fall had arrived without her noticing.

"Can't wait to hear this story." Lisandra's curt formality vanished. She sounded like the woman Zoey had met at various gigs. "I'm trusting that you didn't kill anyone?" She paused. Eyed Zoey's shirt. "If you did, don't tell me."

"It's not a one-beer story," she said. "More like a six-pack."

"I'm ready to drink a six-pack all by myself." Lisandra pointed to a white Leaf, an all-electric vehicle. "That's me over there. Give me a call when you're ready to talk." She handed Zoey her card. *Lisandra Gomez, Esq.*

"Don't you want me to fill out paperwork?" Zoey asked. "Pay you a retainer or something?"

Lisandra flapped a hand. "My pro-bono for the year." She pinned Zoey with courtroom eyes. "You could tell Kath she's a fool for leaving."

"Exactly what I think, anyway," Zoey said, surprised the split had been Kath's idea.

"Over a guy, no less."

"Ouch." She felt uncomfortable, drained of any reserve of compassion with which to comfort the lawyer. "If it's any consolation, Kath sounded pretty broken up."

"No consolation," Lisandra said. "Remember your last gig? He was there in the back, staring at her. Good thing I didn't own a gun or I might be the one down here."

Double ouch. She knew exactly who Lisandra meant—the man Zoey had thought was staring at her. He'd been looking through her to Kath on her drum set. And why not? In Zoey's opinion, Kath's muscled arms and short black hair swinging to her rhythms made her a lot hotter than Sabrina.

Lisandra held up an index finger. "One caution. If law enforcement believes you're involved in a homicide, they might follow you." She quirked a brow. "Speaking of which, do you need a lift back to your car?"

Zoey shook her head. She hadn't considered the idea they could tail her, but if so, it might be better if she weren't in a vehicle. If law enforcement could follow her, they could have followed Harvey when he left the station. The idea alarmed her.

A ride would speed up what she needed to do, but she didn't want to do any of it in front of a someone connected to the law. "Do they really have the manpower to tail people?"

"For a homicide, maybe."

"Thanks for the offer, but I need to walk—clear my head." She smiled grimly at the thought of a patrol car rolling along slowly behind her.

"That's a long walk."

"When I'm sick of walking, I'll call Lyft."

Lisandra barked a laugh. "Have you seen yourself anytime in recent history?" The lawyer retreated down the broad steps. "No one in his right mind would pick you up. Follow me."

They moved toward the crepuscular edge of the parking lot. Lisandra pulled a wipe from her glove compartment.

Zoey mopped her face, the tissue coming away dark with dirt and soot. Lisandra opened the back of the car and trawled out a black sweatshirt. "Take this."

Zoey zipped the sweatshirt over her blood-stained top. "Thanks."

"No need to return it. It's just a rag I keep in case I'm in my lawyer clothes and need to deal with a sticky situation."

As soon as Lisandra committed to driving away, Zoey texted Harvey. *Where are you?*

She didn't expect a response, at least not a quick one, Harvey being Harvey.

His answer came immediately.

Safe dont worry Ill fix this

Her heart lurched. The sentence "Don't worry" should be banned. When had it ever helped someone not worry? And *fix this*? With his military background, he must've had some idea how dire her mother's outcome might be. How could he possibly fix that?

She typed back *WTF* but as soon as she sent it, she realized Harvey might not know what that meant.

She waited a beat but nothing came back, and she knew nothing would.

Chapter Forty-One

In his office, Ray slumped on a barstool, sipping a second vodka tonic. He took a moment to lick his lips, to relish the bite of Ketel One and fresh lime. If you were going to go through all this shit, you had to enjoy the fruits of your labor. He drew a deep breath and sighed it out. Otherwise, what was it all for?

His finger touched the barrel of the Colt resting on the dark lacquered wood. He spun it like a wheel of fortune, not quite believing where life had led him. Where Harvey had led him, he thought. First to Vietnam. Then into this business. He wouldn't be here if it weren't for Harvey. He swallowed a gulp of the bitter tonic and smacked the glass down too hard.

What would you have done instead? Gone into your dad's refrigeration business?

He snorted. *Fat chance.* He'd hated his dad, always griping about long-hairs and *young people nowadays*, literally dragging Ray to the barbershop. If he was being honest, he'd enlisted as much to get away from his dad as to follow Harvey. He'd enjoyed slinging open the back door, tipping his shaved crown toward his dad, and asking, "Short enough?"

But then he'd witnessed the journey on his dad's face, the World War II vet's eyes traveling from surprise to anger to fear. Seeing his dad's retreat paralyzed Ray. He'd stood dumbly in the kitchen, the enormity of his decision weighting his feet like concrete.

And the pot business? He couldn't really blame Harvey for that. They'd parted ways a long time ago because Harvey was an idealist, not a business-man.

Ray took a slug of his drink. What good had the money done him? It wasn't like he had a corner office in a high-rise. Needing to blend in with the other farm buildings, his office was a shithole, cobwebs up in the rafter beams, weathered unpainted exterior and drafty interior. And here he was, sitting in it at night, because it wasn't like he had anything to go home to.

What did he have to show for his life except a twisted gut and two kids who'd gotten older without ever growing up? They hadn't even produced grandkids.

He rattled the ice in his glass and stared morosely at the stained-glass lamp on his desk, made by Suzette, his first wife. She'd been a friend of Rachelle's. He closed his eyes against a stab of pain in his stomach.

Suzette and him had gone to hell slowly. At the end, Suzette blamed him for Rachelle's death, claiming if he'd been a better friend to his sister, if he'd listened to her arguments against the war, if she'd felt validated, that she might not have been at the march. The whole argument was ridiculous. He'd been in Vietnam at the time of the march. How could he have done anything? It was just Suzette's grief striking out, and he'd lashed back with his own grief. And maybe some guilt. It was weird how the thing that had drawn them together, eventually split them apart.

At the creak of the door, Ray snatched up the pistol.

The last person in the world he wanted to see was standing in the doorway.

Chapter Forty-Two

Zoey strode through Playa Maria's downtown like she was fleeing, trying to outpace her grief and worry. She threaded through diners and theater-goers—out in force—and dodged around homeless individuals clustered at sidewalk benches.

Sweat beaded on her forehead in spite of the autumnal chill. She unzipped the sweatshirt a few inches, but stopped at the first spot of blood.

In store after store, the display windows confronted her with Christine Austin's poster and with hand-lettered signs of support for the PMPD.

She was a pariah. Any moment someone might point her out. *There she is! The ride-along who killed Stan Austin!* She imagined a vigilante group chasing her down the sidewalk.

Zoey tucked into an alcove of the bookstore to take a breather. The hospital was at least two more miles.

The alcove used to be one of the store's entrances, but there were only so many doors the personnel could watch to prevent theft. Now these glass doors were permanently closed and blocked by backs of bookshelves.

A man leaned on the opposite wall—one shoe sole pressed to the stucco. He was bearded, young, and slightly smelly. Possibly unhoused, but he wasn't toting possessions, so in Playa Maria, hard to tell. Could be a college student.

He pushed off the wall, crossed the alcove, and planted himself in front of her. "Do you have thirty-five cents?"

She could not deal with this. Unzipping the sweatshirt, she let it flap open so he could see her bloody shirt. Let him think she'd used a machete on someone.

Unfazed, he combed fingers through a dark beard.

Maybe the stains didn't register as blood. "I don't have thirty-five cents."

He stood there like he knew she had a twenty and maybe thought she'd offer to break it or give him all of it. "Fuck off," she said.

"Hey," he admonished. "You don't have to be a bitch." He sauntered across the alcove and resumed his position.

She considered moving, but didn't like the idea of being driven away by some dickhead. The former entrance to the bookstore provided a nice spot out of the hustle and bustle of the sidewalk. She took up her own position against the stucco and called Brianna.

Curt answered.

"I meant to dial Bri's cell."

"This is the apartment. The landline. Quaint, eh?"

"Is Bri there?"

"Nah," Curt drawled, sounding stoned. "When she started a band, I don't think she knew she'd become a mom."

"What's up?"

"Kath is having second thoughts about leaving Lisandra. She's realizing for the twenty-seventh time that men are pigs."

"Bri would consider that a grave insult to pigs."

Curt snorted and hung up.

Zoey took a moment to feel hope for Lisandra, Kath's wife, before her own disappointment squeezed in. If Brianna was busy counseling Kath, who could she turn to?

The prickle of the stucco felt like the only thing holding her up. Her mother was dead. *Murdered.* The police had hauled her in like a suspect. Maybe she should have let them keep her at the station where she was safe. Or, at least, accepted a ride from Lisandra.

"Should haves" were a waste of time. She was here, now, out in the open, with someone around who apparently wanted to kill her. Those were the facts. Her greatest protection, really, would be for the shooter to believe he had killed her. Not a powerful argument for returning to her trailer and flicking on the lights.

Near the police department and in the bustle of downtown, there was a modicum of security, but the remaining two-mile stretch would take her along Scenic Drive, a main artery across the county. It bridged ravines and sliced through undeveloped riparian corridors. Walking there alone at night would be foolish, even when someone didn't want her dead.

Lyft?

She thought of her SUV—Harvey slamming on the brakes at the ER entrance. *A red zone.* Would her car even be waiting for her when she reached the hospital?

Scrolling down her contacts, she hesitated. Her finger hovered, then tapped the name.

When she said that she needed a ride to the hospital, there was no equivocating or questioning.

"I'll be there in five minutes."

A little late but otherwise true to his word, Jimmy pulled up in a light-colored sedan.

She exhaled in relief and plopped into the passenger seat. The interior was silent, odd for someone who managed a record store. "Thanks for doing this."

He shrugged. "I wouldn't leave a woman stranded on the streets at night."

That was less than what she'd hoped for and more than she deserved given the way she'd blown him off at Kamea's.

He took in her hair, her face, her exposed shirt. "Holy cow." He pulled into the street. "To the hospital then?"

"My car's there." Zoey checked the side mirror and then craned her neck to look out the rearview.

"Okay," he stretched the word and then waited for her to fill him in.

Zoey checked again to see if any car seemed to be tailing them. "Are you really allowed to drive?"

Jimmy's left hand traveled to the strap of his eyepatch. "Allowed to drive?" he mused.

"Do you have a California Driver's License?"

"No."

"Didn't that come up the night of the shooting?"

"I have a license. Issued by the State of Arkansas." Jimmy turned on to Scenic Drive and shot forward, the rush hour over, but traffic too thick for Zoey to gauge if any driver seemed overly interested in them.

"Do you have an address there?" she asked.

"My dad does, and the property will be mine someday. He's already put some stuff in my name."

They were making speedy progress. With luck, she could forestall his questions all the way to the hospital. "No siblings?"

"Just my brother Seamus. He had Down Syndrome."

Zoey noted the past tense. Even though people with Down Syndrome could live normal life spans, it was fairly common for them to die young. Now Jimmy was alone. *Like her.* Except he had parents, at least a dad. "How about your mom?"

"She lives here."

"But you use the Arkansas address, and it only requires one good eye?"

"If it covers a one-hundred-forty-degree range. And before you ask," he said, lifting the patch, "it was poked out by a dart."

Zoey flinched.

He turned his head toward her. The lid over the damaged eye puckered with a star of scar tissue, and the iris had a slightly filmy look. It wasn't grotesque—no Poe "vulture-eye"—not even something a person would notice with a casual glance.

Jimmy quickly returned his focus to the road and slid the patch into place. "My brother threw the dart. It ricocheted off the board." He expelled a long breath. "The accident messed him up more than me." He tapped the steering wheel once in finality, like typing a period. "Now it's my turn to ask questions. Why is your car at the hospital?"

"My landlord and I drove my mother there."

"Because…?"

She fisted her hands and squeezed them together with her thighs. "Because she was shot and killed."

They were two blocks from the hospital, but Jimmy swerved into a driveway and screeched to a body slamming stop. "What?"

"Pull into a space." The auto-repair business was closed. It was unlikely anyone would want to enter the lot, but blocking the entrance with the car made her uneasy.

Jimmy drove forward and stopped alongside a roll-up door, closed and padlocked for the night.

The streetlight revealed a black graffiti scrawl on the corrugated metal. *Seeker.* There were two more service bays for the auto-repair shop, and then the narrow drive disappeared into darkness.

Jimmy unclipped his seatbelt and turned to her.

As her hands unclenched, she released the story she'd been gripping.

It didn't fly out like a magician's dove in a graceful arc. It sputtered without any organized beginning, middle, and end, starting with, "I thought I hated my mom." Then she burst into tears even as a tiny part of her acknowledged *that's not a bad first line*.

Jimmy unlatched her seatbelt. He put one hand on her shoulder. He raised the hand and used the warm palm to smooth back her hair.

"People think I'm a killer," she said.

Oh, that was overdramatic, worthy of Camille. Harvey's words came back to her. *You know the thing about parents? One day they're gone.* She sobbed.

Harvey wished he'd known if he was like his ancestors. Zoey wondered if she was more like Camille than she wanted to believe.

Jimmy's thumb brushed away a tear as she tried again with "that morning, before I saw you at Kamea's, a man came to the farm with a gun." Even though every fiber of her being wanted to believe Jimmy was a good guy, she still watched for his reaction.

"What farm?" He was truly confused.

In fits and starts, she managed some of the story.

* * *

Jimmy didn't tell her not to cry or that everything would be okay or any other stupid platitude. He listened and waited.

Gratitude overwhelmed her. She could fall for a guy like this big time. She wiped under her eyes with a fingertip.

Jimmy started the engine. "I'll take you to your car, but you can't go home by yourself."

"I'm worried about Harvey's dog."

"I'm worried about you."

The words slid under a barrier and pierced her heart.

They drove the short distance in silence until she needed to direct him through the labyrinth of the parking lot to the ER in the back.

Her car was gone. Not too surprising since it'd been parked in the red zone, but then she remembered. Harvey had driven. Harvey had the key fob.

What now?

Chapter Forty-Three

Ray pointed his gun at Harvey. Queasiness overtook him, but he didn't dare reach for his pills.

Harvey stretched his arms to his side. "I'm not armed, Ray." He took a step forward. "You wouldn't shoot a defenseless man."

"Defenseless? Where's your dog?" He stabbed the gun, but Harvey didn't flinch.

"Guarding the fort." Harvey inched toward him, eyes on the Colt. "We go back a long way, my friend."

"Don't come any closer." Sweat gathered on Ray's forehead and the back of his neck. That idiot—Jimmy, Justin, Jared, whatever the fuck his name was—must have done the deed, in spite of his message. Otherwise, why was Harvey here? He threw out his best gambit. "Is this about the car?"

"You were prowling around my place." Harvey narrowed his eyes but stayed put. "Why *did you* torch that car, Ray?" He tilted his head. "You could have set the whole hillside on fire."

Ray's shoulders released a fraction. So Harvey wasn't here about a shooting. "It was a controlled burn," he said. "We were careful."

"Right."

Harvey was giving him that look like he did back in high school whenever he suspected Ray was lying; it was as if Harvey saw him, physically, but his vision of him was retreating into his skull. When they were young, Harvey's cockiness had made sense. He'd been good-looking, a graceful runner, and a decent student, with Rachelle, undoubtedly the prettiest girl in their high school, as his girlfriend. But now? Harvey didn't have a family or girlfriend or two nickels to rub together.

The grayness of Harvey's mustache struck him, the slight stoop in his shoulders, his face parched in spite of the hat Ray had gifted him.

Ray heaved a sigh. "We're getting old."

"That's what I've come to discuss."

Ray relaxed the gun to the bar counter but kept a hand on the grip. "How about you sit over there?" He tipped his chin toward the stool at the other end of the bar.

Harvey circled the desk in a wide arc and took a seat.

Ray considered offering him a drink, but that would involve occupying both his hands. He wasn't sure why Harvey had suddenly dropped by. Maybe the fire. Maybe not. Harvey could be cagey.

"Do you mind if I pour myself one?" Harvey said.

Without looking, Ray reached under the counter and produced a shot glass. "That okay?"

"Sure."

Ray slid the glass along the glossy wood and nudged the bottle of vodka toward Harvey. It was weird, he thought, how when you saw strangers who were nearly seventy, they looked old, but when you looked at someone you'd known practically your whole life, a magic filter erased wrinkles and gray hair. Most of the time, when he looked at Harvey, it was like they were still kids, ready for the next adventure. But the events of the last week had stripped away any illusion.

Harvey poured a drink and studied it. "I want out," he said. "I can't keep running my farm by myself."

"I've been wondering about that." Ray added some tonic water to his remaining ice. He carefully took a sip, watching his old friend. "What do you have in mind?"

Harvey clipped the shot glass with his thumb and index finger, but didn't lift it. "I don't know what you've got going on, Ray, but I know it's not good." He lowered his eyes as if embarrassed for him, and then raised a steely gaze. "Now you've involved my farm."

Ray waited, trying to assess Harvey's expression. Harvey had always been better than he was at everything—sports, women, lying. "What do you propose?"

Harvey hammered his drink and placed the shot glass on the bar. "I want you to take over all my harvest—all the packaged product and my plants."

Ray pursed his lips and examined Harvey. *Damn it all to hell.* After all these years, he couldn't read him any better than when they were in high school. His friend produced primo weed. So that part made the deal tempting. But the offer was sudden. Unexpected. Had the car fire freaked him out? Could something positive really be emerging from this shit storm?

"This is a one-time offer." Harvey rested his elbows on the bar, stretched his legs into the room, and crossed them at the ankles.

A little too casual? Ray followed Harvey's gaze down to worn leather work boots. They looked like they weighed a ton. The lace of the top boot was double-tied below several vacant holes. The scuffed tongue rested askew in the loose grip.

Harvey put the other ankle on top as though he could tell Ray was judging his footwear. "Half my going rate on the packages."

"What's the catch?"

Harvey pulled in his legs and sat up. "The offer is time-limited."

"What's the deadline?"

"Now."

Ray calculated. Harvey would not screw him over on a business deal. And he'd been wondering for some time how Harvey could keep running his farm without help. His face puckered with worry. He didn't want to be a sucker, either falling for a trap *or* missing an opportunity. "Why the hurry?"

"Cover of night is a good time, don't you think?"

"But why all of a sudden like this, Harvey?"

His friend turned toward him. "You know the answer to that."

Ray flinched. *Damn Harvey and those eyes! Knowing. Judgmental. Sanctimonious.* He looked away and scratched his itchy scalp. How much did Harvey know? He'd always been a secretive son-of-a-bitch, getting together with his sister behind his back. It had taken him months to catch a whiff of their relationship. But one thing was for damn sure—Harvey wouldn't be working with the cops. Whatever had put this bug up Harvey's ass, Ray could be safe on that front.

"It'll take me a while to round up a crew."

"Time-limited. One hour." Harvey tapped his watch.

"One hour! How am I supposed to gather a team and get to the farm in an hour?"

"I'll help you dig and load." Harvey stood and strode to the door.

As soon as the latch clicked, Ray popped a pill and picked up his mobile phone.

Chapter Forty-Four

Zoey pointed to a wide-open stretch of curb. "Park there."

"Whose house is this?" Jimmy asked.

Her heart thrummed in her neck. "Christine Austin's."

"And we are here, why?"

She wished she could coherently answer that question. Maybe to confirm the woman was at home and not up in the mountains with a Doberman attached to her arm.

They sat in the silent capsule of Jimmy's car, night pooled around them. The street was quiet. A porch light illuminated the distinctive red door of the Austins' house. It matched the Pinterest image. Lights were on behind the big downstairs window, presumably the living room, and in one upstairs window.

"So?" Jimmy finally said.

She cracked the door. "I want her to know someone murdered my mother, and that same someone most likely murdered her husband."

"Should I come with you?"

She drew a deep breath of cold air. "I don't think she'll attack me in front of her neighbors."

"You might want to zip up the sweatshirt."

On the way to the door, Zoey tried to work the zipper and failed. She stabbed the doorbell. When she didn't hear any footsteps, she rang the bell again. Then again. Footsteps bounded down stairs, and the door yanked open.

A tall, annoyed-looking teenaged girl stood before her, cellphone to ear.

"You must be Grace or Elizabeth."

The girl's eyes narrowed. She looked Zoey up and down. "Hold on," she said into her phone.

"Is your mom here?"

The girl remained mum, staring at Zoey's shirt. Then she slammed the door. The deadbolt *thunked* into place.

But the lack of any appearance by Christine, or even a shout from Christine to find out who was at the door, told her what she wanted to know. Unless she was on the toilet or in the shower, Christine was not there.

So where was she?

* * *

"She's probably at the movies or having a glass of wine with friends," Jimmy said. On the narrow mountain road, he flicked the car's lights to bright. His hands gripped the wheel at ten and two.

"She just lost her husband."

"Drowning her sorrows?"

"There's a hairpin turn ahead." Zoey worried anew about how well he could see.

He slowed, maneuvering carefully, his head turtled forward. "Now I know why you don't come to town much."

Even though she was riding up a twisty road with a one-eyed driver, that danger barely ranked in her pantheon of worries. Who had killed her mother? Were they coming back for her? Where was Harvey? What had happened to Rambo?

Her trailer finally rose into view.

"You live here?"

"Yup."

"Cool."

"It would be cooler if my car were here." The area in front of Harvey's house was empty, too. She tried to remember if his old GMC had been parked there that morning, before her mother was shot, before she was hauled to the police station, back in the Iron Age.

"Go left," she said.

"Into the trees?" Jimmy slid up his eyepatch and squinted.

"There's a dirt road tucked on the other side of that farmhouse. Leads down to a barn."

The car crawled across the bare yard. Jimmy turned onto the rough road.

"Stop!" Down the road, dim light spilled from the barn. "Looks like a party."

Jimmy killed the engine and lights.

Their elevated position provided a panorama of the scene. Her car, Harvey's pick-up, a huge black truck, and an unfamiliar gray truck jammed into the area beyond the burnt hulk of the sedan. The black truck looked like the Ram she'd seen the day before.

Past the vehicles, redwoods towered, with nothing in between. Zoey sucked in her breath. Harvey's plants were gone. A black, pot-holed swath scarred the landscape. She squinted. The Ram's extra-long bed heaped with a load. "We may have field thieves down there." In which case, what had they done with Harvey? Her stomach clenched.

"What's our next move?" Jimmy asked.

"I wish we had a weapon."

He stretched down under his seat and came up with a box. "Sometimes wishes come true."

"You have a gun?"

"Remember my dad in Arkansas?" He gave her a wry smile. "Of course, I have a gun. I'm a good shot, too."

If he kept a weapon in his car, it was no wonder the cops had shown so much interest in him the night of Austin's murder. No wonder they'd done a GSR swab.

Jimmy unlocked the metal case. He lifted out a small box of ammo and a Smith and Wesson six-shooter with a dark wood grip. It was a sexy looking gun, but, she feared, no match for what might be down in the barn.

"Being California, it's not loaded," Jimmy said as he slipped bullets into the chamber.

Below, three men emerged into the light. Two of them were using both hands to push loaded dollies, which meant they didn't have immediate access to a weapon. The third man trailed, talking, hands free and gesticulating as though directing a symphony.

None of the figures was tall enough to be Harvey. Was he inside? Dread crawled up her spine. His truck and her SUV were both here. If they'd overpowered him, they would have his Glock as well as whatever firepower they'd brought with them. And where was Rambo? Not seeing the dog made her worried and sad. Had they sent Rambo to his death when Harvey sicced him on the shooter?

Clicking the cylinder into place, Jimmy put the remaining ammo back in the lock box and sat it on the center console. Night and silence engulfed them. How much did she know about the man beside her, now holding a loaded gun? Had her attraction to him clouded her judgment?

In the tableau below, the man supervising was stocky, like Harvey's friend Ray. "The guy in the back," she said, "is most likely armed."

The troop of men moved out of sight.

"Is your overhead light off?" she asked.

"Yup."

"Will your car ping if we leave the doors open?"

"Too old," he said.

She carefully cracked her door and swung it open. Muted music drifted from the barn. "The End" by the Doors.

Carrying his revolver in a SUL position—close to his chest and barrel down—Jimmy followed suit. To avoid noise, they left the doors winged out. More cover and a faster escape if needed. The gibbous moon lit up the road, so they hugged the tree line as they crept forward.

Thumps drifted up the slope toward them—weight hitting into the back of the truck cab. Bits of conversation ricocheted toward them. Swearing. "Careful not to rip them!" She recognized the voice. *Definitely Ray.*

The men didn't seem concerned about their noise or the volume of their voices.

With her Element and Harvey's truck both at the barn, Harvey must be around. Who'd put on the music? Could Harvey be in cahoots with them? Was he out of sight working in the barn? And if he was, what did that mean? Had his story about the stashed vehicle been a lie?

Zoey stopped behind the twisting branches of a shrubby manzanita. Jimmy tucked up behind her, close enough that his breath puffed warm on the back of her neck and his gun radiated cold to the back of her heart.

Ten feet ahead of them, the spent flare lay sideways in the road, a marker to the entrance of a crime scene, a scorched track running down to the burned vehicle. The putrid stink of the fire lingered, blotting out the fragrance of the forest.

A handcart rattled. Zoey crouched, and so did Jimmy. The three men paraded back to the barn. The music stopped.

Behind her a twig snapped. She and Jimmy turned in unison, a move worthy of *Dancing with the Stars*. He landed in front of her.

A tall figure scuttled toward them from up the road, knees bent, arms extended, pointing a semi-automatic in a very professional manner. "Drop the gun."

Jimmy complied, the revolver plopping and rustling in the undergrowth. "Easy now."

Dressed in black like a cat burglar, Christine Austin stepped forward. "What were you doing at my house?"

"Shhhhhhh."

"You're shushing me?"

Zoey shriveled at the loudness of her voice. Glancing nervously back to the barn, she whispered tersely, "You followed us?"

"That's not an answer."

Jimmy stayed rooted in front of Zoey, his hands slightly raised in surrender.

"See that?" Zoey gestured to the crispy metal remains. "The person who killed your husband drove that car."

"So now you know more than the police department?" Christine didn't move into the trees or lower her voice.

"Yes. I do."

"You're something else." Christine slid silent as a shadow down the road, coming closer, but remaining in the open. Even in black clothes, her blonde hair tucked under a watch cap, the moonlight exposed her. Her gun's aim was no longer ambiguous. The barrel pointed over Jimmy's shoulder at Zoey's face. "Stay away from my family or I'll fuckin' kill you."

Zoey couldn't tell if Christine had even glanced at the burned vehicle, if she believed a single word out of Zoey's mouth. The scene at the barn didn't seem to interest her.

A twisted grin sliced Christine's face. "And now I know where *you* live." Her voice dripped with condescension.

Zoey chinned toward the farmhouse. "I don't live here."

"Right."

This volatile woman had tailed them up a lone mountain road without being detected. She wielded her firearm like a pro—a great marksman, according to both her husband and Millard Cranston. Christine Austin was not a person to mess with.

But, Zoey realized, if Christine had just learned where she lived, and thought it was inside Harvey's house, Christine had not shot her mother— had not attempted to shoot her. Zoey tried to ignore the gun, which had swiveled from her face and back to Jimmy's center mass. Peeking around his shoulder, she met Christine's eyes. "At least one of the men in that barn is armed."

Christine snorted. "Anybody takes a crack at me better be a damn good shot."

Still, Christine crabbed over to the tree line, nearing them, pistol in hand. From the barn swarmed the cadre men. She and Jimmy were trapped. Christine on one side of them, criminals on the other.

"Who's your one-eyed human shield?"

"My name's Jimmy." He lowered an arm, as if to step forward and offer Christine a handshake.

Christine jabbed the gun forward. "Reach for the sky."

Jimmy's hand flew back into the air.

Zoey felt relieved, but cowardly, to have Jimmy in front of her. But he wouldn't provide any protection if the men finished their work and took off up the road in their trucks. Which could be any time. The plants had been dug up and loaded. The crew seemed to be wrapping up. She needed to persuade Christine to move out of sight.

Zoey slowly turned to look into the woods, the dense undergrowth, wild berry bushes full of thorns, poison oak, and who knew what kind of terrain.

Family was obviously important to Christine; maybe that was the way to reach her. She peeped around Jimmy's shoulder again. "Look, I didn't come to your house to harass you or your family. I came because someone shot and killed my mother. I wanted to make sure it wasn't you."

"Someone murdered your mother?" Christine swayed like a cobra, which seemed threatening until Zoey realized the woman was just trying to get a good look at her. She sounded confused and genuinely alarmed. Christine closed the gap to a couple of feet, but didn't lower her weapon. "Why on earth would I shoot your mother?"

"The bullet was meant for me."

Christine guffawed. "Now that, that is understandable."

Anger flared in her. "If you want to know who's to blame for Stan's death, if you're interested in the truth at all, you might work with us here." Zoey dipped her head to indicate the barn.

"You're saying Stan's killer is down there?" Christine shook her head.

"They'll know who the killer is." Zoey didn't know if that was true, but she hoped her words carried conviction.

Below them, past the cluster of vehicles and the void of Harvey's field, the brush at the edge of the forest stirred.

Christine swung her weapon.

Chapter Forty-Five

A dog bounded into the clearing. *Rambo!* Relief shot through Zoey. The sleek Doberman moved gracefully, clearly unharmed. He circled, attention focused back into the redwoods.

Christine's new target allowed Zoey to move to Jimmy's side. Christine glanced toward them but kept her weapon pointed at the tree line.

Jimmy gave Zoey's shoulder a reassuring bump. They seemed to be gaining an ally.

After a moment, two figures emerged from the trees. Sandwiched together, they bent forward, struggling up the incline.

"Are they the ones?" Christine growled. "Did they kill Stan?"

"Stop," Zoey hissed. "The guy in the back is my friend." Even at the fringe of the barn's light, it was easy to identify his familiar movements. She hoped in the tableau below that Harvey *was* a friend.

Christine grunted. "Like I give a flying fuck." Her body looked spring-loaded, but she held fire.

On the phone, the last thing Harvey had said was that he planned to *fix this*. Zoey wished she knew what *this* was. He certainly couldn't fix her mom's death, so he must mean the clear and present danger to her life.

Harvey frog marched his prisoner over the torn-up field, emerging into the barn's light, Rambo leaping and barking around them.

At the ruckus, the stocky man strutted from the barn like a bantam rooster. He headed toward Harvey. Then, as though his spidey sense had kicked in, he spun and looked up the road. Zoey froze and felt Jimmy stiffen.

Now that he faced them, it was certain. The man was Ray, brother of

Harvey's long-lost love, Rachelle, the man who'd paid a visit to the farm. *Yesterday*. It seemed like an eon ago.

Abruptly, Ray swung back to Harvey. Zoey released her breath. But beside her, Christine coiled tighter. "Is he the one?"

Dread gripped Zoey. She prayed Christine didn't go off half-cocked. Didn't shoot someone. Didn't start a gun fight when they were out-manned and out-armed.

"Look what I found." Harvey pushed his captive in front of him. He stumbled and fell flat in clods of earth. Prone, the young man covered his head with his arms and begged Harvey not to sic the dog.

It was too late. Rambo chomped onto his forearm. The man howled, but Rambo kept his jaw clamped on the appendage. The dog might be trained not to tear flesh, but it had to be terrifying to have a one-hundred-pound beast attached to one's body.

Seemingly unperturbed, Ray crossed his arms over his chest.

"I believe he's a pal of yours." Harvey's voice had lowered, and Zoey strained to hear him. The only positive was that Christine stilled, as though also intent on the conversation.

Ray vigorously waggled his bald head. "No friend of mine."

The man on the ground cursed, much easier to hear. "You're not going to make a fortune, Boss, while I go to prison. You told me to kill her!"

A gun whipped from Ray's pocket and pointed at the head of the flattened body. The man fell silent. Zoey dismissed the thought of moving closer to hear better.

"Boss, huh? But if, as you claim, you don't know this guy," Harvey said, "there's no need for the weapon, is there, Ray?"

The gun barrel remained pointed at the man's head. "You tell me, Harvey? Is there? Why do you have Rambo pinning this piece of shit to the ground?"

"*Piece of shit*," Harvey echoed. "Definitely sounds like you know him."

From the dirt, the man raised his head toward Ray and spat, "You're the one wanted the witness gone.

"Shut up!" Ray shouted. "I called that off. The only one guilty of murder is you." Ray changed his concentration from the body to Harvey. "This stupid shit is the one who killed that cop."

Without warning, Christine moved like a stealth bomber. She zipped in front of Zoey and took up position, crouched in the cover of the charred vehicle only yards from the action. She hunkered there, inside the reach of the light, her body looking wound tight, but not afraid. An inspiration.

Was she, Zoey, a crime writer, really going to let another woman beat her to a good story? Without picking over the wisdom of the action, she bounded like a gazelle and landed beside Christine. The woman gave her a curt nod, eyebrows lifted in surprise, her weapon at the ready.

Jimmy remained in the trees. Retrieving his gun, Zoey hoped.

A handcart rattled from the barn, and two other men appeared. They stopped short. "What's going on, Boss?" one of them said. He released his load with a thump and strode over behind Ray.

His helper, head on swivel, parked his load, too. "This is the last of it," he said. "I'm outta here."

No one challenged him. A flannel shirt flapped open as the young man beat a retreat to his truck, the gray one Zoey hadn't recognized. He jumped in and fired up the engine.

Christine flattened to the ground before Zoey could think *busted.* The driver was executing a tight three-point turn. In a second, he'd be roaring right by them.

Zoey dropped next to Christine. Jockeying, they wriggled under the burned car frame, not quite hidden.

But at the sight of Ray's gun and a person in the vicious grip of a dog, the driver seemed intent on getting the hell out of Dodge, his eyes glued to the road, the dust spinning from his tires into their faces.

"Good," Christine muttered. "One fewer to deal with." She spat on the ground and started to worm free of the wreckage, the gun still in her hand.

Zoey caught hold of Christine's pants and whispered sternly. "What are you doing?"

Christine jerked free and kicked sideways, landing an MMA-worthy blow to her pelvic bone. Zoey clamped teeth over her bottom lip to prevent a scream. Something between a whimper and a gasp escaped, anyway. Her eyes teared. Wiggling out behind Christine, she kept her eyes locked on the woman's boots, considering for a nanosecond the option of revealing their presence and allowing Ray to shoot her.

Christine remained behind the car. Zoey stuck to her side. With the roar of the truck, they'd lost the last minute of crucial dialog. What kind of negotiation was taking place among the remaining four men? The scene hadn't changed much. At the far edge of his field, Harvey stood at the feet of the prostrate man pinned by Rambo. At the man's head, Ray maintained the downward aim of his gun. Behind Ray, but near him, stood a henchman who looked more like a youth pastor.

To Zoey's surprise, Christine popped free of the car frame. However, she didn't charge toward the action. Instead she ducked and dashed silently to the trees. Damn, the woman moved like a superhero. Strong. Lithe. Athletic.

Zoey considered the short, but lit span, took a deep breath, and quickly followed. When she reached the darkness of the trees, Christine was already talking to Jimmy, strategizing, frowning skeptically at Jimmy's eyepatch, and acting like there wasn't a revolver pointed at her.

"First step, neutralize the armed threat," Christine said.

A sly smile slid over Jimmy's lips. "Isn't that you?"

Zoey blinked, her earlier doubts about Jimmy flooding back, although he'd never seemed more appealing than he did at that moment, his light hair luminescent against a redwood trunk, his calm unfazed by Christine Austin.

"We're all on the same side here," Zoey said.

Keeping his focus on Christine, Jimmy said, "You sure about that?"

She wasn't, but she said, "Yes."

"So what's the plan, Zoey?"

If the situation had been different, she would have flown over to lock her lips on his at the easy way he handed the power to her. *Smitten*—a word she'd known since the age of twelve—filled almost painfully with meaning. In spite of her fear and the hot blush on her face, she said, "Harvey, the tall guy with the dog, is probably our ally, so we just have to worry about the other three, and Rambo has one of them under control."

"Probably?" Jimmy remarked at the same time Christine asked brusquely, "Rambo's the dog?" Christine hadn't lowered her gun away from Jimmy, but in all fairness, he hadn't stopped pointing his at Christine.

"Yes," Zoey said, leaving the two of them to work out their impasse. She struggled to hear what the men below were saying. Now that she and Christine had moved back to the trees, the forest swallowed the conversation. Ray made dramatic stabbing motions of his gun toward the man on the ground, while Ray's sidekick kept pointing back to the dolly and black truck as though trying to persuade Ray they should take the goods and jam.

Christine and Jimmy remained squared off, each unyielding. The only way to end the stand-off, Zoey figured, was a plan that put the two on the same team. "The main person we have to worry about," she said, "is Ray—the one who's armed."

"Do we know his cohort isn't?" Christine asked.

"No, we don't, although it seems like if he had a weapon handy, he would have taken it out."

"So," Christine interjected, "your one-eyed bandit—"

"Jimmy."

"Jimmy and I can approach from different directions and cover—"

"—while I call out to Harvey from behind the burned car."

"A bullet could penetrate that," Christine objected.

Well, at least the woman now seemed not to want her dead. *Progress.*

"Or, we could call the police," Jimmy said.

"By the time they arrive, everyone and everything will be gone," Christine objected, "including my husband's killer."

They stood in silence for a moment, and then, as if by an agreed-upon signal, Zoey scuttled to the charred car frame. Christine shot to the other side of the road, flattening in the weeds.

"Harvey!" Zoey shouted.

Ray reeled about. Zoey pancaked. A bullet zinged into the metal over her head. She didn't say another word. Ray had nothing to aim at except the sound of her voice.

"Get him, boy!" Harvey shouted.

Oh my god. She hadn't factored in the dog. Her insides flipped. She shivered against the ground, hiding her face between her arms and expecting Rambo's fangs to rip open a limb, no matter what Harvey claimed about the dog.

She heard a bellow of indignation. "Christ, Harvey, call him off! Rambo! Shit! Rambo."

Zoey peeked around the wreckage. Rambo had shifted to Ray's gun arm, causing him to drop his weapon. Harvey drew his Glock before his captive on the ground could scramble up. Staying away from the man's hands, Harvey stamped his upper thighs, sending the young buck back flat, his face in the dirt. Ray's sidekick backed away, hands in the air.

Harvey kicked Ray's gun into the ravine.

"Hey, now, buddy." Ray's tone was wheedling. "Think of Rachelle. She wouldn't—"

"Drop your weapon!"

Harvey and Ray's assistant wheeled toward the new voice. Ray turned as much as he could with Rambo on his arm. Even the guy on the ground lifted his head. But Harvey didn't drop his gun.

That, Zoey thought, was vintage Harvey. "It's me! Do what she says," she hollered.

At the same moment, Jimmy shouted a repeat of Christine's order.

Her heart hammered. *What if the old fool doesn't comply?*

And he didn't exactly. He turned the barrel back toward Ray.

"Now, Harvey," Ray spluttered, "you and me—"

"Shut up." Harvey held out a demanding hand. "Gimme your keys."

"Come on, bro—"

"Now."

Ray dug awkwardly in his pocket with his left hand. "What are you going to do?"

"Just taking what's mine." Harvey poked his gun at the henchman. "Throw the last stuff in the truck."

The guy looked up the hill in their direction, but Harvey's gun was the closest and most real. He hustled to the dolly and heaved packages into the already opened door.

If her mouth weren't plastered shut with dryness, Zoey would have smiled. *The brilliant old coot.* Without lifting a finger, he had his plants and his product loaded and ready to go. He was going to drive off with evidence of his illegal grow and leave the other three to face the music, provided, of course, neither Christine nor Jimmy shot him. Their appearance was obviously not part of his master plan.

Christine rose from the weeds with her firearm at chest level.

"No!" Zoey shouted. Her body was moving, but felt frozen in time. "No!" She put her head down to bulldoze the woman. "No! He's not Stan's killer."

Christine sidestepped her.

Zoey barreled past and stumbled, latching on to a tree branch to stay upright.

"Geez, Louise, I wasn't going to shoot your friend."

Harvey glanced toward them, hurled a few more packages from the dolly into the truck, and climbed into Ray's black Ram. "Come on, boy."

Rambo released his hold on Ray's arm and sprang into the truck, crawling over Harvey's body. As the two of them rumbled up the road, Harvey threw a two-fingered salute in Zoey's direction. The tarp over the heaping truck bed flapped a fragrant cannabis goodbye.

Only Harvey's GMC and her Element remained, and presumably, the men didn't have a key to either. They were stuck right here with her and Christine and Jimmy.

Sometimes there was justice in the world.

Chapter Forty-Six

From her position against a laurel tree, Zoey watched the scene unfold. Christine commanded the men to put their hands in the air. On the other side of the road, Jimmy emerged from the woods to cover her.

Ray and his cohort thrust their hands up.

"You, too!" Christine snarled.

The young man on the ground placed his hands a short distance over his head. But instead of lying still, he pushed into one hand and then rolled like a baker's pin.

Christine fired. The bullet spat dirt onto the man's face. He tumbled across the footpath and dropped over the edge, the spot where Zoey had hidden from Ray.

"Watch them!" Christine shouted to Jimmy. She dashed past the two vehicles, her long legs flying over the holes in the field.

Zoey ran after her, screaming, "Stop, Christine! There's a drop!"

Christine disappeared over the ledge.

The scream stopped Zoey's heart. In spite of Jimmy's six-shooter aimed their way, Ray and his Kiwanis lackey turned toward the redwoods. The dark, ominous spires responded with silence.

After a few seconds, the brush rustled.

Christine huffed up into sight. "There's a drop, all right."

"The kid fell?" Ray asked.

"Yeah," Christine said. "That's what happened." Her eyes locked on Ray. "Was he the one who killed my husband?"

"I wouldn't know."

"Sounded before like you did."

Mr. Kiwanis's head was swiveling between Ray and Christine. "What are you talking about?" he asked. "Who's her husband?"

"Up here, it's easy to understand how accidents happen," Christine said, directing her speech to Ray. "Night time. In the woods. A steep drop."

"And, this area is famous for dumping bodies," Jimmy's deep voice added. "Down the ravine they go. Dinner for the coyotes and insects. Bones might not be discovered for years. Maybe not ever."

Zoey thought she was seriously falling in love.

"What the fuck," Mr. Kiwanis said. "I don't know anything about a murder." He put his hands higher as if to prove his point. "I just came up here to get some pot plants. All agreed upon by the owner, who just left. A business transaction—"

"Oh, shut it, Stuart," Ray snapped. "These people are not law enforcement." He lowered his arms. "If they shoot us, they'll be charged with murder. And they're not going to hurl us down a cliff, either."

When Christine didn't immediately shoot Ray, Stuart lowered his hands, too.

Ray and Stuart inspected Christine and Jimmy as though calculating the odds if they went *mano a mano*. Zoey edged forward so they'd see the match would be three to two.

The two men assumed back-to-back positions for maximum coverage of the threat. Ray was old, but stout and powerful. Stuart was much younger, fit, and indignantly angry, weight forward on the balls of his feet, ready for a fight.

"Hey, Ray!"

Ray turned his head toward Zoey. She slowly neared the two men, giving them three places to focus.

"Little Red Riding Hood," Ray said. "How'd you know my name?"

"I'm the witness you wanted killed."

"Now, wait a minute—"

"My mother is dead because of you."

"I didn't kill—"

"Save it, Ray. I believe the kid." She took her cell phone from her pocket. "You ordered the hit. And now that Harvey has removed all his product, I can't see any reason not to call the cops." She glanced at Jimmy and Christine. "Any objections?"

"None here," Christine said, "as long as the motherfucker who killed my husband is the one who went over the drop.

"And you," Christine trained her weapon on Ray, "if you think I'm afraid to use my firearm, just try me."

Chapter Forty-Seven

Zoey cranked the volume on her piano, set to the rock organ voice, and banged the E7 chord on a piercing high octave. People in the audience swayed their bodies as Sabbie closed their set with *Check Mate.*

At a bar stool directly in front of the band, Lisandra bopped her head. The lawyer exchanged a smile with Zoey before returning her gaze to Kath on the drums.

Sabbie did a final twirl and a mic drop. Hoots from the crowd. Before people finished applauding, the band splintered. Brianna rushed over to tell Sabbie for the fifth time not to do that; the mic was not hers to dent. Andrea headed out back for a toke. Having her tribe act the way it was supposed to act sent a wave of bliss over Zoey.

Toned arms glistening with sweat, Kath scooted from her drum set. She made a beeline for Lisandra, bent down to kiss her, and then took a proprietary guzzle of Lisandra's beer.

Zoey didn't want to intrude, but she was dying to hear the latest from Lisandra. The district attorney was her buddy from law school. Lisandra had been able to eke out bits of information not in the media, although Zoey had to give Millard Cranston kudos for his coverage. It seemed lately that he was writing the entire *Playa Maria Reporter* by himself. He'd even done a feature article on her mother, *The Innocent Second Victim.*

Her mom, as it turned out, had a living trust with her send-off planned down to the nth degree—the obit, the site, the music, even the caterer. She'd made this chapter of Zoey's life as easy as possible. At weak moments, like now as she stepped away from her piano, Zoey wondered if Camille could have been thinking of her. Could have wanted to make her life easier. She shrugged to herself and turned off her amp. More likely Camille's motive was to control everything to the very end.

Her neck pinched with guilt. Camille was dead because of her. She tipped her head side to side, vertebrae cracking.

No, not because of me. Because of Jared O'Keefe.

Across the crowded room, Jimmy leaned against the wall. Zoey flashed him two fingers and mouthed *two minutes.*

She edged closer to Kath and Lisandra. Kath was bending over the bar to tuck a strand of Lisandra's hair behind her ear, but Lisandra glanced up at Zoey. "Great set."

"Thanks." Zoey didn't want to waste Lisandra's time or to bushwhack Kath. "If you have an update on the case, maybe later?"

Lisandra grinned. "Sure thing, Detective."

Zoey moved quickly away to prevent a clam jam, Lisandra's and Kath's faces close together and eager. People had trickled outside for fresh air, but the fall nights were getting nippy, and much of the crowd remained in the room, milling about, drinks in hand. Zoey threaded through them, the bar air warm and fusty from bodies and beer, her new She Cats shirt glaringly bright.

When she neared Jimmy, his hand reached out and grabbed hers. He towed her the last three feet, smack up against his body. He wrapped both arms around her. *Yum.*

"I'm with a rock star," he murmured into her hair.

"And I'm with a long-haired, gun-toting, he-man." She sang a few bars of "I Wanna Be Like You."

"Wanna go outside?"

"Yes."

Jimmy led the way to his white Honda Accord and sat on the hood. Standing, she nestled back between his legs, swathed in soft orange corduroy. He encircled her with his arms. "Anything to report?"

"I think you're up to date. They found a gun in the woods—a ghost gun—

covered with the fingerprints of the kid—Jared O'Keefe—who went over the cliff. Ballistics matched it to the bullet taken from my mom. They're working to connect it to the shooting of the police officer."

Jimmy shivered. "A couple of nights we'll never forget." He gave her a squeeze, meant to comfort, but its tenderness pressed her heart, and a tear rolled down her cheek. She twisted and looked back up at him. "Did I tell you my mom has this hulking Living Trust, all bound up in leather?"

She wiped away the tear. The Living Trust listed all her mom's assets, which, except for a few endowments, would pass intact to Zoey Perfect Kozinski. But she didn't say anything about that—wasn't even sure how she felt about it yet. The money could liberate her from her tiny house and her contract, but she wasn't sure she wanted out of either.

Instead, she said, "Stuart is out on bail. He's made a plea agreement and is going to roll over on Ray. According to Lisandra's source, Ray has hired the best criminal lawyer money can buy and isn't saying squat, but because he's linked to the death of a police officer, they're doing everything they can to keep him in jail."

"Without any connection to the weapon, what are they using to hold him?"

"There's the car. Stuart admits that he hid it at Ray's behest and later burned it."

"That car is toast."

"True," she sighed. "But there's the conversation we all heard where Jared accused Ray of ordering him to take out the witness."

"Yeah," Jimmy murmured, "we heard it, but how will the D.A.'s office prove that Jared was telling the truth? And even if they can prove it, is it a crime to say you want someone dead? I think he's going to walk."

"You sound like a crime writer."

"From you, that's quite a compliment." Jimmy nuzzled into her kinky hair and kissed the top of her head. "How about your friend?"

"Harvey?"

"Yeah."

"He texted me to say he's fine, but he hasn't shown up."

"The police haven't located him?"

"He's not their priority. And knowing Harvey, he has a secret hide-out somewhere and a whole truckload of pot to sell."

"But that's not his truck, right? Isn't it stolen?"

"*Stolen?* First, I don't think Ray's made that accusation. It's not like he currently needs the truck, anyway. And second, Harvey's no doubt in another vehicle by now." *Like, from time to time, a green Honda Element.* Not a fact anyone ever needed to know.

Zoey turned to face him and raised her head. Her hands snaked along the corduroy, up the sides of his fuzzy jacket, and around his neck. There were other things in life besides this case. She'd finally unloaded the whole story to Brianna the day before.

Brianna, of course, asked, "You going to write about it?"

"Nope." One time through had been enough.

Jimmy's lips met hers, and for the moment, the horror of the last month melted away. Then Kath pounded on her drums, calling Zoey back to life.

Acknowledgments

My fear in acknowledgments is always that I will leave someone out as the creation of a book is long while my memory is short.

The early stages of *Crime Writer* involved research. Neither of my cannabis sources want to be named but if they ever read this, I hope they will know their help was invaluable. Thank you to Eileen Magill and her sister for the insights on hypnotherapy, a big shout out to Ellen Kirschman for her shared expertise on PTSD, and gracias to Edward Martinez, former firefighter, for the bits about car fires.

Before the Capitola Book Café Writing Group fell apart during the epidemic, members, especially Mary Flodin, provided feedback on embryonic chapters. My husband, Daniel Friedman, also provided ruthless and helpful criticism along with heavy doses of support.

Once I had a first draft, Shannon Esposito, offered a critique. As did Shawn Reilly Simmons of Level Best Books. Happily, Shawn liked the manuscript enough to offer me a two-book contract, which included the re-release of *One Gun*—the companion book to *Crime Writer*—and *Crime Writer*.

Five beta readers gave generously of their time: M.M. Chouinard, Crystal Edwards, Mary Ann Miller, Gary Cunningham and Pat Morin. As a psychiatrist, Pat Morin added even more insight into the effects of stress. I appreciate all of you.

Out of the generosity of her heart, fellow mystery author Karin Fitz Sanford designed a gorgeous flyer for me.

Blurb writers, I bow down to you. As someone who has written blurbs, I understand what a big task it is. Thank you so much!

And most of all, thank you to booksellers, librarians, and readers. Without you, we are dust in the wind.

About the Author

A Claymore and Silver Falchion finalist, Vinnie Hansen is the author of the Carol Sabala mystery series, the novels *Lostart Street, One Gun,* and *Crime Writer,* as well as over seventy published short works.

She is a member of Mystery Writers of American, Sisters in Crime, and the Short Mystery Fiction Society. A retired high-school English teacher, she lives with her husband and the requisite cat in Santa Cruz, CA.

Learn more at www.vinniehansen.com

Also by Vinnie Hansen

One Gun (LBB, 2024)

Carol Sabala Mystery Series (misterio press):
   Murder, Honey
   One Tough Cookie
   Rotten Dates
   Squeezed & Juiced
   Death with Dessert
   Art, Wine & Bullets
   Black Beans & Venom
   Smoked Meat (prequel novella)

Standalone novel (misterio press)
   Lostart Street

And over 70 short works

www.ingramcontent.com/pod-product-compliance
Lightning Source LLC
Chambersburg PA
CBHW030129010826
48973CB00002B/477